A Gift From Edil

A Novel By

Tina Bauer

ISBN (hardcover): 978-1-7375675-3-0
ISBN (ebook): 978-1-7375675-4-7

Illustrated by
Harley Dallojacono

Edited by
Christine Weimer of Our Galaxy Publishing

Formatted by
Lindsay Tisi of Our Galaxy Publishing

For my little brother and my two kids:
Just when I thought I was outgrowing the childlike wonder of Christmas, they came along and made me a kid again.

For my husband:
He always encouraged my love for Christmas, to where some might call it an obsession.

For my mother:
No matter how hard times were, she always made sure every year was the best Christmas ever.

And for my father.
He always said, "You should write a book about Santa's Elves."
Well, Dad, here it is.

Prologue: The Lost Letter

What seemed like ordinary snow drifts on an extraordinary ice ridge was more than meets the eye. Under the bright winter moon, chimneys peeked out from the snowdrifts, and dark smoke rose into the silver night sky. A warm, yellow glow dotted hundreds of drifts in the shape of tiny windows. Where the snow cleared or blew away, there would be a small gate, a lamppost, or a sign declaring what business would occur beyond the white slopes.

What seemed like ordinary snowdrifts was a sizable village. The houses and buildings were small, sometimes buried within the mounds on the worst of winter days. The people of the village liked that. It was warm and cozy to them and kept them hidden to the average human eye.

The village comprised what all villages did. There was a general store, a bakery, a tanner and a blacksmith, many homes and small stables, various trades of talents- oh, and a post office.

Compared to the other buildings, the post office was fairly large, its second story and roof peeking up from the drifts. At the beginning of the village, it was the first establishment one would encounter as they walked or rode into town. The windows were bright with firelight, and one could see dynamic shadows hustling and bustling. Under the whistling wind, voices were heard coming from inside the post office.

Being nighttime, the post office was closed to the public but inside was a disarray of people working diligently. Some were doing the heavy lifting, moving furniture and boxes. Others had rags and buckets of warm soapy water. And still, more had brooms. Dust was floating, causing some to sneeze and others to swat it away as if it were a fly.

Remus and his brother, Echo, ran the post office. Despite being twins, the two looked and acted nothing alike. Remus stood taller than most in the village with a "strictly business" scowl always upon his face. His head was shiny and bald, with just a rim of reddish hair growing long from ear to ear. His brother, Echo, was thinner and smaller, a youthful questioning look twinkling in his blue eyes. He had a full head of red curls that he was always tossing or blowing out of his eyes.

Remus was barking the orders; what needed moving, what needed careful packaging, what needed washing. Every year, in January, they did their annual cleaning. It was the only time of year they had to slow down the processing of the letters and concentrate on cleaning up the previous year's mess. It was a matter of weeks before the flood of letters would begin again.

They processed the letters differently at the post office than in the rest of the world. Only a slight percentage of the letters were personal, inter-village mail. An even smaller rate was outgoing mail beyond their private, hidden village. The incoming mail, however, was enormous- tons of letters from around the world. The post office had separate rooms for each continent. They then broke each room down into rows of wooden file cabinets. Each row was a country. The rows were arranged by cities and towns, then streets and avenues, and onto to a specific house of a particular child with a special wish.

Remus was diligent in how he and Echo ran the post office. They organized every little thing right down to the inkwells and quills. He ran the place like a general ran an army. This year, he was even more strict because this was the first time they since building the post office that they'd repaint it. The old, worn, broken shelves and cabinets were going to be torn down and replaced.

He stood above everyone, hands on his hips, eyes on everything, making sure not a letter or file was missed as they were packed up and moved. He shouted orders, shook his head, mumbled under his breath, and at times, slapped his forehead under stress.

"No, no, no!" he would shout. "You can not put Africa's files with Italy's! Africa is a continent! Italy goes with Europe! Label it! Label it right!"

He went from room to room delegating. The others did not mind his grumpy tone of voice. Remus was who he was, and they accepted him. They followed his orders with a knowing smile and glance among themselves.

He found his twin in the main room by the entrance. Echo sang a little ditty to himself as he folded the burlap sacks that the mail came in. It was in this room where the mail first came. All along one wall were slots where they sorted mail a bit before being filed down by Remus' strict organization.

"We need to move the mail slots from the walls. The carpenters are coming tomorrow to rebuild bigger ones," Remus reminded him.

Echo stopped singing mid-note, put the sacks neatly to the side, and motioned to others in the room to help him pull and slide the slots from the wall. The slots came apart in sections. They slid and pulled them with careful movement, then carried them one by one out the door into the snow. Someone would be by in the morning with a sled and team to take the old cabinets to see what someone could salvage and reuse and what they could turn into firewood.

Echo went back to humming his song as he and another pulled the fifth cabinet away from the wall. He stopped with a gasp when he saw it. It was up against the wall, covered with dust. Others peeked behind the cabinet and let out a collective gasp, causing Remus to look at them with a scowl.

"Oh, dear. Oh, dear!" Echo said, bringing his fingertips to his chin nervously.

"What is it? What is going on over there?" Remus wanted to know.

Echo's eyes went wide, his mouth moving, but no words could come out. Instead, he just pointed frantically to the gap between the wall and cabinet.

"Don't be a fool! What is it?" Remus asked with frustration.

"A lost letter," Echo squeaked.

"Impossible! Move the cabinet! Let me see!"

Echo slid the cabinet out, and everyone gathered behind Remus as he looked towards the floor. It was his turn to gasp. It was indeed a yellowed envelope with a gray coating of dust. They could see someone addressed it with a blue or green crayon.

"No," Remus whispered. His immaculate record was tarnished. There had never been a lost letter. A child's wish never went unread.

"Maybe it's nothing," Echo said. "Maybe it's just a little note to say hello. Or--or a vacation letter saying they wish we were there."

Remus glared at Echo.

"A birthday card? Perhaps a resume? An invitation?" Echo

continued with hope.

"Nonsense. No one ever writes here without wanting something! It's always a wish."

Remus bent down and picked up the envelope. He shook it to break the dust free, then looked at it closely. All the others in the room crowded around him, peering over his shoulder if they could, to get a better glimpse of the lost letter.

Someone indeed addressed it in green crayon, the carefully printed handwriting belonging to a child. In big letters, right in the center, it said *Mr. Claus*. In the corner was the return address from Claire Whitfield of Deer Plains, Indiana.

"Open it. Open it," Echo said, but Remus shook his head. He was still trying to figure out how this letter ever got lost or what to do with it.

"I think we should let Nick open it," Remus finally decided out loud.

"Shall I fetch him?" Echo asked.

"No. We'll bring it to him. Everyone else, back to work! We will settle this soon enough. Nick will know what to do," Remus said, then motioned for Echo to follow him.

They bundled up in their coats, scarves, hats, and mittens. Remus put the letter in his pocket for safekeeping against the wind and snow before opening the door and trekking it to Nick's house.

Nick's home was a bit of a hike from the post office. He lived apart from most of the village in a much larger house. His door was taller than the others, his gate higher. The windows were grander and seemed brighter. Despite having only one floor, the roof stood almost as tall as the post office's two-story building.

It was cold and bitter as they walked up to Nick's path, but the twins did not mind. They were used to the cold. It was all they knew.

They glanced nervously at each other before Remus took off a mitten and knocked hard on the thick, tall, wooden door.

It was only a moment before the door opened, and they looked up at Effie, Nick's wife, smiling down at them. The smells of firewood and home-baked cookies wafted from the open door. Remus felt his nervousness easing away. Nick would know what to do. Nick could make anything better.

"Why, Remus and Echo," Effie greeted, "What a pleasant surprise. Come in. Come in."

They stamped the snow off their feet and removed their hats to show good manners as they entered the large home. They could see Nick was sitting in an oversized wingback chair by the roaring fire, a cookie in one hand, and two dogs sitting with begging eyes by his feet.

"We are so sorry to interrupt your evening," Remus began, "but something came up at the post office."

"Please, sit," Effie said, motioning to the sofa by Nick. "I'll bring out some tea."

Nick smiled at them, his blue eyes curious, as he brushed cookie crumbs from his white beard. The twins climbed onto the sofa and settled in. Nick held out a plate of cookies to them. Remus politely declined, but Echo beamed, taking one, thinking about it, then grabbing two more before Nick placed the plate back on his side table.

"Well," Nick said, his voice deep and soothing. "Something came up?"

"Oh, yes," Remus said. "It's a discrepancy of sorts at the post office."

Remus became quiet again, not knowing where to begin. He looked at Echo for help.

"Go on. Go on," Echo urged.

Remus sighed and reached into his pocket, pulling out the sealed envelope. He looked at it one last time, the lost letter that would forever blemish his impeccable system, then handed it to Nick.

"What is this?" Nick asked, reaching for his glasses.

"A lost letter," Remus admitted with a quiet voice.

"Ahhh," Nick nodded, understanding the dilemma.

Without another word spoken, Nick carefully ripped the envelope open. Effie had come back with a tray with the twins' tea on it as he read it. Nick read it once. Twice. Three times to make sure he understood. He even let out a chuckle as he read it, bringing great relief to Remus.

"What's it say? What's it say?" Echo asked innocently over his cup of tea. Remus elbowed him gently.

"Maybe it's not a wish," Echo whispered to Remus. "Perhaps we won a cruise!"

Remus rolled his eyes and shook his head, but Nick laughed at Echo's childlike imagination. He took off his glasses and carefully put the letter back into the envelope.

"No, Echo," he said. "It is indeed a wish. An old wish. And it is quite a problem that needs a solution."

"How old?" Remus asked.

"Sixty."

Echo let out a low whistle. "That's old, alright."

"But, young enough to maybe still be fulfilled," Nick smiled.

"That can't be possible," Remus said.

"Really, Remus? Look around you. Remember where you are. Anything is possible here," Nick reminded him.

"Then how do we go about solving the problem?" Remus asked.

"It's an odd wish- one that requires something I might not be capable of," Nick thought out loud. "There is only one person who can do justice to this wish."

Nick suddenly stood up, causing his dogs to jump up excitedly, tails wagging. He went by the door and pulled on his boots, dressing up for a cold walk.

"Come on, boys," he smiled down at them. "I know just the person who can handle this."

"Who, who?" Echo asked, pulling his hat back on and down over his ears.

"Edil. Let's bring the letter to Edil. He'll know what to do."

Remus felt confused but would not question Nick. Everyone respected Nick in the village. He was smart and thoughtful. If Nick said Edil was the solution to the lost letter, Remus would not question that. He trusted whatever idea Nick had going on in his head.

Nick towered over Remus and Echo as they walked back to the village with Jingles and Bella, Nick's dogs, playfully circling them. It was another long walk as Edil's house was at the edge of the village, perched close to the ice ridge. Edil built it there because he liked to look down into the valley.

They walked through the streets quietly, only shouting a greeting to people who were coming or going to the village tavern. The buildings became fewer and fewer, the houses more and more spaced apart. Finally, they came to Edil's house.

It hid in a snowdrift, but a cleared path led to the front door. A decorative wreath hung on the door, encircling a small, red-stained window. Remus nodded to Echo to knock. They could hear shuffling as someone neared the door. Then, Edil answered.

Edil smiled with a look of confusion, seeing the twins, Nick, and two dogs outside his house. It was not typical for him and his wife to have visitors late in the evening.

"Hello," he greeted as his smile turned into a worried frown. "Is everything alright? Did something happen?"

"No, no, Edil," Nick said with reassurance. "We just came across a slight problem, and I think you might be of great help."

"A problem?"

"It's nothing, really. I wouldn't call it a problem," Remus said, finding his nerves getting unsettled again. "It's a hiccup."

"A burp!" Echo joined in as Remus rolled his eyes.

Edil glanced at Echo and returned to smiling. He opened his door even wider. Nick's dogs ran in, noses to the ground.

"Do you mind?" Nick asked.

"No. Please, do come in," Edil insisted.

Nick bent down to fit through the small doorway, and Remus and Echo followed. They could hear Edil's wife, Lottie, laughing in the kitchen at the intrusion of the playful dogs. Edil insisted they remove their coats and scarves and hats and mittens to make themselves comfortable. Being taller than the rest of the village, Nick did not quite fit on Edil's chairs or sofa, but he did his best. He was used to it. He sat on a wooden dining chair, his knees folded up by his chest.

Lottie came in, her voice dotted with giggles as she wiped her hands on her apron. "How good to see you all," she exclaimed. "Can I get you anything? Tea? Cookies? I just got some fresh gingersnaps from the bakery this morning."

They declined the tea, but Nick could never turn down a good cookie. She headed back into the kitchen, only to reappear within minutes with a plate of gingersnaps and two meaty bones leftover from dinner for Jingles and Bella.

Lottie sat on the couch next to Edil, and both of them looked at Nick, then to Remus and Echo.

"So, this hiccup," Edil finally said.

"Yes," Nick nodded, reaching into his pocket and pulling out the envelope. "It's a lost letter."

"Oh," Lottie said, her eyes opening wide. "I never thought that was possible."

"Trust me," Remus said, his head hanging in shame. "Neither did I."

"I want you to read it, Edil. I think you might be the one that can handle it with the care it needs," Nick said.

Edil nodded, taking the letter from him. He pulled out the letter and read it with Lottie's eyes on the letter as well. Echo interrupted them by clearing his throat.

"Ah, yes," Nick said, understanding the look on Echo's face. "Perhaps you can read it out loud, Edil?"

Edil nodded again in agreement, bringing his eyes back to the top of the letter. He glanced at the date, written in the same green crayon as the front of the envelope: *December 1st, 1953*.

Edil sighed, then read the letter with a crisp voice.

"Dear Santa,

My name is Claire Whitfield, and I am 9 years old. But you probably already know that. Christmas is coming soon, and I have been a very good girl all year. I help my mother with the chores, always listen to my father, try very hard not to fight with my brother, and get good grades in school.

I know most little girls want a Tiny Tears Doll or a Mrs. Potato Head set, but I truly and really want an Elf. I just love Elves. I think they are the cutest things ever. Would you be able to send me an Elf from the North Pole? I promise to take very good care of it. I will love it forever and ever and make sure it is very happy. I will feed it and make sure it has comfortable clothes and shoes. I even have the perfect doll bed that he can sleep in!

Please, Santa? If I get an Elf for Christmas, I promise to be good to it. And I'll be a good girl forever and ever.

Thank you, Santa!

Merry Christmas!

Love,

Claire Whitfield"

Lottie giggled, and Nick chuckled. Remus looked confused, but Echo smiled. Edil, however, fumed.

"She wanted an elf for Christmas? Like a pet? Like a child wants a puppy dog or a pony? That's- that's—"

"That's a child," Lottie said with amusement.

"No! That's not normal!" Edil insisted. "And what am I supposed to do with this?"

"It is an unanswered wish," Nick reminded him.

"And? It's been unanswered for sixty years. Do you suppose I am to be wrapped in a big red bow come next Christmas and placed under some old lady's tree? Because I don't know how we are to give a seventy-year-old lady an elf on Christmas morning!"

"If she's even still alive!" Echo chimed in with a big, innocent smile on his face. The room grew quiet, and Echo realized what he said, his smile fading. "Oh, wait. That's sad."

"Well, that solves that," Edil said, folding the letter. "We just let it be. Mistakes happen. No one will be the wiser."

"No," Nick said, snapping his fingers with an idea. "We head over to the Records Office."

"It's closed," Edil said.

"Well then, we will go to Pell's home and ask him to open it."

"And then what?"

"Step by step, Edil. Step by step," Nick smiled. "First, we see if Claire is still with us. If not, it is what you said; a mistake. We let it be."

"And if she is still with us?" Edil asked.

"Step by step," Nick winked. He stood up, needing to stretch his joints after sitting in the tiny chair. Then he clapped his hands together and rubbed them. "Who's up for another walk on this fine night?"

"More walking," Echo groaned.

Once again, they piled on their winter garments and bundled up. This time Edil and Lottie joined them out into the night. Jingles and Bella abandoned their bones, excited for another brisk walk.

The walk to Pell's house was not that far. His house connected to a large storefront. If the window were not covered in frost and snow, one could read the painted gold letters that said *Records Office*. That window was dark, but the house windows were glowing.

A quick rap on the door bought Pell out. And just like Nick, then Edil, he looked surprised to see the company on his doorstep. Nick explained quickly that they needed to get into the Records Office, and they required Pell's help to locate someone.

Pell nodded and went back into his house only to grab a shawl, put on boots, and take the office keys. Then, they followed him next door.

Once inside the Records Office, Remus and Echo helped Pell light the lanterns and start a small fire in the wood-burning stove for warmth. Pell went behind the counter, adjusted his glasses, then looked up at Nick with a smile that meant he was all business.

"Now, how can I be of help, Nick?" he asked.

"We need to find a child- only she is no longer a child," Nick started. "Her name is Claire Whitfield, and she is from Deer Plains, Indiana. But, this was back in 1953."

Pell stopped writing the information Nick was giving him and looked up over his glasses.

"A lost letter?" he guessed.

"Unfortunately, yes," Nick nodded.

"Well, that is a tough one," Pell said as he looked back down at his slip of paper and started writing with his quill again. "Claire Whitfield. Deer Plains. Indiana. Anything else?"

"Just tell us what you can."

"Very well then," Pell said. He turned to the shelves behind him. Like Remus, Pell had his efficient system to keep track of all the children in the world. But, instead of files, he used books. He developed his method of cross-references with these books a long time ago. They trained very few select people in the village to follow Pell's system.

The books were massive tomes lined over twenty feet of shelving from ceiling to floor behind Pell's counter. Pell had steps on wheels that could pull and push back and forth so he or his assistants could get to the very top shelf. Nick, the brothers, Edil, and Lottie all watched as Pell busied himself. Pell would glance at the paper where he wrote the information, then walk along the shelves, fingering the spines and muttering to himself quietly.

He pulled out one tome and carried it to the counter. It made a loud thud when he put it down. He flipped through the pages, nodded, then made a notation on his paper.

"She moved by 15," he said to no one in particular. "Her father relocated. Let's see…."

He was off again, looking for another book. This time, he needed the stairs to climb up to a high shelf. He brought the second book back to the counter and laid it next to the first one. He once again flipped around through the old pages of the thick book.

"Married at 20. No longer a Whitfield. We are now looking for Claire McIntyre."

Once again, Pell wrote this down and looked among the shelves, following a code only he knew. Edil shook his head, still not understanding, and took a seat on a small sofa in the corner. He still did not know what ideas Nick could have if they found this Claire. He ran his fingers through his dark, shaggy hair and sighed.

"Last one. This should do it," Pell announced, lugging the last book to the counter. "Gator Springs, Texas. That's where she is."

"She's still with us?" Remus asked.

"Oh yes. Very much so. Mother to three children. Grandmother to seven. She's a retired nurse but actively volunteers," he read out loud from the book.

"Volunteers doing what? Cleaning cages at the Elf Rescue Shelter?" Edil said with sarcasm.

"Edil, shush," Lottie frowned.

"I'm sorry, but where exactly are we going with this, Nick? What was all this for?"

"Well," Nick said, stroking his beard as a grin appeared on his face, "I thought perhaps you could answer her wish."

Edil looked up at him, eyebrows raised. He threw his hands in the air and shook his head, meaning he still had no idea what Nick wanted to do.

"You can tell her about the elves," Nick said.

"Tell her? Tell her how? Tell her what?"

"Perhaps in a letter," he suggested. "A well-written letter that will tell Claire where you came from and how this delightful town began. Tell her your story. Tell her you are really not an elf. Not a pet, but a person- a wonderful person. And how you all are amazing people here in this village."

"Now there's an idea," Remus agreed as Echo nodded.

"That sounds lovely," Lottie said. "Can you do it?"

"A letter? That's it?" Edil asked.

"Nothing more. We can't give Claire a pet elf," Nick chuckled. "And her letter will no longer be unanswered."

"I don't know," Edil sighed. It was all so overwhelming and even a bit confusing. They always lived a private life.

Nick nodded, seeing the look in Edil's eyes. He sat next to him, squeezing himself on the sofa, and patted Edil's shoulder to comfort him.

"They sing songs about the reindeer and snowmen," Nick finally spoke. "They write poems and myths and legends about me, but it should be about you- all of you. Perhaps now it's your turn."

"The letter will no longer be lost," Remus reminded Edil with a smile.

"Can you do it? Can you?" Echo wanted to know. "Can you tell her your story? Our story?"

Edil rose from the sofa and walked to the small, iron, potbelly stove. He crossed his arms to give himself more warmth. Everyone remained silent to give him time to think. Finally, he sighed. Then he spoke.

"Well, there are things I've been told. And there are things I remember."

Part One: Things Told

Johan's Journey

The one, lone road into the small town of Bluster was covered with hard, packed, dirty ice and snow. The street was lined on both sides with small huts, cabins, and shacks. Bluster was a small village way up in the northern part of the world where people mainly kept to themselves, went about their lives, and braved harsh, cold winters and mild summers. There was no fall or spring.

On the day Johan arrived in Bluster, it was unseasonably sunny. The glare bouncing off the ice and snow caused Johan to squint from atop his seat in his sleigh. He kept the reins of his large, black draft horse loose in his hands and let him walk at ease. Johan was not in a rush. If anything, Johan was apprehensive. His stomach was a mess of broken knots.

It was Johan's first time away from the comforts of his village, which was a good five days ride from the east. It was his first time out on his own. He had gone on many hunting and fishing trips with his father, but his father had told him he must make this trip independently this time.

"You're a man now," his father had told him. "It is time for you to start your own life and have the comforts and happiness of any other normal man."

Normal man. Those words echoed in Johan's mind over and over. He knew his father wanted that for him. His mother too. They tried their best to ignore Johan's small stature and ignore the staring eyes and occasional taunts of others. They tried to raise him as if that was what he was--a normal man. Aside from the physical appearance of Johan, they succeeded.

Johan was smart and inventive. From an early age, he could piece items together that would help him live the average life. A small fishing net attached to a stick helped him reach things on high shelves. An old wooden crate turned upside down gave him height at the table. He modified a boy's saddle to make riding more comfortable and manageable for himself and even taught horses to kneel before him so he could easily mount and dismount.

When he came to Bluster's only tavern, Johan pulled the reins to make the horse stop. People that were walking by stopped and watched as he stood up and unwrapped himself from blankets. He stretched a bit, then leaned over to the side where he unlatched a set of steps that unfolded down to the ground with a clatter- another one of his modifications to make getting in and out of the sleigh easier.

As he climbed down, people whispered to each other. They gossiped quietly behind their hands and in each other's ears. Johan avoided looking at them. He concentrated on tying his horse to a post, trying to ignore the knots in his stomach and the burning sensation in his cheeks and ears. He tried to remember that this was something his parents wanted for him. Something they considered a miracle. Something they never imagined would happen for their son.

He headed into the tavern, pushing the heavy door that was lopsided and made of splintered slabs of wood. It was dark, and it took a few seconds for Johan's eyes to adjust before he could see it was nothing special. There are just a few tables and chairs with a bench here and there and a fire going in a large hearth.

Whatever boisterous conversations were flying about before Johan entered ceased to exist. Everything became quiet as all eyes were on him. The only sounds were from the fire crackling and some sort of stew bubbling in a pot.

Johan began to regret the trip. He regretted not questioning his father's reasons. He was not a normal man. He was nothing but a speck of a man compared to the men in the tavern. Men that leered at him with drunken eyes and snarling grins.

One man slowly rose from his table and walked up to Johan. He eyed him up and down as Johan swallowed hard, trying to keep his stomach under control. Then, he thrust his large hand in Johan's face, palm open.

"Johan," he said with a gruff voice. He did not have to ask. He knew who he was. He was expecting him. It was not every day a man only as high as his hip came into Bluster.

Johan stared at the man's hand for a second before placing his small one in it. They shook in a formal greeting, and Johan's nerves quieted down.

"Come," the man said, leading him back to the table where three other younger men were sitting. "Please, sit."

Johan climbed up onto a chair as the man waved to the tavern keeper to bring over fresh steins of ale for their table. The man waited for him to settle before speaking.

"I am Frederick," he said. "Amelia's father. These are my sons; her brothers Antoine, Henrick, and Willem."

Johan nodded politely with each introduction. The three sons were looking at him with just as much curiosity as the bystanders that were outside. But their curiosity was different. Kinder. Nothing was leering and gossipy in their eyes.

"I hope the trip was an easy one for you," Frederick continued.

"Yes. Yes, it was. Thank you," Johan said.

"You know, when I first met your father last spring, it took a lot of convincing that this was the right thing. We spent many late nights here in this tavern at this very table discussing the fate of our children. It's a hard world out there. Even harder for you and my Amelia, beingdifferent."

"Well, sir, I am going to do my best to do right by her," Johan said quietly.

"We wanted to meet you first before we go ahead with this. My boys and I are very protective of Amelia. She's a tiny thing, fragile thing," Frederick explained. "I need to know that aside from not being a tall man, you are otherwise perfect for her. She's quite bright. She needs someone who will encourage her smarts and stimulate her thoughts. I will not give a dowry to just any fool who comes along."

"No, sir. Of course not, sir."

"Your father tells me you are a smart man yourself and that you are hardworking, tough of mind and spirit. That you can provide Amelia with all the comforts of a warm, loving home."

"I am. I can."

"Then tell me. Tell us, Johan," Frederick said, leaning over the table. "Tell us about you and how you live your life."

Johan was taken back. He knew what he was getting into when

he left for Bluster. His father had told him he was going to Bluster because of a young girl named Amelia, a very similar girl who was his only chance of ever having a wife, a home, and maybe even a family.

His father told him he would meet Amelia's father first at the tavern when he arrived at Bluster. His mother told him to be polite and not to worry. It was tradition for a bride's father to want to know his future son-in-law and make sure he was worthy of the dowry. However, nothing could prepare Johan for the intimidation he felt as Frederick stared at him, waiting for him to tell him about himself.

It was not a menacing stare that Frederick looked at him with. Just a probing one, causing Johan to feel once again nervous. Johan let out a scared little chuckle, then took a long drink from his stein.

"I'm sorry," he finally said. "I'm just a bit nervous. I'm not sure what scares me more, getting married or you."

Frederick broke out in a big grin as his sons laughed. His eyes suddenly became kinder. He leaned back, more relaxed.

"Tell us anything," he said. "I want to make sure you were not coddled. As fragile as our Amelia is, we never coddled her."

Johan shook his head and told the first story that popped into his head. He spoke of a time he and his father were fishing on an icy lake. Johan mentioned how large the fish was and how he struggled to bring it in without the help of his father. He spoke of working hard to plant, then harvest his father's modest crops, how he had a knack with horses and trained them to kneel for him and how he loved to ride them. He felt mighty and tall from a horse's back.

He kept talking. Johan did not know where all his words were coming from. He wondered if it was nerves that kept him talking or the ale. Frederick and his sons never interrupted. They just listened with smiles on their faces, entertained by Johan's stories.

Finally, Johan's stein was empty, and he realized he had been talking for almost an hour. He blushed with embarrassment and hoped Frederick did not think he was a bore or a braggart.

Frederick glanced at his sons, and they all nodded knowingly to each other.

"Looks like you are getting married today," Frederick said to Johan. "Come. Get your sleigh and follow us."

This time Johan's stomach slammed down, and his heart skipped a beat. *Married*. The whole reason he was there. He had to admit to himself that a small part of him hoped it would not happen. He was quite comfortable with his life at home with his parents. He never imagined any girl would marry him. That any father would see him as a fit husband for their daughter. He never saw anyone of his kind, so he never thought there might be a girl out there with a similar stature as his. He thought he was the only one. For the longest time, he was.

It was not until his father came back from a trading trip in Bluster with exciting news. There was indeed a small girl who was born with whatever Johan was born with. Like Johan, she, too, had not grown past childhood height. Then his father made the most shocking announcement: this girl was to be Johan's bride.

Frederick and his sons had come to the tavern by horseback, so Johan followed them in his sleigh. They made small talk as they rode away from the village and headed to Frederick's home. They talked about the weather, commented on each other's horses, and predicted the future of crops.

When Frederick's home came into view, Johan was surprised. It was a rather large home, built mainly from stone. A man rushed out of the house, bowed slightly to Frederick and his sons before taking the horses' reins as they dismounted. Johan realized he was a servant. He did not know his bride came from wealth.

"Come on," Frederick said, waving at him to come down from the sleigh. "We've had the bishop here since morning. I suspect he's half crocked by now."

Johan took a deep breath before climbing down and standing next to Frederick. Frederick looked down at him and once again offered him a friendly smile and patted him on the shoulder.

"It'll be fine, son," he assured him. "We are all nervous here."

That made Johan feel better. He followed Frederick into the house, their footsteps echoing on the stone floor in the entryway. Johan had never seen a home that had an entryway before--a room just for stamping snow off boots and hanging cloaks up to dry. He could see a staircase that went up to another floor. There were also two separate doorways, one to each side of him. Another door was across from him that led to the back of the house.

Frederick walked to the door on the left and opened it. Johan could see shadows from a fireplace dancing about. He peeked in and immediately saw her. Amelia. His bride.

Amelia was indeed small like him. She was shorter than him by a couple of inches, but that was not the first thing he noticed about her. It was her eyes. They were a brilliant green that sparkled in the firelight. She was busy talking to someone who Johan guessed was her mother. She had not noticed that her father had arrived with her groom.

He watched her as she smiled and laughed. Her hands were fluttering about to emphasize what she was saying. Occasionally, she touched her brown hair, which was gathered neatly into an ornate, crocheted net at the back of her neck.

Johan liked her immediately. He could feel a sense of ease come over him. Only minutes before, he could not imagine himself married. Now, he could not imagine never having this animated, lively girl in his life.

Frederick cleared his throat, and Amelia stopped what she was saying mid-sentence. Her eyes grew wide, and her hand covered her mouth lightly before she let out a little giggle when she saw Johan.

Her father made quick introductions. He introduced his wife, who looked as if she was about to cry, and the bishop, who seemed to pass the day away with a jug of wine. There were some other people in the room, mostly neighbors and business associates of Frederick's, but Johan faded them out. He was focused entirely on Amelia.

"Perhaps you two would like to go for a walk," Frederick suggested. "Before we decide to go on with this. Maybe Amelia can show you the dowry?"

"No need," Johan said as Amelia smiled. "I mean for the dowry. No need to show me the dowry. But, if you would like to go for a walk…."

"That would be lovely," she said, her smile matching his.

Johan watched as she exited the room, back into the main entryway. He felt Frederick's hand upon his shoulder.

"She's the one with the final say, Johan," he said. "I will not marry her off if she doesn't want to. I am not marrying her off because we have to. It's because she wants to. Just trying to do right by my daughter."

Johan nodded with understanding, then followed her into the entryway, where she was wrapping a cloak around her. She just smiled gently and motioned for him to go with her out the back door.

At first, their walk was silent. Johan let Amelia lead the way along a path. They passed a pen with some pigs in it, grunting as they walked by. Another pen had horses in it, including his draft horse.

"Yours?" she finally said about the horse.

"Yes. That's Onyx."

"He's so big. How ever do you harness him?"

"He kneels for me."

"Does he now? I would love to see that!"

Johan let out a low whistle. Onyx perked up his ears and trotted over to them. His large head bent down as he playfully butted Johan. Johan rubbed Onyx's soft, velvety muzzle for a minute and smiled over at Amelia.

"Onyx, down," he commanded, with his right hand out, palm facing down, then lowering in a swift motion. Onyx immediately backed up from the wooden posts that corralled him in before he slowly but surely brought himself down with his front legs bent under him. Johan could not help but smile with pride.

"Good boy. Onyx, up," he continued. This time, he flipped his hand, so his palm was facing up, then raised it just a touch. Again, the horse followed the command and pushed up from the ground.

"Incredible," Amelia clapped. "Clever trick! You taught him that?"

Johan smiled sheepishly and shrugged with modesty. He wished he had a treat for Onyx in his pocket. He made a mental note to remember to bring him an apple or carrot from the house later in the day.

They continued to walk, climbing up a hill and ending at the stable. Even the stable was large by usual standards. It was larger than the small cabin Johan grew up in. He frowned, looked at it, and then turned to look at the large stone house at the bottom of the hill.

"Come. I'll show you the dowry," Johan heard Amelia say as she pushed the stable door open. He turned back around and followed her in.

In the middle of the stable was a pile of items unlike he had ever seen. He walked around it in amazement and fingered items here and there. There were bolts of fabric, sacks of seeds, tools, a plow, some furniture, blankets, pots, pans, and on and on. It had everything a home would need to get started. Everything for farming. Anything for hunting. He and Amelia would want for nothing for a long, long time.

"My father tells me that your father had purchased some land for us," she said. "It was all part of the agreement; the land, the supplies, and so forth."

Johan remained speechless.

"It's a bit much, I agree," she laughed. "I am not sure we have enough room on your sleigh."

Johan shook his head.

"No worries. I suppose we could take my troika? Tie it onto the back of your sleigh and tie up some items on it? Do you think that would work?"

Johan looked over at her troika. It was a small sled built for leisure riding in the snow. He nodded.

"I didn't need all of this," he finally spoke. "I would have taken care of you without any of this."

Amelia smiled as he walked back to the doorway and once again looked down at the house. Amelia was born to wealth and privilege. He did not doubt that she spent her nights in a warm, ornate bed and woke up to clothes laid out for her and breakfast cooked for her. He could tell by how she spoke and how she carried herself that she was a girl of education and culture.

"I can't give you that," he said, motioning to the house. "I can't give you this. I am just a simple man with simple means. I am a farmer. A hunter. The house I will build for you will be small, made of wood and mud."

"Will it be warm?" she asked.

"Very."

"Will our farm be bountiful?"

"God willing," he replied.

"Are you a good marksman?" she asked.

"Quite good," he admitted.

She walked over to him and stood by his side. She, too, looked down at the house she had called home all her life.

"I never asked to be born here," she said. "I never asked to be of wealth or to have servants. I never asked to be born small either. All I ask for is a normal life."

"What is normal, really?" Johan asked.

"Perhaps there is no such thing," Amelia suggested.

Johan glanced down at her hand and smiled. He could not believe that such a stranger could feel so comforting, so right, standing at his side. Johan never thought he would see the day when another adult would be equal to his height. He could look directly at her and not up at her. He gently reached over and took her hand in his. Her hand felt soft and warm.

"This feels normal," he said to her quietly.

"I think you and I are going to be good friends for a long, long time," she smiled.

White Out

The wedding ceremony of Johan and Amelia was immediately following their walk. It was a short and simple union performed by the bishipin front of the large fireplace in the main sitting room. Only a handful of people stood about to witness the vows, all of them Amelia's family and friends.

Amelia's mother spent most of the time stifling the sobs that kept catching in her throat and dabbing her eyes with a square of lace cloth. Amelia's brothers' faces twisted, lips pursed, jaws clenched to keep from letting their emotions get the better of them. They could never imagine that their little sister would get a chance to be a wife and be taken from them.

Frederick stood with pride, having faith in himself and Johan that the right thing was being done for Amelia. She needed this. She wanted this. She deserved this. Like all little girls, she grew up dreaming of a home of her own, a husband, and maybe even children. It was hard for him to let go, but he knew that Johan coming into their lives was a sign that she must move on, and Johan alone could give her the life she always wanted.

Johan could not believe he was someone's husband. More than that, he could not believe how comfortable he felt with that title. Amelia's green eyes constantly looked at him with confidence and happiness, her smile soothing and knowing. He did not know someone could make him feel that way.

After the ceremony, they gathered in the dining hall for a feast to celebrate the nuptials. For the first time all day, Johan's stomach growled with hunger when he could smell the roasted meats, simmering sauces, baked bread, and boiled vegetables. He had never seen such dishes or knew such spices and flavors existed.

It was a festive table with laughter as they told stories by candlelight. They poured wine and ale, men became boisterous, and servers brought out more food. The celebration went on into the night.

When morning came, things were somber. As excited as Johan and Amelia were to start their journey as husband and wife back to Johan's village, the rest of the family was sad.

Her brothers had packed up Johan's sled high, with room for two piglets crated in the back. Amelia's troika was also packed and covered with burlap to protect the goods and items under it. They hitched the troika to the back of the sled. Onyx was harnessed to the front.

Johan unlatched his makeshift ladder of steps and helped Amelia climb up. Together they settled themselves with blankets around them. Amelia and her family cried out farewells and promises of visits and letters with bittersweet waves and kisses blown. Johan clicked his tongue and gave the reins a light snap, letting Onyx know it was time to go.

They rode towards Bluster, a sudden awkwardness between the two. They would glance at each other, smile, and let out the occasional laugh.

"Are you sure you are alright with this?" Johan asked.

"I could not be happier," she insisted.

She wrapped her shawl tighter around her to block out the cold and looped her arm in his. She could feel him straighten up with pride when she did this. Her husband had a handsome face with dark hair and brown eyes. She liked his smile best. It always seemed to start as an unsure smile asking for encouragement, and when he found it, she loved how his smile grew strong and brave. It became a proud smile.

It was when they entered the town that Amelia felt dread. She never did like going to the town and usually avoided it. She did not like the staring eyes or gossiping tongues and hated the occasional comments or teasing taunts.

Her first morning as a wife was no different. Because there were now two of them, the stares seemed even more intense. People laughed and pointed. She could see that Johan was trying hard to remain focused on the road in front of him, his jaw clenched, his eyebrows furrowed. He was trying to block out the people of the village that had gathered on walkways and in door frames.

"Look at the wee little bride and groom!" a woman shouted. "Have you ever seen such a sight?"

"Can it be? I've heard rumors, but has Frederick's daughter found a matching-sized suitor?" another woman giggled.

Their sled became surrounded, and people's curiosity got the best of them. Names were called, and words were slung, causing Johan and Amelia's hearts to sink. Their happiness had vanished.

"She's a bride now, ain't she?" a man laughed. "Is it not custom to get a kiss from the bride?"

"Good luck it is!" another man joined in. "Though not sure how much luck a little bride like that would bring."

"Do you reckon he'd mind?"

Amelia yelped as the man grabbed her arm and tried to climb up into the sled and lean in for a kiss.

"OFF!" Johan yelled, not knowing where his bellow came from. He stood up and lashed at the man with a crop he had but never needed before.

Laughter ensued as the man fell back away from the sled. The cheering and taunting continued as Amelia and Johan grew red with embarrassment. Onyx continued to trot down the road, never stopping. Eventually, as they neared the end of Bluster, the crowd fell away, and they left them behind.

Bluster became smaller and smaller behind them in the distance, but they could not shake the incident. Johan grew angry. He was used to teases and jokes about his height. It always hurt, but he was taught to shake it off and move on. This time, it was different. He did not like that Amelia was the brunt of their jokes and laughter.

He looked over at his wife, her eyes downcast and red-rimmed from tears. She let out a sniffle. The way she looked hurt him more than any time he was ever teased.

"Are you alright?" he asked gently, the anger fading away into sadness.

"I never did like going to town," she admitted.

"I'm sorry."

They rode on for miles in silence. Snow began to drift from the grey sky. Amelia pulled her shawl up and around her head.

"Is it like that in your village?" she finally asked.

"Like what?"

"The people. Do they point and stare?"

"Yes," he admitted. "Sometimes worse."

"Oh," she said quietly.

"It'll be like that no matter where we go," Johan reminded her sadly. "We will always be some source of entertainment. People will always see us without getting to know us."

It was quiet again for a bit before she spoke.

"How long to your village?"

"Five days," he told her.

"At least we will have five days in peace. Just you and me," Amelia smiled. Johan could still see the sadness behind her smile.

Johan gazed out into the distance. There was nothing before them but the long ride home with snow on the ground and grey-white skies above them. Everything was flat.

"I wish it weren't like that," he mumbled to himself. "I wish I could take you to a place where people would leave us alone so we could live in peace."

A wind came in, cold and rigid. It blew Johan's hair into his eyes. Amelia reached up and brushed it away gently.

"Me too," she agreed.

Another blast of wind came, harder than the first, rocking them in their seats. Onyx let out a whinny, breaking them out of their sad thoughts. They looked in the direction the wind was coming from. The light snow flurries were becoming more intense, and the flakes larger.

In the distance, they could see a dark wall building down from the sky. More and more gusts of wind and flakes rushed around them as they watched this wall move towards them.

"Johan?"

The incident with Bluster was quickly forgotten. Never had Johan seen such a furious change in the weather. A storm was bearing down on them quickly.

"Get in the back," he told Amelia. "Under the covering!"

The wind was now howling and whipping. Snow was not only coming from the skies but was being blown up from the ground as well. With incredible speed and strength, the storm was upon them, enveloping them in blinding snow. Amelia took one last look at Onyx, who was now nothing but a dark shadow amidst the swirls of white. She climbed over their seat and lifted the flap of the covering to get some protection from the icy wind.

"Stay warm!" Johan hollered over the loud wind. Amelia sat down on some pillows and a mat, gathering blankets around her. She could hear the piglets squealing with terror. The sled's covering whipped and rippled as the sled itself rocked from the wind and the movement as Johan continued to urge Onyx further.

Amelia suddenly missed the comforts and securities of her big, stone house and her family. Gone was the excitement and sense of adventure. The open tundra left them unprotected against the beast of nature. She had never been so frightened. She closed her eyes and prayed that the storm would not get the best of them. It horrified her to think of freezing to death in the middle of nowhere.

The flap opened, and Johan climbed in. He blew into his hands and rubbed them together before crawling over next to her and getting under blankets.

"Can't see anything out there," he told her. "It's nothing but white. A complete whiteout. Ain't never seen anything like it."

Amelia could feel the sled still rocking and lurching forward.

"Are we still moving?"

"I trust Onyx," he nodded. "He'll sense the way. He'll bring us home. Or at least to safety."

He rummaged around near him and pulled a basket towards them. Opening it, he saw leftovers from their wedding feast packed neatly.

"Might as well have a bite," he said, offering her some bread. "Get comfortable. Who knows how long the storm will last."

"Where did it come from?"

"I don't know. There were no signs of a storm. Came out of nowhere."

With the wind howling and the snow pelting the covering of the sled, they shared a meal and took comfort in trading stories and just talking with each other. Onyx continued to trudge on into the cold, white nothingness. It was hours before they succumbed to the rocking and fell asleep among a pile of blankets and pillows.

The silence woke Johan up. He sat up and rubbed his eyes. He looked around him, realizing that the sun was peeking through the flap, and the wind and snow were no longer lashing at them. He could feel that the sled was still in motion. Onyx had walked through the night.

He gently nudged Amelia awake before climbing out and back into his seat. He grabbed the reins and pulled Onyx to a stop, knowing his poor horse needed a break. Looking around, he saw there was not much to see, as usual- just white, flat land, and blue skies. He tried to judge where they were by the position of the sun.

He climbed down to walk around to the back of the sled and made sure everything was still intact, and the troika survived the storm. Everything looked good. He grabbed Onyx's feedbag and walked to his horse.

Onyx nickered and nudged him as he scratched him behind his ears. Johan looked again around as Amelia came out of the sled, shielding her eyes from the sun's glare upon the snow.

"Where did you bring us?" Johan whispered to his horse.

"Everything all right?" Amelia called out.

"Fine. Just fine," he assured her.

"Where are we?"

"A little more north than we should be, I think."

"You think? I thought your horse knew his way home."

"Or somewhere safe," he reminded her. "He most likely took a safer course. Shouldn't be a problem."

Amelia climbed down from the sleigh and walked over to Johan and Onyx. She could not help but giggle at Johan's confused look as he continued to search the horizon for signs of direction.

"I trust him," he said. "Onyx has never failed me."

"Then I trust him too," she smiled, patting Onyx.

Amelia walked around, mainly to stretch. She looked out, seeing nothing. No hills or forest. No mountains or lakes. She let out a sigh and laughed.

"What?" Johan asked. "What is it?"

"Oh, just not exactly how I thought married life would start."

Johan shook his head and laughed with her.

"They said marriage would be an adventure," she giggled.

"Well, it can't get any worse than this, right?" he said.

He put his arm around her shoulders, and together they looked into the bleak distance.

"Right," she agreed. "It can only get better."

SHADOW

Johan did not want to admit it to Amelia, but the snowstorm threw off his sense of direction. He knew they were miles off course and way more north than they ever should have been, but every time he turned Onyx south, both he and the horse would become disoriented. He would think they had headed south again, relax on the reins, enjoy the ride with his wife, and then realize that they somehow circled and headed north.

Even though he did not want to admit it, Amelia could sense something was wrong, but she bravely trusted her new husband and horse. For two days following the storm, she ignored the occasional bewildered look on Johan's face. She just submerged herself in the role of a supportive wife.

She rode by his side, no matter how cold or windy. She sang songs with him and told stories, both real and fairy tales, to help pass the time. Occasionally, she would bring out the Bible gifted to them from the bishop who married them. She would read aloud from the pages.

Before the sun would set, Johan would pull a tired Onyx to a stop, and Amelia would help set up camp. She tried to keep a home for them as best as she could with just a sled and troika. The piglets needed tending to, their crate cleaned out, and some room to run around in the snow, and Onyx needing feeding. They built a small campfire so she could heat some leftovers from the feast for supper. Then, snow would melt over the fire in a pot to wash hands, faces, and dishes.

Just before they would climb into the little makeshift bed in the sled, Johan would put the fire out with snow. Huddled together for warmth, they would spend the darkness of the night under layers of blankets, sleeping away until morning.

Many crisp nights and cold, bleak days passed them. Amelia was packing away their items into the sled, and Johan was tending the fire when she noticed how little food was left in the basket. She took a quiet count of the few pieces of meat, the stale bread, some cheese, and a small jar of jam that was more than half empty. If they sacrificed, they might make the food stretch for another three, maybe four days, and that did not include the crate of root vegetables and the sacks of coffee, sugar, and flour that were packed up. The trip to Johan's village was only supposed to take five days, and she knew they were lost, despite Johan never saying it out loud.

She looked around into the darkness. She knew what was out there- more bare tundra. The same thing that they had been traveling through since they left Bluster. They had not passed a single bush or tree nor another living thing. There were no signs of game to be hunted or even a lone cabin that could have offered warmth and food for a night or two.

She decided not to think about it anymore. What will come will come. She had to believe that something would lead their way. She had to have faith that they would not freeze to death or starve to death. If she lost her faith, she just might go mad.

Once again, as they did the nights before, they settled in for a long night's sleep. The nights were getting longer and longer, the sun rising later and later. There was nothing to do but sleep it away.

Not long after they fell asleep, Onyx let out a nervous whinny and stamped his hoof on the icy ground. Johan half-heard it in his dreams but did not awake. He turned to his side, pulling the blanket up over his head. Somewhere in his foggy sleep, he heard Onyx whinny again. This time, the piglets squealed and thrashed about in their wooden crate, bringing Johan to the surface of reality. He sat up and rubbed his eyes.

He could tell it was still nighttime. From the silvery light that shone in through the flap, he guessed it was a full moon. Johan heard Onyx outside the sled, restless. Amelia slowly sat up next to him, her head tilted with curiosity.

"What is it?" she asked.

Johan shook his head, not sure what caused their animals to stir up. Onyx continued to stamp his hoof and nickered, and the pigs would not stop squealing. Then, they heard it.

"Was that—" Amelia began, but Johan cut her off with his finger to his lips. Together, they listened carefully for another moment.

It came again. Somewhere, in the distance, a lone howl. It sent chills up Johan's spine and caused Amelia's eyes to fly open with concern. It was a sorrowful sound.

They jumped up and climbed outside to their seat. Standing there, Amelia and Johan looked around. The full moon reflected off the snow and ice, giving the night an eerie, shining glow. On their right, in the distance, they spotted him.

The wolf was just a speck of a shadow against the sliver night, but they could make him out. He sat there and seemed to watch them for a minute or two. No one moved. Johan and Amelia could not speak. They watched as the wolf lifted his head, pointing his snout to the moon, and let out another howl. The cold wind seemed to carry it across the distance, making him sound closer than he was.

"What do we do?" Amelia asked with a whisper.

"I suppose we keep an eye on him. Perhaps he will move along."

As if the wolf could hear him and understand him, he let out another long howl. Then, from the darkness behind the animal, two more wolf shapes appeared. They sat next to the first one, appearing smaller than him. Together, the three of them howled as if to call more of their pack.

"Perhaps we should move along?" Amelia suggested.

Johan nodded. They quickly climbed down to get Onyx hitched to put some distance between themselves and the wolves. When they climbed back up and settled in their seats, they noticed the three wolves were joined by four more.

"That's not good," Johan muttered under his breath. He clicked his tongue but held Onyx back a little. Johan did not want him to run and give the wolves a chase. He just hoped that if they rode away calmly and quietly, the wolves would lose interest.

They rode for a bit and could no longer see the wolves as the darkness grew over them. Onyx seemed to calm down and stopped fighting the urge to run. Johan and Amelia breathed a sigh of relief and joked about what could come next on their journey.

"Why don't you get some sleep?" Johan told her. "Might as well ride through the night. Get some more distance under our belts."

"I'm wide awake now. I could keep company for a bit. Would you like me to..." Amelia trailed off as she noticed something behind him.

The wolves were back. This time they were closer and keeping up the pace. Onyx once again pulled, begging Johan to give him the freedom to run.

Johan could see them clearly in the moonlight. Most of them were grey and white. There was a brown one. The biggest one of them all was the one that was black as night. He was a few steps ahead of the pack, trotting to keep up with Onyx's pace. He was the largest wolf Johan had ever seen, his green-yellow eyes glimmering in the moonlight and his tongue lolling out of the side of his mouth.

The wolf pack continued to grow. It was too many for Johan to get a good count. If he had to guess, it was between twenty and thirty. He never knew of wolves to travel in such a large pack, especially in a desolate environment where their food was scarce. Most of the wolves from Johan's home were lone wolves. Very few traveled in packs.

Johan still held Onyx back, trying to calculate the distance between them and the pack. He tried to figure out what their next move should be when the pack split. A good number of wolves disappeared behind the sled, only to show up on Amelia's side. He could feel them slowly closing in.

The huge black one continued to stay on Johan's side. He could feel his eyes on him, and his open, panting mouth seemed like a grin. It was an evil grin, daring Johan to escape.

"They are shadowing us," Johan said quietly. "They are not going anywhere. Go inside and stay safe."

Amelia did not question him. She wanted to stay by his side, but she knew it was better if she was out of the way. She moved slowly, so she would not startle the wolves and disappeared under the covering.

Johan looked around him again. The pack was getting closer. His mind raced with panic as he tried to come up with a solution. Then, he remembered Onyx and how he always trusted his horse and his instincts.

Leaning forward and bracing his feet on the footboard, Johan did something he had never had to do before. He did not want to give Onyx the reins to run. He wanted Onyx to know the urgency of the situation. Johan snapped the reins on Onyx's back.

"YAH!" he screamed and snapped the reins again.

That was all the horse needed. Onyx flat-out ran, jerking the sled forward. The leader of the wolf pack let out an excited yelp. As if on command, the wolves sped up and closed the gap around Johan.

Johan held on tightly, yelling for Onyx to go faster and faster. He had never seen his horse put out such speed. At times, Johan felt as if the sled was no longer touching the ground but flying over the drifts. Still, the wolves kept up with them.

The large one was only a few feet from Johan, his snarling grin daring him. Despite the terror, Johan could not help but admire the size and pride of the wolf. He snapped the reins again. Onyx pushed on faster.

Where Amelia was sitting only moments before, a grey wolf leaped up, causing Johan to yell in surprise. The wolf growled and bared his teeth as he slipped back down the side, dangling from the moving sled. With his front paws, he kept scrambling to lift himself. Johan yelled and tried kicking the animal off while still holding onto the reins. The wolf became agitated, and still holding on, started snapping at Johan's leg, trying to catch it.

Amelia reappeared from the flap. In the commotion and scuffle between Johan and the grey wolf, a metallic clang rang out, and the wolf howled in pain as he fell off the sled. It took Johan a few seconds to catch his breath and realize that Amelia was standing there with a shovel in her hands. She had swung the blow to the wolf's skull.

Johan wanted to screech in delight at his wife's quick thinking and bravery, but he knew they were still not out of trouble yet. He once again turned his focus to the gigantic wolf that was running beside him.

If Johan did not know any better, he could have sworn the black one had the cold, calculating mind of a human. There was intelligence in the wolf's eyes. He could almost read the wolf's thoughts. Johan watched as the wolf eyed him, then looked forward to Onyx. The wolf took one last look at Johan as if to say, "Watch this," then turned all his focus on the horse. The wolf knew if he could bring down the horse, the chase would end.

"Nooo!" Johan yelled, frantically cracking the reins as the wolf picked up speed and slowly inched towards Onyx. "Quick! The pigs! Throw the pigs to the wolves!"

Amelia shook her head in horror.

"It will save us! It'll give them something to stop for!" he told her.

"They are not getting our pigs!" she insisted. She was no longer scared. Just angry. "These wolves will not win this!"

"There is nothing else to do!" Johan cried out, watching as the wolf gained another inch on the horse.

She put her hand on his, which was wrapped tightly around the reins. Her touch was gentle but light.

"Trust Onyx," she reminded him. "Let him go."

With that, Johan dropped the reins. That was what Onyx needed. As soon as he felt the reins go loose across his back, he tried to pick up speed even more. This did not stop the wolves from chasing him, though. Johan could only hope that eventually, Onyx could outlast them and tire them out.

Another wolf tried jumping up on Johan's side. Amelia thrust the shovel into Johan's hand, and he swung at the wolf without hesitating. Instead of a clang, they could hear something crack as the wolf slumped down. Johan pushed him off with his foot and watched him tumble and bounce lifelessly onto the frozen ground.

Amelia went under the covering again to search for something to help her defend their lives and belongings. She appeared with a cast iron frying pan. Together, she and Johan stood guard as the sled raced across the silver night for miles.

Onyx seemed to gain some distance from the black wolf and his pack, but they did not seem to give up. Johan could see the annoyance on the leader's face, along with determination.

They did not know where the wolves were chasing them or where Onyx headed. If Johan had lost sense of direction before, he was perplexed by how far north they were headed. In the moon's light, far off in the distance, he could see that the white of snow ended and met a dark strip below the silver sky.

He kept becoming distracted by the occasional wolf that would get too close to the sled. He and Amelia would swing and shout at it, getting it to back away a bit. Then he would glance ahead again to see where Onyx was heading. The dark strip was getting larger- taller.

His heart sank when he realized it was a wall of some sort. A very high wall that stretched as far to the east and west as he could see. Johan felt trapped. He wondered if the leader wolf's intention all along was to to chase them in this direction, only to be blocked off by an endless wall, trapping them.

As they approached closer, they could see it was not a wall but a ridge. A great, mountainous ridge, covered in a sheet of ice and some snow, rose from the earth and towered towards the sky. Onyx continued to head straight towards it with no signs of slowing down.

In a panic, Johan reached for the reins, determined to bring Onyx to a stop. It seemed as if the horse was intent on barreling right into the rocky wall of the ridge. With a look, Amelia reminded him silently that if they stopped, the wolves would win.

"What will be, will be," she told him sadly. He nodded and grabbed on to her, bracing themselves for either an impact or the jaws of the wolves. Whichever was to come first, he would not let go of her.

"Look!" Amelia suddenly shouted and pointed. Onyx headed to the ridge without slowing down. With squinted eyes, Johan could see what Amelia was pointing at. A hole. A cave of sorts on the side of the ridge.

Johan realized the horse headed straight for this cave. It was not a large opening, and he questioned Onyx's judgment in size. He did not know whether to be relieved or to continue to panic.

The wolves never gave up and chased them with frenzied yipping and froth bubbling at the corners of their mouths right to the cave. Johan and Amelia collectively held their breaths as they came upon the cave's opening, and Onyx pulled them in.

It was tight- almost too tight for the horse, but he made it into the darkness. The sled was wider, catching on the rim of the cave walls and coming to a screeching halt that yanked Onyx back and tossed Johan and Amelia from their seats with screams.

They could hear the padded paws of the wolves coming to a halt outside the mouth of the cave. One wolf howled, and Johan knew it was the leader, the black one, who shadowed them to the ridge.

"Are you alright?" he yelled to Amelia, helping her up from the sudden jolt. Onyx kept bucking against his harness and frantically tried to pull the stuck sled deeper into the cave.

"Yes. We must seal the cave," Amelia said, pointing to where they could still see the wolves outside. It was only a matter of time before they braved the cave and climbed up and over the sled.

"Look for lanterns," he told her as he climbed up to the top of the sled with his shovel. He peeked out to see the wolves surrounding them. There was no way out. The leader sat there, panting from the long run, but he stared at Johan. He could see the wolf was assessing the situation with confident eyes. Johan saw the panting as laughter.

Johan thought hard and fast. The only way the wolves could get in was over the sled. The sled was jammed in the cave's mouth. He just needed to build it high and quickly to keep the wolves out. If he and Amelia could just wait it out for a while in the cave, the wolves should lose interest. They should tend to their hunger elsewhere.

Johan saw the troika still miraculously tied to the sled and in an upright position. Light danced on the cave walls as Amelia lit and placed a few lanterns around. Onyx was pawing on the ground, wanting to run further into the darkness of the cave.

"Amelia, I need rope! Let the pigs out!" Johan told her as he reached down and tried to reach the troika hitched to the back of the sled.

The black wolf watched him and rose onto all fours. He paced back and forth as Johan untied the rope from the sled. With all his might, he pulled and was surprised with how easily the troika jerked forward. This caused the wolves to jump up and let out a few excited yips. The black one growled deep within his throat. Johan pulled quickly as the troika slid closer to the sled.

"Quick! Toss me the rope!" he yelled. Amelia did as she was told. He quickly tied the troika's rope to the one Amelia gave him. "Unharness Onyx, then tie the other end to him!"

Amelia ran to Onyx's side. He towered over her. She could easily walk under his belly without bending. His stomping and snorting made her nervous. Remembering how Johan had trained him, she walked in front of him and put her hand out with the palm facing down.

"Onyx, down," she said sternly.

Onyx looked down at her and nickered. He watched as she lowered her hand in a quick motion. Without hesitation, he did what he was trained to do and clumsily lowered himself to the ground.

"Good boy," Amelia whispered in relief, and she quickly worked at the buckles in his harness.

Johan threw the rope back to her, and she tied it as best as she could to the horse. He turned back around to see the wolves slowly approaching him, their heads and tails low. Of course, the black one was leading them. He had to think quickly, then called for a lantern.

Amelia grabbed one and climbed up to join Johan. It was the first time she could get a good look at the pack that stalked them.

"Oh, dear," she whispered, handing the lantern to Johan.

"Go. Get Onyx up and have him pull forward with all his might," he told her. Amelia scrambled back down as he threw the lantern with all his strength.

The lantern shattered at the black wolf's paws, and the flames blazed at the increase of air. The wolf yelped and jumped back, glaring at Johan. Johan could hear Amelia command Onyx up and to pull.

With his shovel, he jumped down to give the troika some leverage so Onyx could pull it up.

"Easy! Easy does it," he called to Amelia and Onyx. It was a struggle, but the troika flipped up. Johan climbed up the sled to keep ahead of the troika, helping Onyx by keeping a hand on the rope to guide it. Slowly, it rose the back of the sled. Johan grabbed the front of the runners with his feet braced for extra strength and pulled it forward. It fit.

"Stop," he called out. With the troika stacked on top of the back half of the sled, they felt

secure in the cave with the wolves blocked out. There were small gaps here and there, but

nothing a wolf could squeeze through.

He turned to Amelia with a smile. He could see she was sighing with relief, and Onyx was heavily breathing. He sat down with an exhausted thump and let go of his shovel. Running his hands through his dark hair, he could not believe that they once again survived the wrath of nature.

"Are you alright?" Amelia called up to him. He just nodded. She took a lantern and walked around Onyx, looking at the ground. "The pigs- they are gone."

"Couldn't have gone far," he told her. "Can you untie Onyx for me? Give him a rest?"

Outside, a wolf howled. Johan knew it was the leader. He sounded angry and frustrated. This caused Johan to laugh.

The Tunnel

Johan and Amelia had to pause for several long minutes. They just needed time and silence to catch their breath and their thoughts. Onyx stomped at the hard dirt floor impatiently and seemed eager to move to the back of the cave, away from the blocked entrance. Johan held up his lantern to cast a broader glow on the cave walls, but it could not reach into the deep darkness. There was no telling how far into the ridge the cave went.

He unhitched Onyx hoping it would settle the horse's nerves. Amelia salvaged what she could from the sled and took a quick inventory. They could last a couple of nights in the cave. At least they would have shelter from the elements of the snow and wind, and eventually, the wolves' empty bellies will lead them elsewhere for a hunt.

"Onyx, stop. Onyx, where are you going?" she could hear Johan call. She could no longer see the horse, only hear his hooves clopping softly on the floor and fading into an echoing distance.

"How far can he go? He'll just meet up with the pigs, then turn around," Amelia told him.

Johan nodded in agreement and walked over to her. He felt safe again, and she was safe with him, which was all that mattered to him. He never knew he could feel that way about someone. He smiled and chuckled lightly to himself.

"What? What's so funny?" she asked, smiling with him.

"I was just thinking of how you came out of nowhere and clobbered that wolf good and proper with the shovel," he laughed. "Your father told me you were fragile."

Amelia laughed and shook her head.

"All fathers like to think their daughters are fragile," she told him.

"I don't think I've ever seen any girl with such gumption before."

"That's because I grew up with three older brothers," she reminded him. "A girl must do what a girl must do in a rowdy bunch like that. They taught me plenty."

"I can imagine," he nodded. "So, you will be alright with us bunking here for a couple of nights? Until the wolves go away?"

"I can't think of a better idea," she said, frowning towards the back of the cave. "It's awfully quiet back there, isn't it?"

Johan listened but could barely hear Onyx let out a whinny. The horse sounded so far away.

"Just how deep is this thing?" he wondered out loud.

"Shall we find out?"

"It can't hurt. Grab an extra shawl or blanket or something," Johan told Amelia. "Caves can get quite cold as you go deeper in."

Together, they each put on an extra layer of winter garments. They grabbed rolled-up blankets and tied them onto their backs, just in case, and grabbed a lantern. They walked to the back of the cave, where the animals had disappeared, and held up the lanterns. It cast a light deep into the cave, but they still could not see where it ended. Eventually, the light shifted abruptly with eerie darkness.

"Well, this is exciting," Amelia said as she stepped in further.

"I think I have had enough excitement to last a lifetime," Johan said, half-heartedly joking.

They continued into the cave, bringing their glow of light with them. Every time they walked a few feet, they hoped the newly lit walls would reveal a dead end with Onyx and the pigs standing there. It never did. All their flames showed was more darkness ahead.

The cave walls became high and wide. The dirt floor became bumpy and uneven. Johan bent down to look at it better, taking his mitten off to touch it. The thousands of tiny holes in the rugged, almost stone-like ground fascinated him.

The walls curved upwards, giving the cave the look of a channel or aqueduct of some sort. Johan wondered if water once flowed through this cave.

"A tunnel?" Amelia finally spoke, reading his mind.

"Perhaps."

Amelia and Johan continued to walk. It seemed this cave or tunnel was much larger than they ever imagined. They estimated they had covered over a mile when they realized they were walking on a slight downward slope.

Amelia felt the fatigue from all the excitement they had with the wolves, the chase, the cave itself, and the walking. She wiped the sweat from her brow and took off her knit hat to stuff in her blanket roll. She removed her mittens and put them in her pocket. The air no longer felt icy and bitter. It was cool but soothing to her exposed head.

She noticed Johan had done the same. He was even removing his outer layers. She stopped to remove her shawl and coat and repacked the blanket roll to make everything easier to carry.

"I thought you said caves get cold," she said to him with a teasing look.

"I don't think this is a normal cave," he admitted. He noticed the air getting warmer instead of colder. He saw the vapor from their breaths that had been ever-present the entire trip was gone. The cool cave air was not cold enough for them to breathe out vapors.

"Do we keep going?" she asked.

"I don't see why not. Are you too tired? We can try again later."

She was tired, but she did not want to stop. Amelia just shook her head and continued. A few minutes later, she could hear a slight tinkling sound that echoed off the curved walls. Their fatigue waned as a new curiosity grew. They listened to the sound as it grew to a splashing sound.

"Water," Johan said.

As they headed towards the sound of water, a faint wind came from the darkness, making their hair dance about in their eyes. They came upon the source of the water sound first. It was a small trickling coming from above. It splashed into a tiny pool, then rushed out through a narrow stream that ran alongside the path. Johan put his hand into the falling water.

"Not cold. Not icy at all," Johan commented as he smelled it, then tasted it. He smiled. "Good. It's clean."

Amelia followed suit and cupped her hand under the running water to catch some of it. Even though he had said it was not cold, she was still surprised. She had expected it to be painfully cold, like when water is just about to turn to ice. Instead, like the air and the breeze, it was cool and refreshing.

"It must be a tunnel," Johan said, pointing to where the small stream was running off. "It must go out. The breeze, it's coming from somewhere."

"I think we are close. I smell something," Amelia said. Johan sniffed at the air.

"I don't smell anything."

"It smells like grass or a garden. Dirt, like spring," she told him.

She was right. It was not long before the glow of their lanterns finally met something other than darkness. Instead, a silver light came towards them, making the black walls seem bluish.

The mouth of the tunnel opened up into the moonlight. Johan and Amelia just stood there for a moment, not sure if they believed their eyes. Under the full moon, they could not see everything, but they could see enough.

Onyx was a few feet from them, his head lowered to the ground, chomping on grass. The piglets were not far ahead, making grunting noises as their little noses shoveled into the soil, rooting around.

A meadow with grass and wildflowers spread out before them. They could make out shadows in the distance that looked like trees-lots of trees. Somewhere in the dark forest, an owl called out, and a second one answered him.

Johan and Amelia stepped out of the tunnel. Turning around, they took in as much as they could. They appeared to be on the other side of the ridge, but it was almost as if they had stepped into a different season, unlike the original side.

"Impossible," Johan whispered as he craned his neck up, looking back at the ridge. It was not as icy looking as the side they came from, but it was high and continued in both directions as far as he could see.

"Perhaps we are dreaming? Maybe we fell asleep," Amelia suggested.

Johan shook his head. He removed his blanket roll from his back and untied it. He shook it out and laid it down on the ground, next to the opening of the tunnel.

"Sleep actually sounds good to me," he said, suddenly exhausted. He still felt safe and warm. He found his horse and the pigs. His wife was by his side. "We can see better when the sun comes up. See what is out there and why."

Amelia nodded, his exhaustion becoming catching. He yawned, and she followed. She unrolled her blanket and laid down next to him, pulling her blanket on top of them.

"When the sun comes up," she agreed, looking out into the silver meadow.

Onyx and the pigs continued eating. The horse let out a chuffing sound, and the pigs continued to grunt and snort. Amelia closed her eyes, drifting away. The last thought she had was how happy the animals sounded to her.

The Valley

Johan could feel tickling on his face that brought him to the surface of reality, away from his crazed, exhausted dreams. He opened his eyes to see Onyx gently nuzzling him. He gave Onyx a lazy pat before pushing his large head away so he could sit up.

The sun was up, shining but grey. Johan had to blink a few times to get the last of his sleep from his eyes. Once again, he was amazed at what was before him: the meadow, the trees in the distance. A small bird or two would occasionally fly up, only to land somewhere else and disappear. The stream that they discovered in the dark tunnel continued to flow out into the distance.

He could not figure out how this was possible. How, in the middle of the frozen lands of the tundra, the ice and snow and brutal wintry winds, there seemed to be a paradise where plants could grow and birds could sing.

It was not just birds, he realized, as a brown rodent quickly dodged by and disappeared. It was too quick for Johan to make out what it was. Judging on its speed, Johan decided it had to be a rabbit or a hare of some sort.

He gently shook Amelia's shoulder so she could be awake with him and marvel at all that laid before them. She sat up and, like him, needed to blink and take it all in. Like him, she wondered how it was all possible.

"Magic?" she asked.

"No such thing, is there?" he replied, not so sure anymore.

She rose to her feet and walked out into the meadow, pulling a shawl around her shoulders. There was a chill in the air, but it was not the cutting and harsh-like cold on the other side of the ridge. This was a morning chill with promises of warming up as the day went on.

He followed her, watching as she occasionally bent down to touch a plant or break off a flower. He watched her pop one into her mouth.

"Mmmm..." she smiled as she chewed. "It's borage. Try it. Just the flower petals, though. The leaves and stems are prickly. Might get caught in your throat."

Johan wrinkled his nose but plucked a flower. He sniffed it. It smelled harmless to him, so he placed it on his tongue. He was surprised with a mild, light flavor. It reminded him vaguely of cucumbers from his parents' garden.

"Dandelions, chamomile, chicory, bee balm," Amelia listed as she pointed here and there, all over the meadow. "All edible. So many edible flowers and plants out here."

"And trees," he said, pointing into the distance. "I bet we find some good stuff over that way."

"Shall we?"

Together, they walked in the meadow. Amelia would point out the flowers that she seemed so knowledgeable about. She told him how dill tasted wonderful with potatoes and how bee balm could seep into tea.

She spotted calendula, which she said made broths tangy and golden in color, and she claimed dandelions were not only delicious fried in butter but also could be fermented into wine.

"How do you know all this?" he asked, amazed at her vast wealth of knowledge.

"I had a nanny who was raised to live off the land. She was a forager. We would spend afternoons walking on our grounds in the short summers, and she would point out all the fresh flowers and plants. She'd say which ones were good for us and which ones to stay away from. Like those."

She pointed to a patch of dainty little yellow and black flowers with just a purple hue. They looked like ordinary pansies of sorts to Johan.

"Johnny-jump-ups," she continued. "They look harmless enough. A bite or two might be fine, but too much of them is not a good thing."

"So, we avoid those, then?" Johan said with a snicker.

"Absolutely."

They continued to walk, surprised at the wildlife they spotted from time to time. Occasionally, a deer's head would rise from the tall grass. A rabbit or field mouse would dart by them, birds were always around them, and they spotted many nests in the fields that belonged to quails, pheasants, and grouse.

The meadow merged with the trees. The trees were spaced out at first. Johan recognized some of them as apple trees and rushed over to pick some off the low-hanging branches. He handed one to Amelia, and she closed her eyes as she bit in and welcomed the sweet yet tart flavor.

They recognized pear trees, cherry trees, and some nut trees Johan had never seen before as they continued to walk. The trees eventually became thicker, and soon they found themselves in a forest.

The ground was soft, and ferns grew among the trees. There was an earthy smell in the air, and a light, wispy fog crept around their ankles. Johan kicked at the soft soil then bent down to touch it. He pinched at some dirt and rubbed it between his fingers.

"It's warm. Not cold. Not hard and frozen. It's slightly warm," Johan told Amelia in amazement.

She nodded half-heartedly, heading towards some ferns. She fingered some tips coiled tightly before breaking off a few and putting them in her pocket. They were fiddleheads, another edible plant. They would make an excellent snack for their walk back to the tunnel.

"This is incredible," Johan said. "This soil is perfect for farming. I just don't see how this is all possible."

"Johan, the sun," Amelia suddenly pointed up to the sky. He raised his head and peered among the thick canopy of tree branches. She was right. Even though they were someplace where it seemed like spring, the sun was already setting. It reminded them they were still somewhere, somehow at the beginning of winter, and the nights were becoming longer and longer. The sun was only up for just a few more hours.

"I suppose we should head back," he said. "We'll grab some fruit to help keep us through the night. Tomorrow, we will figure out what needs to be done. Figure out where we are."

"Where do you think we are?"

"North."

"I know. But where are we? What is this?"

Johan shrugged his shoulders. He was just as baffled as she was.

The walk back to the ridge and tunnel was brisk as the sun was setting fast. Johan knew it was only a matter of weeks before the sun would barely peek out during the long winter nights. He had to decide and do what was right. If he were alone, he would not stress as much, but now that he had a wife, his stress level was more pressuring than ever.

They once again made a little bed in the same spot as the night before. They munched on apples and fiddleheads for supper. They did not have to worry about Onyx or the piglets. They had plenty to eat and graze on. The animals would wander a bit but always seem to come back, never straying too far.

"Do you think the wolves are still out there?" Amelia asked as they lay down to settle in for a long night's sleep.

"I don't know. Most likely not."

"If we leave and set out again for home, do you think they will pick up our scent and shadow us again?"

Johan had no answer for her. It was a thought that weighed heavily on his mind. If they left this valley, would the wolves eventually catch up with them again? How long will they be on the path to home? Will they make it home before the days slipped into nothing but long winter nights? Was he even sure which way home was anymore?

He could hear Amelia settle into the soft, deep breaths of sleep. Johan tossed and turned, his mind racing. Finally, knowing he would not get any sleep, he stood up and stretched. He was tired, physically. His eyes and mind were wide awake, but his body was exhausted.

He walked away from the little nest of blankets under the stars and followed the stream a bit. The moonlight reflected gently on the running water. There was a spot where the stream dropped, creating a tiny waterfall before opening up into a wider creek. Johan imagined he could catch plenty of fish in the creek. He envisioned a net at the bottom of the fall to capture leaping fish.

He noticed a family of deer drinking from the creek near him. He watched them quietly. The deer lifted their heads and stared at him, then went about their business back to drinking. It amazed Johan that they did not run or startle at the sight of him.

He headed back to where he left his sleeping wife. Once again, he tried to settle into sleep. Sleep would not come easy for him that night. He had so many decisions to make, decisions that could change the course of not only his life but Amelia's as well.

In the morning, Amelia woke up early, just before the sunrise. Her stomach was growling, ready for breakfast. It surprised Amelia to see Johan gone from her side, and she frowned. She stood up and looked into the distance to see if she could spot him.

Marks in the dirt caught her eye. She walked over to it to see Johan had taken a stick and scrawled a message in it. *Be Back*. A simple message, but she was grateful that he took the time to leave it. It made her feel reassured.

As the sun rose, it reflected off the icy patches that clung high on the ridge. The reflected sunlight beamed down, stronger than it should have been, onto the meadow and slowly grew into the valley. Amelia took the time she had to herself to wash up in the stream. The water was almost warm. There was nothing frigid about it, and it felt good on her arms, feet, and face.

She wandered into the meadow, foraging among the plants and flowers. She spotted so many good things. If only she had fresh meat and vegetables to go with it. The meadow offered an overabundance of ingredients to cook a splendid meal for Johan. She wanted nothing more than to prepare a loving meal for him. Even though they were still strangers and had only been married for such a short time, he had been so kind to her. She loved how he wanted to protect her and provide for her. She loved how he never once made her feel different from the rest of the brides in the world.

"Amelia!" she heard him call. She looked up and waved to him as he waded through the grass towards her. He was smiling. It was the biggest smile she had ever seen on his face.

"Everything alright?" he asked when he reached her. "Did you get my note?"

"Yes. Thank you."

"Finding something for breakfast?"

"Just some more plants, herbs, flowers, berries. There is plenty here. It's just not a meal without some meat. We need some vegetables and maybe bread," she said. "But it's enough to hold us over until—"

"Until?"

"I don't know. Until what? Until we go back to the sled and supplies? Until we reach home? What are you thinking?"

Johan sighed and looked into the distance. He scratched his head for a second or two before turning to Amelia.

"What if this was home?" he finally said. "What if we settled here?"

"Here?"

"Why not? There's plenty here. There's fish and game. The dirt will grow crops beautifully. I am sure of that. The forest will provide us with firewood and lumber for a home," he said. "I've been walking about all night because I couldn't sleep. I found a perfect little spot that we can clear away and build a home. A nice stream runs by it for freshwater. It's halfway between the cave and the forest."

"What about people? There have to be people here," she insisted. "A valley this bountiful cannot be without people. What if they are not friendly? What if someone owns all this?"

"I don't think that there are any people here," he responded. "I don't think there ever were. Have you noticed the deer don't run when they see us? How all the animals just go about their ways and don't skitter in fright when we come along?"

Amelia nodded.

"Well, I've been thinking about it," he continued. "I don't think they know what to make of us. They never set eyes on a man before. Man has never hunted them. So, they are not afraid."

"You think we are the first to discover this valley?"

"I do. I really, truly do."

It was Amelia's turn to sigh and look off into the distance. It was a beautiful place. She could picture herself living there with Johan and making a home with him, raising children.

"But no people?" she finally said. "Is no people worse than some people?"

"No people means no teasing. No staring eyes. No whispering gossip. Just you and me in our world that we create," he reminded her softly.

"And our families?"

"I have no response for that. They will grieve if we don't return home. But we might not return home anyway if we set out traveling again. With the freezing nights coming and the wolves…" he trailed off, giving her time to take in what he was saying.

"Either way, they are going to grieve," she admitted sadly.

"Amelia, we are safe here. Can't you feel that? I know you do. Look at Onyx and the pigs," he pointed. "Look at how relaxed they are. They feel it too. There is something very safe here in the valley."

She nodded. She felt it the moment they stepped out of the tunnel.

It was as if they stepped into a mystical, utopian world, and they left all the worries and fears behind.

"Let's try it for one year, maybe two," Johan suggested. "See what the seasons are like here. See what else there is to offer us. If it doesn't work out, we leave. Return to the outside world."

"Sure," she smiled. "I can do that. I trust you."

Johan let out an excited laugh and clapped and rubbed his hands together. He was eager to get started and ready to take the first step towards a new and exciting life with Amelia.

"I am going to take Onyx back to our sled," he told her as they walked back. "Check on the wolves. I'll Grab some items for Onyx to carry back and come up with a plan to bring everything back and seal the entrance from future predators. Is there anything you want me to bring back today?"

Amelia smiled and nodded. She did a quick mental inventory of what was in the sled and troika and the field and forest.

"Pots and pans. Some tools for skinning and gutting. Something to fish with. Something to trap with," Amelia began as she counted off her fingers and continued to list various items.

She felt the excitement build up inside of her. If they could catch a rabbit or a fish, she could make an excellent meal for him, just like she had been daydreaming.

Johan took the rope he used to tie his blanket up and lead Onyx back into the tunnel. They said quick goodbyes to each other, eager to get the day going, and thrilled to have some plan towards a normal life together.

While Johan was gone, Amelia used the time to clear a spot for a cooking fire. With her blanket, she went to the stream and gathered large stones. Placing them on the blanket, she dragged them back and used the stones to encircle the cleared area.

With the same blanket, she walked through the meadow and into the forest. She gathered branches and small, fallen logs and placed them on the blanket. Once again, she dragged what she found back. By the time she finished, she was sweaty and covered with dirt smudges on her hands and face. The blanket was torn and tattered, covered with dust, soil, and burrs.

She was exhausted, almost too tired to go ahead with her plan to make a delicious supper. She sat down for a bit, her head back on the ridge wall, and closed her eyes. She did not even realize that she had drifted off until she heard the clopping of Onyx's hooves on the hard cave floor. Amelia jerked her head up, surprised she was sleeping. At once, the enthusiasm grew in her heart and chased the exhaustion away.

Johan appeared, leading Onyx with one hand and a lantern in the other. He piled Onyx with crates and bundles on his back and down his sides. Johan also carried a bundle slung over his shoulder. Extra lanterns and a pan jangled from being tied to the bundle.

"So, Wife," he greeted with a grin. "What shall we do first?"

"Catch us our supper, Husband," she smiled back.

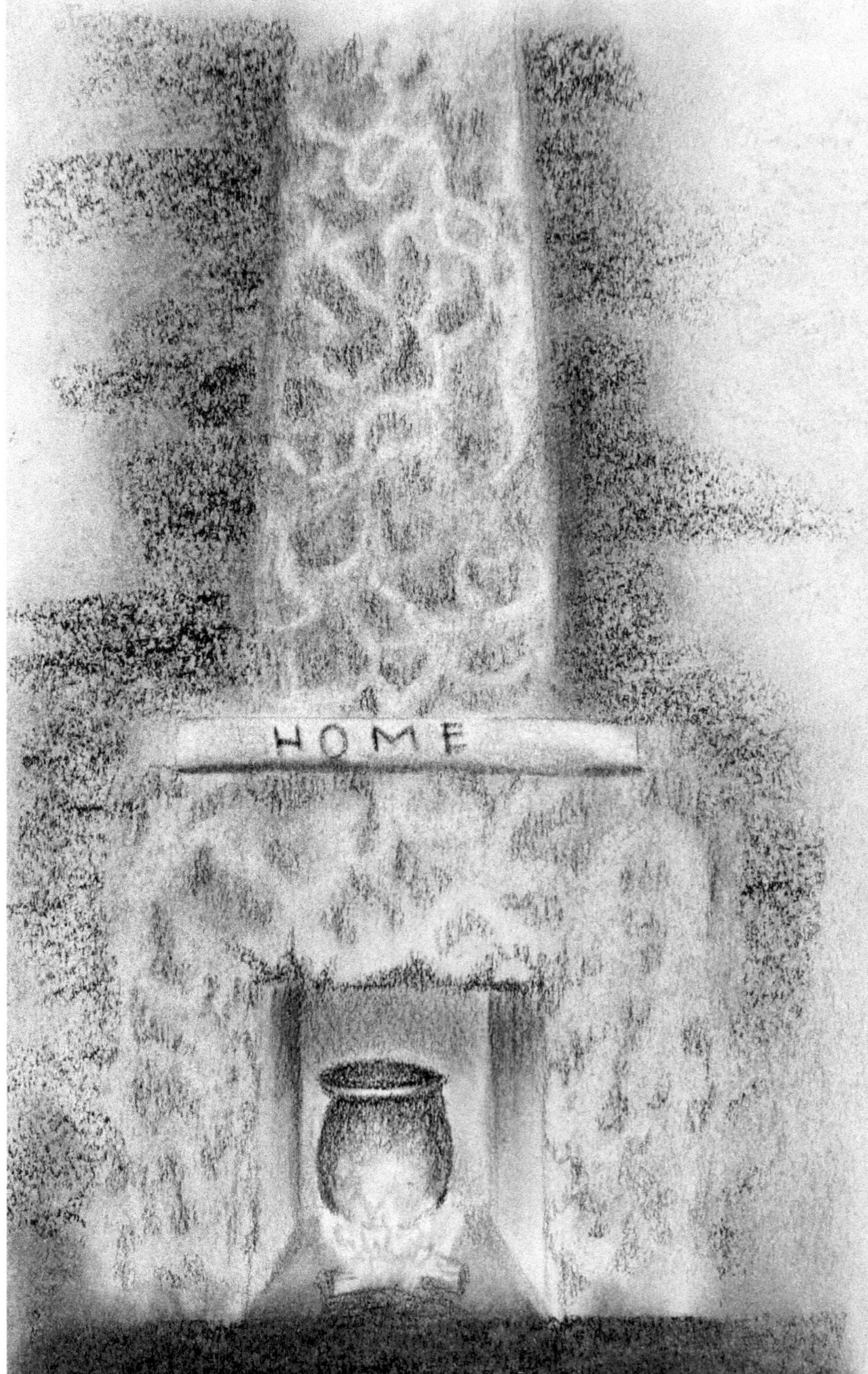
HOME

Settling Down

It took time, but Johan and Amelia had all the time they needed. As they searched the valley and planned, broke down the sled and troika blockade, and built a wooden wall to keep any wolves or dangerous predators out, their lives began. As they cut down trees for lumber and plowed a small field for future crops, they noticed things were different in their valley than in the world they came from.

They headed into the darkness of winter, a time where the sun would not rise. Twilight would appear daily before plunging into the night, but not in the valley. The sky above them was dark, but it would radiate daylight on the sides of the ridges where there were patches of ice. The best Johan could figure out was it was picking up sunlight from somewhere far away and bouncing it back and forth, reflecting it for miles on end. He could not wrap his head around it and just accepted it. Both he and Amelia were grateful for the light.

They discovered hot springs that dotted the landscape. Warm water in small pools that were great for bathing or just leisurely fun. Johan continued to notice that the soil was warm. As he dug his fingers further into it, it seemed warmer. He could tell it was rich with nutrients, perfect for nourishing the seeds that came with the dowry.

The dowry contained many things that were useful as they settled down. Seeds for planting. A plow for breaking down the soil. An ax and saw for cutting down trees. An assortment of tools for filing, sanding, hammering, breaking down and putting together items.

With the tools, he could prepare lumber from the forest. With Onyx's help, they dragged the lumber to the spot he cleared for their home. Just feet away from the clearing was a babbling brook, perfect for fetching water. Together, he and Amelia built a small, cozy home.

It was just a tiny, one-room cabin with a pantry room on the side. Sacks of flour, salt, and sugar, a few jars of spices, a couple of jugs of ale, and a small barrel of coffee were all that went into the pantry. Soon, Johan built a small smokehouse to the side, and together he and Amelia made sausages and smoked, cured meats from the game they caught.

Being inventive, Johan had created traps throughout the meadow and forest. Mostly, he caught rabbits and fowl in the traps. Eventually, cured meats and sausages ended up hanging from hooks suspended from the ceiling of the pantry.

Eggs were also plentiful in the meadow. Quail eggs were small but perfect for them. Amelia would collect them along with herbs, berries, and flowers when she was foraging. Eventually, everything ended up stored in bowls along a shelf in the pantry.

By the time the black sky had become light again, showing that spring was coming in the outside world, the pantry was well stocked. Amelia and Johan had everything they needed, from dried herbs to meats. Johan's crops grew just as he predicted, even though the air was always mild and the sunlight was weak. Yet, it worked. It was all coming together.

He loved being out in the field or working to better his home. He built a table and chairs for them to have meals on. He created a bed frame to elevate the straw tick mattress they had from the dowry. He crafted wooden bowls for Amelia to store her foodstuff in, little containers with fitted lids to keep the field mice out.

He built a pen to keep the animals from wandering, though they never went far. The piglets were no longer piglets but growing big and fat. Johan had mentioned only once to Amelia about bacon and chops coming from the pigs, and she quickly cut him off.

"They survived the storms with us, the wolves, the cold. No," she had told him. "We don't need to make meals out of them. We have plenty here. They are family now."

So, Johan never mentioned it again. The pigs even gained names, indeed making them part of the family. Hock and Chop they became known as and even answered to them when called. They had their little hut that Johan built, right next to Onyx's small lean-to stable.

It rained in the valley but rarely snowed. They could see the flakes coming down if they looked up at the grey skies, looking like a swarm of insects descending upon them. By the time the flakes reached into the depths of the valley, the warmer air had turned them to rain. If the atmosphere were chillier than usual by chance, the flakes would light upon the warm soil and then melt away.

Rainy days became Amelia's favorite days. It gave Johan an excuse to stay indoors and relax. She would prepare a big, comforting meal in the large, beautiful hearth that Johan had built for her from the river rocks and clay-like mud he found near the hot springs. The fire kept them warm on chilly days, gave them great smelling and tasting foods, and provided light to read.

Johan and Amelia only had one book with them, the Holy Bible, given to them by the bishop. They would take turns reading from it, mainly on the day they assumed was a Sunday. They would rest from their daily routines and come together in prayer with gratitude, blessed to feel safe.

It was late spring when Johan noticed the mountain goats on the walls of the ridge. With thick, white coats, it was easy for them to blend with the ice and go unnoticed for so long. He and Amelia watched them for days, nannies bringing kids down to snack in the meadow before heading back up the rocky terrain of the valley. Amelia gathered their shedding fur that would catch on the plants and store it in hopes of one day using it to make yarn.

They realized there was a path that the goats were traveling on as they would disappear above them. Packing a picnic, Johan and Amelia climbed the path to see where it would take them. Up they went, higher and higher, over rocky trails and climbing boulders. With labored breathing and sweat, despite the chill, they reached the top.

Looking down, they had a bird's eye view of the valley. Seeing it took their breath away as they realized just how vast it was. It went further than they could see. Meadows, forests, lakes, rivers- it was all laid out below them.

They sat for a bit, eating their picnic of dried meat, berries, and boiled potatoes that Amelia seasoned with wild onions and dill. Then they walked across the top of the ridge to the other side that faced the outside world.

It took some time as they strolled across the snow. It was warmer than when they first arrived but still cold. They almost forgot what cold felt like since the valley maintained a comfortable mild temperature every season.

On the other side, they looked down. The bleak, flat, grey tundra. Nothing but land and sky. A barren land that reminded them of just how harsh the outside world was. There was some movement in the distance, a herd of reindeer, most likely looking for any grass that might peek out from the thin snow. That was it--no sign of wolves or other arctic animals that might roam about in the spring.

They turned around and headed back, wanting to leave the bleak world behind. The valley was so colorful and safe, and it did not matter that there were no others there with them. They felt no need for other human interaction or to be reminded they were not "normal." In the valley, everything was normal.

Spring quickly turned to summer. The air became a little warmer, but the crops and the meadow were blooming in the strong sun. The sun now shone all day and most of the night. Bees buzzed about, and animals seemed to dance as they frolicked and played.

Johan would come back from the field, sweaty and filthy. He loved walking into their home. There was always a supper being made in the hearth with a delicious aroma welcoming him home from a long, hard day of labor.

Amelia seemed tired those days, but she still smiled and greeted him as if he had been gone for weeks instead of hours. She would place her hand on her back, supporting it from the aches. Her other hand usually had a wooden spoon that she was just using to stir a stew or ladle juice over the roasting meat.

Johan would accept her kiss and then gently place his calloused hand on her swollen belly to greet their unborn child. Everything was coming together as it should be.

Part Two:

Things Remembered

A Day and A Night

Over the years, things changed, but much remained the same. The cabin grew as extra rooms were added on. They built a third pen and hut to contain some nannies, and their kids caught coming down from the ridge. It was a ritual to keep them during the time they nursed the tiny, white baby goats. It was a struggle, but they were milked, and Amelia used the milk to make cheese. When the nursing season was over, Amelia and Johan released the goats since they could not tame them.

The valley itself was always the same. It never failed to provide for Johan and his family. Some things were long gone from their pantry. Items that could not be grown or foraged. There was no more flour or salt or sugar. The coffee and ale disappeared ages ago. With no flour or sugar, there had been no bread or cakes or sweets of any kind.

Amelia and Johan missed those items, even longed for them on dark, sleepless nights, but then they would count their blessings. They replaced their old tastes. Dandelion was used to make wine. Many different plants were brewed and seeped into teas to replace their coffee. Honey was used to sweeten the teas and the wine.

On one of the last days of summer, as the nights were slowly coming back, Johan was tending to his potato garden when the front door of his cabin burst open, and a small child ran out. Her long, dark hair trailed about behind her as her little, bare feet pumped against the ground. She held one of the many wooden bowls her father had fashioned over the years in her hands.

"Be careful, Karina!" Amelia called out from inside the cabin. Johan watched as his daughter ran towards the field to pick whatever herb or flower Amelia needed. He knew Amelia most likely needed nothing and just needed the active child out from under her feet, so she gave her a chore to do.

Karina was seven years old and always ready and willing to go, go, go. She was a small child, more along with the size of a three-year-old. She was observant and bright, always filled with never-ending questions. Johan would never forget her first word.

"Why?" she had asked at just over a year old. She had this great need to know everything. Johan had never met a more inquisitive child.

His oldest was the opposite of his youngest. Gregor, his firstborn, was always content. He did not need to know how things worked or why things were. He accepted their world for what it was.

Like his father, Gregor was a hard worker. He followed Johan's footsteps and learned how to tend to crops and build snaps and snares. He knew how to smoke meats and how to care for Onyx, Hock, and Chop.

Gregor was also inventive. After watching the goats from season to season, it was his idea to catch them and provide the family with something he had only heard about: milk. Johan claimed it was not as good as milk from a cow, but it would do. Gregor had no idea what cow's milk tasted like or what a cow even looked like.

Gregor would have loved to keep the goats, but they were not friendly and hard to maintain. It was always best to release them and take a much-needed break from the kicking and butting.

He was mending part of the pen that had rotted over time. Johan watched him from a distance and could see he was struggling to get the job done on his own.

"Where's your brother," Johan called out.

"Who? Edil?"

"Do you have another?"

"Where do you think he is?" Gregor sighed. "Up on the ice again."

Up on the ice referred to the flat top of the ridge. Johan shook his head and went back to pulling weeds around his potatoes. He should have guessed. Edil was almost always up on the ice. Or in the forest. Or down by the lake.

Edil was younger than Gregor by two years. Edil has yet to let go of his childhood notions of adventure and daydreaming at eighteen years old. He was as smart, if not smarter, than his older brother and younger sister, but he still loved to wander. His favorite place was on the edge of the ridge, looking out and wondering where the flat land led.

As a child, Amelia would tell him and Gregor fairy tales about the Land of the Giants, where she and Johan came from. It was a place where everyone towered over them, and they were constantly underfoot. Some giants could be quite nice, but many of them were very mean.

In this Land of the Giants were also different animals that they had never seen but could only imagine. Loyal puppy dogs that guarded homes and hissing cats that kept the mice away from the pantry. Some cows gave milk, and sheep were like their mountain goats, yet different.

They tried to imagine this far away land, this fairy tale picture Amelia would paint for them, but it was hard. Edil wanted to see it for himself. He wanted to see a dog and drink cow's milk. He wanted to talk with a giant and taste things like coffee and beef. More importantly, he wanted to find people that were just like him.

His parents warned him, though. It was too dangerous outside the valley. The cold was bitter, and the wolves would chase you. There was nothing for them out there in the grey Land of the Giants.

Edil would always come down just in time for supper; long after Karina had gathered the wildflowers, Gregor had finished his chores, and Johan had finished his gardening for the day. They set the table and sat down, ready to say their prayers when he would come walking in.

"Could have used your help, brother," Gregor said to him.

"Sorry," Edil responded, his head low and his dark hair in his eyes.

"Tomorrow, Edil. I expect you out there helping us," Johan told him.

"Yes, Papa."

"Good," Amelia smiled. "Now would you like to recite your numbers, Karina?"

Every night, during supper, Karina would recite what she was taught that day. Amelia did schooling with all three children. Everything they were taught was from Amelia's own memory. They learned their numbers, letters, words, and figures by scratching them into the dirt or reading the Bible. Then, they would proudly show off what they learned to Johan at night. Edil and Gregor finished with schooling, being much older than Karina, but they patiently listened to their little sister rattle off equations in between bites of stew.

The evening ended with Amelia sitting by the fire, working goat hair yarn through a loom that Johan had built for her. She dyed the yarn with a mixture of berries, wildflowers, and warm spring water. It was going to be a multi-colored blanket for Karina's bed.

Dishes were washed by Edil in a large wooden bucket and dried by Gregor. Karina would stack them away neatly on a shelf. Johan would put his feet up on a stool and lean back, closing his eyes. He would sing an old tune, and his family would join in. Everyone did their part in the small, cozy cabin. Everyone had their place.

When the fire burned out, they turned in for the night. Amelia and Johan had their room that Karina shared with them. She slept in a trundle that slid out from under their bed. Gregor and Edil shared a small room, just large enough for their two narrow beds. Eventually, Johan planned on building a third bedroom for when Karina came of age.

Edil liked to open the shutters of his window and lie in bed, looking up at the sky. It was finally getting dark again, letting the stars shine through and warning them that winter nights lay ahead. He wondered if you could see the same stars in the Land of the Giants.

The Battle

The young, snowy white mountain goat was not happy. Edil had wrestled with him as he slipped and latched a harness around his middle. The goat bucked and kicked, bleating out to his mother, which only made the mother agitated. She was pacing and stomping her hooves, butting her head against the wooden wall in the stable that kept her separated from her baby.

Gregor and Johan watched, their arms folded with a slightly amused look on their faces. This was a familiar scene. Every year, during the summer months, Edil tried his best to train and domesticate a goat. Johan did not know why he was so determined to have a goat harnessed to a small toboggan. Originally, Edil's idea was to have goats pull toboggans up the ridge and on the ice. The idea failed and failed again. The goats were born wild, and they could not train the wild out of them, but Johan concluded that Edil just wanted to prove that he could do it. Edil was just as stubborn as the goats.

The goat calmed down but still huffed and pawed the ground. Edil gently ran his hand along the kid's back, walking around him and talking to him in a soft, calming voice. He came around to the goat's face and continued baby-talking to it, looking into its black eyes. It was a beautiful little creature, all white and fluffy with two nubs of horns growing from its head. Its eyes were curious, young, and innocent.

"There, there," Edil smiled. "See? Nothing to hurt you. Just a silly ol' harness."

With that, the kid rose suddenly on its hind legs and danced and jumped around. It ended the little show with a loud popping sound as its head met Edil's. Edil went sprawling back, pain spreading from his nose and up into his forehead. He grabbed his face and rolled onto his side, groaning.

"Saw that coming, didn't we?" Johan laughed as he and Gregor went to grab the wildly jumping goat. They held onto the goat and struggled to remove the harness before letting it go so it could run back to the panicked mother.

"How many times we have to tell you, goats just don't want to be tamed," Gregor said, pulling Edil off the ground. He could see dark rings forming under Edil's eyes from the impact with the goat.

"Mama says there are tamed goats out there," Edil reminded him.

"Different breed, son," Johan called out. "Whole different breed and world out there."

"It didn't work with the pigs. It will not work with the goats," Gregor chuckled, remembering a summer when a young Edil kept harnessing and trying to get Hock and Chop to pull a small wagon.

"At least the pigs just laid there. None of this head boinking nonsense," Edil groaned, gingerly touching his nose.

Johan looked over at Hock and Chop in their muddy pen. They were lying in the sun, filthy and content. Occasionally, they let out a grunt. They were huge, weighing in over 600 pounds each, Johan had to guess. They had come a long way from the days when they were small enough to be crated and carried in the back of a sled.

That was over twenty years ago. Hock and Chop should not even be around anymore, and Johan and Amelia knew this. They knew the pigs should have died years ago, if not from being turned into bacon, then from old, natural causes that might befall a pig. However, there was something about living in the valley that kept the pigs relatively young in health. They grew up into adulthood, then just stopped aging.

The same mystery seemed to have befallen Onyx as well. A horse his age should have slowed down a few years ago, but Onyx was as fit and spry as the day Johan's father gave him over.

It did not escape Johan and Amelia as well. They aged a few years from when they first came upon the valley, but then it was over. The small wisps of grey hairs that grew from their temples never spread. The laugh lines never turned to wrinkles.

They never questioned it or even bought it up to the children. They just accepted it. Their only worry was the unknown. Did the aging suddenly kick in at once? Would they somehow age overnight? Did this mean they would never die? And the children? They were growing, the boys reaching adulthood. Would they eventually stop aging too? Or would they surpass their parents and eventually fade away, leaving their parents alone? Would the blessing become a curse?

Johan shook his head to clear his mind from worrying thoughts. He reminded himself that they just had to take each day as it came. He looked at his sons and smiled. They were growing into fine young men.

"The nursing season is pretty much over," he said. "The milk is turning sour. You might as well let the goats go. Then you two can go up on the ice and bring back some ice and snow for the cold box."

The cold box was another one of Johan's inventions. It was a chest made of stone and clay. Inside he lined it with goat fur for insulation, then another wall of clay. Every so often, Edil and Gregor would go up on the ice with the toboggan pulled behind them, and they would dig and break away at the snowy ground. They would pile up the snow and ice in the toboggan to bring back to the cabin, where their mother would line the chest with it. It helped keep the goats' milk and cheese and even some meats and fish from spoiling.

They released the goats. It was nothing more than opening the stable door and the gate and yelling "Yah!" behind them. They ran out, happy to be free and be where they belonged as they headed towards the rocky wall.

With rope, they packed up the small toboggan with extra layers of clothing for the cold air above them, a shovel and pick, and a picnic that Amelia and Karina made for them. Together, the two boys promised their mother to be safe and headed up the same way the goats ran.

Edil and Gregor liked the time they spent alone together. Two young men up against nature, helping provide for their family. They joked and teased. They argued about whose turn it was to pull the toboggan. They discussed ideas of how to make a living in the valley more productive to them.

When they reached the top, it was no longer rocky. It was nothing but pure snow and ice. They argued for a moment about where to harvest the ice. Edil wanted to go to the edge that overlooked the tundra and the outside world. Gregor did not see the need to walk the extra miles when they could get ice right there. In the end, Edil won because he was the more persuasive of the two.

They walked to the other end and found a spot to sit and rest. Edil, being daring, liked to sit where his feet would dangle, and the ledge was not as high as other spots. He felt closer to the rest of the world there.

"One of these days, you are going to slide right down," Gregor commented as he handed Edil a package wrapped in a scrap of cloth.

"Would that be such a bad thing? To end up down there? On the other side of the valley?" Edil responded, unwrapping the cloth. Amelia had packed up some berries and dried deer meat.

"You'd never survive the fall."

"But if I did, I don't think I would mind being down there. Take a walk around a bit. Maybe even venture into the Land of the Giants."

"The Land of the Giants," Gregor muttered with a chuckle and shook his head. Edil's fascination with the world their parents came from always amused Gregor.

Edil ripped at the jerky with his teeth and gazed into the distance. He pointed at a dark spot on the horizon.

"Reindeer herd," he said.

"I wonder why we don't have reindeer in the valley."

"Maybe because they like the cold," Edil shrugged.

"Maybe because Papa sealed off the tunnel," Gregor joked.

Edil laughed and continued to look down and around him. The world seemed so big from the top of the ice. So empty, too, but he knew of the oceans and the jungles. He knew there were deserts and islands. His parents had told them tales, and they had read repeatedly from the Bible. As much as he longed to travel into the world, his father convinced him there was no reason. The valley was safe and met all their needs. Amelia likened the valley to God's Garden of Eden in the Bible.

He noticed the darkness that was the herd of reindeer break up.

They were no longer one mass but specks moving quickly about in disarray. He and Gregor watched, wondering what caused the herd to become frenzied.

"Old Shadow," Gregor said, pointing to the right.

More specks, in the tiny shape of wolves, were running in. It was a large pack, and it was not the first time Gregor and Edil had seen them. As children, Johan had pointed them out in the distance from the top of the ice. Johan told them the tale of a large, black wolf called "Old Shadow" and how this wolf led an army of smaller wolves. This army of wolves was dangerous and bloodthirsty and had chased Johan and Amelia into the valley. That was why Johan had sealed off the tunnel with a large door he made from lumber in the forest. That was one of the first things Johan had done when they stayed to live there. He sealed the tunnel so the wolves could not get in and remind the children that they should not go out.

They stood up, watching the scene unfold before them. The wolves were getting closer to the reindeer. A haunting bellow trumpeted across the land, followed by chuffing honks from the herd. The terrifying sound caused the hair on the back of Edil's neck to stand. He had never heard such a racket from reindeer before.

The bellowing continued as the wolves became closer. The herd broke up, most running into the distant horizon. Some reindeer fought the wolves, using their antlers to stab at them and fend them off. Occasionally, Edil and Gregor could hear a wolf yip in pain.

Eventually, most of the herd had escaped, but the wolves were not finished. They had focused their attention on a small group. Edil squinted and could see it was four reindeer that were running towards the ridge.

"They'll be trapped," Edil realized out loud. "Why are they running this way?"

Old Shadow led his pack, his tongue lolling from his mouth in delight. Edil could see that the wolf knew there was no way out for the reindeer. The reindeer were running at full speed, and as they came closer, Edil could see that two of them were young, just babies.

"They are headed straight below us," Edil said excitedly. He looked around, then focused on the toboggan.

"Edil—" Gregor warned, knowing his brother's mind was off and racing.

"They'll die if we leave them."

"Papa always said to never interfere with nature," he reminded him.

Edil sighed, knowing Gregor was right. He looked back down. The reindeer were almost upon them. They were so close, Edil could see that one of the young ones had the tell-tale nubs of the beginning of antlers, just a baby born that spring. He could see the other one was not fully grown, and his antlers were not as large as the adults. He was only about a year old. One adult let out that sorrowful bellow again, gripping Edil's heart. It was the last cry for help to the herd, but they were abandoned. The herd was long gone, and they would not risk coming back and facing the wolves again.

"Quick!" Edil shouted. "The rope!"

He ran to the toboggan and untied the rope that was holding everything down. He frantically unwrapped it, round and round, as Gregor stood there, shaking his head.

"Edil, no! There is nothing to be done!"

"Come on, now! We have to try!"

"How?

"The rope. You lower me down. I'll figure out a way for you to pull them up," Edil said breathlessly.

"Pull them up?!" Gregor yelled. "Are you mad?"

Yet, somehow, Gregor helped Edil unwrap the rope. Muttering under his breath, Gregor pulled the rope from the toboggan. Edil grabbed an end and wrapped it around his waist.

"You'll lower me down," Edil instructed. "Hopefully, I can hold off Old Shadow and tie up the reindeer, and then you pull and pull hard."

"Hopefully? Edil! You are asking for the impossible! I can't pull up those gigantic beasts!"

Edil looked around quickly, trying to come up with something that would give Gregor some leverage.

"There!" he instructed, pointing at a small boulder. "Run your end of the rope around that. Place your feet at the base to give you support. I'll do what I can from below."

Gregor was shaking his head, but he followed Edil's instructions and looped his end of the rope around the boulder.

"Where's your sense of adventure, brother?" Edil grinned.

"Edil," Gregor put his hand out to stop him from beginning the climb down. He looked down below them. The reindeer were there, trapped. The wolves were approaching, the pack in an arc to surround them.

"You can't save all four," Gregor said quietly. "You won't have the time. Not if you want to save yourself."

Edil nodded sadly. He knew his brother was right.

"The babies then. We can save the babies," he said as he climbed down.

"Wait! Take this," Gregor stopped him, grabbing the shovel.

"Good idea!"

With his feet on the ledge wall and a rope around his waist, Edil climbed down as Gregor lowered him. He would push out and drop a few feet quickly before swinging back towards the wall. He would brace himself for the impact using his legs, only to spring back out and drop again.

The wolves were only feet away from the reindeer, standing there, surrounding them in a semicircle. Their sides swelled in and out, breathing hard from the chase. Old Shadow was grinning, a low growl coming from the back of his throat.

The two grown reindeer pawed at the ground and lowered their heads threateningly. They would not give up without a fight, as frightened as they were. They kept the young ones behind them, protecting them.

Old Shadow put his head down, and his eyes narrowed. His pack followed suit, their haunches high and tails low. Slowly, cautiously, they approached the reindeer. Their padded paws inched forward, almost as if they were teasing the reindeer.

The wolves were almost upon them when Edil dropped from the sky onto the ground right between both breeds of animals. Startled, Old Shadow and his pack jumped back and yipped. The reindeer bucked in surprise to see a man standing there with them. Edil's heart raced with fear and excitement.

He quickly untied the knot with one hand as the wolves took a minute to reassess the situation. They never expected an intruder. Old Shadow stared at him for a minute before throwing his head up and howling. Then he stared back at Edil, his eyes boring into him, his lips curled back in anger. The wolf was angry that their chase had been interrupted.

Edil held on tightly to the shovel, not sure what the next move would be. Suddenly, the adult reindeer trumpeted at the pack in anger. This time it was not a cry for help but a threat. It was as if the reindeer knew Edil was there to help them. Edil did the next thing that just came naturally to him and tried to imitate their sounds as he roared to show the wolves he stood with the reindeer.

Again, Old Shadow took a pause, confused at the animal-like noise the man was making. Old Shadow barked out a command as if to say *enough of the games,* and one of his wolves jumped out from the pack towards the reindeer.

"Oh dear," Edil whispered as he jumped back between the two babies. The larger of the reindeer put his head down and, to Edil's amazement, scooped up the small, brown wolf and tossed him aside with his antlers. Another two wolves approached them, and both adult reindeer battled them. It was teeth and claws against antlers and hooves.

The noise was deafening; the growling, snarls, bellows, grunts, and the occasional sounds of pain.

Using the distraction, Edil quickly grabbed one baby reindeer and wrapped the rope around its midsection. Using leftover rope, he grabbed the other and also wrapped him before tying it securely. He pulled and yelled up to his brother.

"PULL!!" he screamed as he saw a wolf coming at him from the corner of his eye.

He grabbed the shovel, and like his mother so many years ago, he swung as hard as he could at the wolf's head. The sound of metal against the skull made his stomach churn as the wolf collapsed at his feet, not moving. Not even his sides moved to show signs of breathing.

He turned back around to the babies who were crying out as they dangled. He could tell Gregor was having trouble up above, getting his footing to pull the weight up. Edil reached out to the reindeer and turned them around to face the wall of the ridge. Then he tried with all his might to lift them so their small hooves would find footing on the wall, to ease some of the weight on Gregor's end.

It worked. By some miracle, the babies understood they needed to walk up the wall with the support of the rope. The rope moved up, guiding the babies.

Edil turned back around to focus his attention on the wolves and the adults. With his shovel, he jumped in, his fear being pushed aside and replaced with will. He swung and veered, the shovel clanging and thudding with contact. He yelled and shouted as loud as he could, hoping the noise would make the wolves back up.

The wolves backed up a bit again but had no intentions of leaving. Old Shadow would not let it end so quickly. He growled as he sat down for a moment, his eyes never leaving Edil. All the fighting came to a standstill, an invisible line drawn between Edil, the reindeer, and the wolves. They all panted, catching their breaths. Edil knew it was just a break; the battle would continue. He knew Old Shadow was thinking, trying to come up with a better strategy.

Edil could see some wolves were bleeding from where the antlers had gouged them. The reindeer themselves had claw marks and scrapes on them. He heard the rope land behind him with a small thump. The babies made it up to the top.

"Come on! Get out of there!" he could hear Gregor shout from the top.

He looked at the adults sadly. *Just the babies*. It kept ringing through his head. Slowly, he walked backward, never taking his eyes from the wolves. He bent down and picked up his end of the rope.

One of the reindeer turned back and looked at him. If Edil did not know any better, he could swear her eyes were talking to him and thanking him for saving her babies. He saw her udder was swollen with milk for the younger of her two babies. She looked back at the wolves and stomped the ground, grunting. She was letting them know she was ready for another battle now that her babies were safe. It was a battle she was sure to lose.

"Aw, heck!" Edil groaned. "What's another fight, right? He ran to the mother reindeer, and she yelped in surprise as he threw the rope across her back.

"Easy, girl. Babies need their mama," he said as he worked furiously and fast. He knew the wolves were getting ready for another round.

"Are you crazy?!" he heard Gregor shout from above.

"Pull!" he yelled, pushing the reindeer towards the wall. His sudden yell caused the wolves to become frenzied, attacking the army again.

The mother reindeer bellowed and bucked in confusion as she was slowly raised. Like he did with the babies, he spun her around to help her gain footing on the wall and prayed it would work again. She was heavier than the two young calves. She was more work for Gregor.

He left her to fight off the wolves once again. He stood side by side with the large buck. Distracted from watching Old Shadow, a grey wolf hit him from his side with such an impact that he went tumbling and rolled away onto his stomach.

Edil flipped onto his back only to have the grey wolf pounce on him, his giant paws on Edil's shoulder. The wolf's face hovered above Edil's, his lips curled back, revealing yellow-stained teeth and pink and black gums. Edil could smell the hunger on the wolf's foul breath, and he could hear the low growl.

He closed his eyes, not wanting the rancorous face to be the last thing he would ever see. He quickly offered a prayer before he heard the growl grow into a vicious cry. Something made him open his eyes in time to see the wolf's mouth open and come down for a bite. Teeth snapped against teeth, catching nothing but air as the wolf was suddenly lifted and thrown. Hooves slammed down on the ground next to Edil.

He looked up, the male reindeer standing over him, just for a second before going back to fight and throwing another wolf, tossing him as if he weighed nothing, with his antlers. Edil had no time to comprehend what had just happened. He had no time to think. He just needed to survive long enough for Gregor to drop the rope one last time.

He crawled over to his shovel quickly and pulled himself up to his feet. He looked around and noticed they had once again come to a standstill, catching their breaths. The wolves paced back and forth, stalking Edil and the buck. The buck stood firm. His mighty head held high with pride. Edil slowly walked towards him and stood next to him.

Edil reached out, unsure of the buck's reaction, and placed his hand on his shoulder carefully. To his surprise, the buck did not even flinch. He accepted Edil's touch.

The rope thudded down again in the snow. The mother had made it up to Gregor and reunited with her young.

"Don't be a fool!" Gregor shouted down. "Hurry!"

"Me and you, friend," Edil said gently to the buck. "Me and you."

The semi-circle of wolves tightened around them, becoming smaller and smaller. Edil quickly grabbed the rope and once again wrapped it and tying it around the reindeer's midsection.

"NO!" Gregor screamed down.

Edil let out yells and swings of his shovel, and the buck stamped his feet to get the wolves to back off a bit. He continued to secure the buck, with just enough rope left from under the furry belly to wrap around his wrist.

"Hope this works," he prayed out loud as he began shoving the buck towards the wall. "PULL! NOW! PULL!"

The rope became tense from the top down to the buck. Using all his weight, pushing with his left shoulder while swinging the shovel with his right hand, Edil did his best to give Gregor help and get the reindeer off the ground.

Old Shadow had enough. He leaped to the front of the pack, his teeth snapping.

"Faster!" Edil screamed as the buck rose, bellowing in confusion.

Edil could feel the tension being created on that last bit of rope wrapped around his left wrist. He held on tightly, and his feet rose from the ground.

Old Shadow looked up at the long rope coming down from the ridge. The buck was above Edil, too far for the wolf to reach. Edil was dangling by one arm from under the deer. He was scrambling desperately to gain footing on the wall while holding onto the shovel with his free hand. He was not too far from Old Shadow's grasp.

The large, dark wolf ran towards the wall with remarkable speed before jumping up, jaws open, at Edil. Edil swung his shovel right for Old Shadow.

He felt the connection but heard no sound. There was no thud or clang, no yelp or yip- just Old Shadow landing on his feet. Edil was yanked up another couple of feet to safety. He looked down, surprised to see blood around Old Shadow's feet. He glanced at his shovel and saw blood along the edge. He watched as the wolf shook his head in confusion, then raised it to look at Edil above.

A gash ran along the side of Old Shadow's face. Blood took the place of the wolf's left eye. Only one yellow eye could focus on Edil as he was raised higher and higher, away from the pack's reach. Edil's shovel had connected with Old Shadow on an angle, causing it to slice rather than hit.

Edil beamed and let out a loud laugh at the wolf's injury. It was not life-threatening, but it was severe. The fear had left Edil as he looked down with a bird's eye view of the battlefield below them. Wolves were limping, some licking their wounds. A few wolves laid about, barely moving. Edil could not stop laughing.

"Dear Lord!" Gregor shouted at him as he pulled the buck and his brother to the top.

Edil could not stop shaking, his adrenaline rushing through his veins. He finally dropped the shovel as Gregor unwrapped the rope from his wrist, revealing burn marks. He had to quickly let the buck loose as it was eager to rejoin his family, waiting patiently but unsurely away from Gregor.

"That was insane!" Gregor scolded Edil, his finger shaking in his face. Gregor felt upset. His nostrils were flaring, and he looked grey from both the physical act of pulling up the four deer and his brother and from the emotional act of watching his brother fight the wolves.

"No, brother," Edil grinned. "That was an adventure."

THE REINDEER

Edil and Gregor took a few moments to compose themselves, sitting on the edge of the toboggan. Edil became very aware of the injuries while fighting the wolves once the excitement wore off. It was bad enough he had a headache and a sore nose from the goat's head-butting incident earlier in the day, but his shoulder was aching from being pulled up by the rope. His hip and knee were throbbing from being slammed, and he had cuts and scrapes all over. Still, he felt good.

Gregor was in a state of disbelief. He could not believe his brother risked his life for a family of reindeer. Edil going down the icy wall into such danger broke their parents' only cardinal rule. Edil had left the boundaries of the safe valley, and Gregor did not know what he would have told his family if something had happened to him. Gregor was so relieved that Edil had come back safe, yet, he had the urge to slap him in the head for being so stupidly brave.

Gregor looked up at the reindeer. This was the closest he had ever been to such a breed of animal. They stood only a few feet from them, the buck eyeing them suspiciously as the female nudged and sniffed the babies, checking them over to make sure they were all right. They were magnificent-looking animals, their antlers larger and more powerful looking than the deer in the valley. The male reindeer had a thick, greyish mane growing under his throat and chest, making him seem more prominent and broader than he was. The female was more of a brown shade, and both babies were light.

"Now, what becomes of them?" Gregor finally spoke. The sound of his voice made the reindeer step back a few steps, skittishly. "There is nothing up here for them. If they don't find the valley, they'll starve."

"We'll have to lead them down somehow," Edil said. He stood up to stretch the aches out of his bones. The reindeer once again stepped even further away, unsure of what was going to happen next.

"Come on, now," Edil said gently. "I thought we were friends."

The buck let out a chuffing sound.

"I don't think he trusts you too much," Gregor told him.

Edil had to think. He knew Gregor was right. They could not leave them up on the ice. There was nothing for them to eat. All that fighting and struggling to get them away from the wolves would be for nothing if Edil could not get them down into the valley.

"Let's try roping them again," Gregor suggested.

Edil nodded and bent down to pick up the rope. He hoped to harness them somehow and lead them down, but the buck stamped his hoof and let out an angry-sounding trumpet.

"No. I don't think they like that idea right now," Edil said, putting the rope down. He spotted his long-abandoned package that his mother had carefully wrapped. The cloth that held Edil's leftover dried meats and berries were still sitting on the ground where he had left it.

"You deer hungry? Eh?" he asked with a smile. "I bet you are. After all that fighting, I bet you worked up quite the appetite, eh?"

He slowly picked up the cloth bundle, careful not to startle them. He picked out a couple of berries and tossed them on the ground in front of the animals. Gregor figured out where his brother was going with his idea and reached for his bundle.

The reindeer eyed the fallen berries suspiciously at first. Gradually, the buck sniffed at it, rolled it around with his large snout, and then nibbled at it. This was a sign for the others to eat the remaining fallen berries.

"Yes, very good," Edil nodded. "There's more. Come on. Have some more."

He plucked a few more berries from the cloth and tossed them. This time he made sure they landed closer to him, forcing the reindeer to step closer as they ate.

"Start walking back," Edil told his brother. "We'll drop some berries here and there. They'll follow."

They crossed the top of the ice, the sled trailing behind them. They often dropped some berries and looked over their shoulders to make sure the reindeer were following. After a while, it surprised Gregor when something nudged his hand. The youngest of the family had become brave enough to walk beside him and was begging for more berries. He laughed with delight and amazement as he fed the baby berries from his hand.

It was Karina who first spotted them on the goat trail, coming down. She was sitting outside where she used tree stumps for a table and chair, acorn shells for cups, large leaves for plates, and her imagination for the invisible meal she was serving to a make-believe family. She had looked up to see her brothers slowly coming down the path with the four reindeer.

"Papa! Mama!" she yelled with excitement. "Quick! Come look!"

Her mother came out of the cabin where she was preparing supper. Johan was in the garden, tending to potatoes when he looked up. At first, he could not make it out. Johan put his hand to his brow to shield the sun's reflection and squinted. He could see that Edil was not walking as steadily as he should have. The worry of his son's injury went in and out of his mind when he made out the reindeer family. Two larger ones were following his sons. Two smaller ones were walking alongside them and seemed to play with them, butting them and frolicking.

"What has he done now?" he muttered to himself. He knew this had to be Edil's doing.

He rushed, along with Amelia and Karina, to meet them at the foot of the trail. He could not imagine the story behind this. How they even acquired reindeer from the other side of the ridge was beyond his imagination.

Amelia was the first to gasp when they came closer into view. She could see that Edil had been roughed up. A bloody gash was on his cheek and a scrape on his chin. His hair was more disheveled than usual, and his clothes were filthy from dirt and mud. He walked with tenderness and looked exhausted.

"The mud," Johan mumbled. Amelia detected anger in his voice. "There's no mud up on the ice. That's on the other side."

As they became closer, the reindeer became skittish again and stopped walking when they saw the others. Karina went running up, but Amelia reached out and held her back. Gregor was the first to come down and greet them.

"Just remain calm," was the first thing he said. "We don't want to scare them back up the trail. Let them find the meadow and the forest."

"How? Where? Why?" Johan sputtered, not sure where to begin.

"Edil will tell you. It's his adventure. Come. Let's leave them so they will come down," Gregor said.

They walked back to the cabin, filled with questions. Gregor just wanted to wash up, eat, and drink. All the excitement and pulling on the rope had drained him. He answered most of their questions with shakes of his head between bites of stew and gulps of water.

Finally, Edil appeared, looking worse for wear. Amelia jumped up and helped him to his seat at the table. Edil told the story while Amelia set a bowl of stew in front of him and fussed around him, cleaning his wounds. Karina was on the edge of her seat, hanging on to every word, every detail of Edil's fight with the wolves, and rescuing the reindeer. Her eyes were huge and sparkling in the firelight.

Johan sat there silently. Inside, he was brewing with anger. He was angry at Gregor for allowing Edil to do such a stupid thing. He was mad at Edil for coming up with such a foolish idea. It upset him that Old Shadow remained out there after all those years and caused a threat to his son.

Johan was also proud. Pride swelled as he came to realize the bravery and strength of his son- at Edil's smarts and quick thinking. Edil was a son that any man prayed to have.

He could not let Edil know that, though. He could not condone leaving the valley. However, he did not want to scold him either. Edil was eighteen years old and a man now. So, Johan just sat in silence while Edil went on. It made Johan sad to see how excited Edil was- animated as he talked, his voice racing. It was then that Johan knew perhaps Edil was not meant to stay in the valley.

He pushed that thought aside and sipped his tea. He could not think about that now. He was not ready to think about that.

"Where are the reindeer now?" he asked calmly.

"Gone. I led them as far as the meadow before they took off. They'll find a place here, don't you reckon?

Johan nodded.

"They seemed happy," Edil smiled. "Like they were dancing among the flowers."

"Good. Glad to see you think it was worth it," Johan said. "But, it's been quite a day. I think we need to rest. Since you boys failed to remember to bring back ice for the cold box, Gregor, I am sending you up first thing in the morning. Edil, you need to rest and tend to yourself. Harvesting is just a matter of days away. We need you at your fittest."

Edil agreed he needed the rest. As soon as he laid his head on his pillow and closed his eyes, he was sleeping soundly. He dreamed of wolves and smiled in his sleep.

In the morning, he could hear the bustling of his mother as she prepared a breakfast of fried apple slices in honey, quail eggs, and deer sausage. He could smell the tea brewing behind his closed eyes. It was Gregor that nudged him awake. He opened his eyes to see his brother standing over him, smiling.

"Come. They are back," Gregor told him

Confused, sleepy, and sore, Edil limped to the front door. He rubbed the sleep from his eyes and blinked away the sand to see the reindeer standing only a few feet from the cabin, where the clearing ended and the meadow began. Their stubby tails flicked the summer flies away as they quietly ate their breakfast of moss. The buck looked up at Edil and his family that gathered in the doorway to watch them, then lowered his head, greeting them with a bow. Then he went back to calmly grazing.

"Can I pet them?" Karina asked.

"I don't know," Edil admitted. It shocked him to see them again and so close to his home.

Karina darted out. This time, no one stopped her. She ran up the path but stopped short when she was close to them. Carefully and slowly, she put her hand out in greeting. She held her breath as the baby stepped forward and sniffed. Karina could not contain herself as she giggled. She tried to pet the baby, and it pleasantly surprised Karina when the baby allowed it.

"What do we do with them?" Edil asked his father as they watched Karina scratch the back of the baby's neck.

"Do with them?" Johan responded. "I suppose we just let them be. They don't seem to bother us. We don't seem to bother them."

Edil nodded. It seemed the reindeer were going to keep close, and he was happy about that. All the fear and injuries that came with rescuing them were worth it.

The reindeer became a daily sight. Every morning they were within the view of the cabin. Karina was smitten by them, and they with her. The youngest reindeer loved to follow Karina into the fields, where they would chase each other and play. The others tolerated Karina's curiosity as she would pet them and hug them.

Karina took it upon herself to name them: Buck, Mimi, Junior, and Baby. Along with Onyx, Hock, and Chop, the reindeer became permanent members of their little farm.

Amelia was shocked to find Karina milking Mimi one morning. Karina was under her belly with a small bucket, and Mimi just grazed as the little girl milked at her udders.

"It's good, Mama!" Karina beamed as she held up the bucket.

Amelia raised her eyebrow at Johan. Perhaps now they would not need those annoying mountain goats anymore.

It was also Karina that had climbed up on Junior's back and grabbed onto his antlers. He bucked just a little, but she laughed, squeezing her legs to hold on tight. Then, he grew bored with her and stopped resisting. When Edil saw that, he realized the potential in the reindeer.

He started slowly. He knew they loved to snack on little mushrooms, so he would feed them mushrooms by hand as a treat. Then, he whistled two quick notes every time he gave them a mushroom. Eventually, all he had to do was whistle the two notes, and they came running in from the meadow or wherever they were.

Harnessing them was a different story. The reindeer shied away from the rope, remembering the burns it caused when they were pulled up the side of the ridge. Edil convinced the younger ones to tolerate leather straps with treats of mushrooms. Eventually, the older ones gave in too.

After a time, he hooked them to a log to get them used to pulling weight. He figured by the following spring they could help plow the fields. Between Onyx and the reindeer, Edil, Johan, and Gregor could get the work done quicker.

When fall settled in, Johan woke up one morning to hear creaking and a rhythmic clopping of hooves on dirt. He could not believe what he saw when he went outside. Hooked up to a small push wagon that Johan had built years ago were Buck and Mimi. In unison, they pulled, trotting round and round the cabin. Edil stood on top of the wagon, reins in his hands, laughing with victory.

Letting Go

The long winter came and went. Most things remained the same. Johan and Amelia noticed Edil went up on the ice more than ever before. Buck usually accompanied him, the two of them making the oddest pair of friends. And yet, the friendship worked. They had built trust and bond between man and animal.

In the spring, Johan and Gregor rigged up two extra plows. Along with Onyx, Buck and Junior helped plow the small fields. Edil was right. They completed the plowing season in a fraction of the time as the years before.

On a stormy spring night, Mimi gave birth to rare twins. They gave the tiny fawns the names of Dunder and Blixem. Their reindeer family was growing.

There was no need for the goats that spring. With Mimi nursing the twins, there was more than enough milk and cheese in the cold box.

When the planting was done, and the fields showed a little green, Johan and his family took a day to celebrate and pray for a good bounty come the harvest season. They packed a picnic and hiked to the hot springs where they could splash and play. As always, the reindeer followed them.

Johan sat on the blanket, one arm around his wife, the other digging in the basket for something to snack on. The parents watched as their older sons teased their youngest and tossed her back and forth in the water. Karina squealed with delight.

"We have to let them go," Johan said quietly to Amelia, his voice sad. "We can't keep them here forever. It's not fair."

"I know," Amelia smiled as she kept her eyes on her sons. She felt the tears building up. "We have to give them the chance we had. Maybe there are more of us out there. They deserve to have love."

"Love. A family," Johan nodded. "I know Edil just wants to see what's out there. He's aching to get out and experience new things."

"Ever since he bought the reindeer home—"

"Yes. Ever since Edil stepped on the other side, he's been dying to get out and keep going."

Amelia wiped away her tears with the back of her hand and took a deep breath to chase the sob that caught in her throat.

"They'll come back," Johan nodded, trying to convince himself more than Amelia. "We can send them on a trading trip. They will get news of the outside world. They will have experiences, maybe meet someone, and then they'll come back."

"We didn't go back," Amelia reminded him.

"That's different," Johan huffed. They dropped the conversation as Edil rose out of the water and walked to them for a drink, drying off in the sunlight.

That night, after everyone was asleep from a fun-filled holiday, Johan snuck out into the stable. Onyx whinnied as Johan walked past him to an empty stall that they used for storage.

He stood there with his hands on his hips, looking around at over twenty years of odds and ends they had crafted, mainly to keep their hands busy and try new things. It was a creative outlet on long winter days to build a bench or chair. They wove blankets, carved bowls, and whittled animals from wood.

Johan walked out and looked at his fields in the moonlight. They always harvested more than enough. There was always plenty of cabbage, potatoes, carrots, turnips, and other vegetables. The meadow itself was a bounty of herbs and spices just waiting to be picked and dried.

He did a quick calculation in his head. Johan knew the villages south of them did not provide the lush crops and plants that the valley did. He knew that they could sack and crate plenty of goods that they would not need come harvest with hard work and extra time. Edil and Gregor could then load up the old sled and take it south for trade.

They could also put their talent for crafting to use. Perhaps trade furniture, blankets, and carving pieces for a night in an inn or a meal at a tavern.

Slowly, Johan's plan came together. He did not mention it right away. He spent the next two nights up on the ice, alone. He would study the stars, stare off into the distance, and do more calculating. Occasionally, he would scratch some figures into the snow with the tip of his walking stick. He had to figure every little detail out. He could not just send his sons into the unknown.

On the fourth sleepless night, he was ready. He had all his calculations figured out. After supper, he took Edil up on the ice and crossed the edge above the sealed-off tunnel.

"What's going on, Papa?" Edil asked, concerned. "You have not been yourself, and you've been wandering at night."

"See the stars, Edil?" Johan began, pointing up at the sky. Edil looked up to see the millions of stars twinkling down at them. "God put those stars in the sky for a reason. They give us direction. Seafarers learn to read them, so they know where to sail without getting lost. Travelers learn them so they won't become lost on great, barren plains with no landmarks.

"There are no landmarks out there," he continued, now pointing out into the dark distance. "There is nothing but flat land and flat sky for days and days. If you are going to venture out there, you are going to have to learn to read the stars."

Edil's heart skipped a beat.

"Read the stars?"

"Read the stars and the moon and the sun. They will lead you to Bluster. It's your mother's village. It's where we married."

"Why?"

"Because—" Johan sighed sadly. "It is time. It is time for you and Gregor to go out there and see what it offers.

Edil was speechless.

"We'll fix up the old sled. We'll get Buck and Junior to pull it. I'll keep Onyx here. He might be fit as a fiddle, but he's still up there in age. We'll make items for trade. Harvest crops and plants for sale. After your battle with Old Shadow, I think you proved you could hold your own out there."

"Does Mama know this?" Edil asked.

"We've spoken a few times. It's not an easy subject to approach. Parents don't like saying goodbye to their children," Johan said sadly.

"But we are coming back, no?"

"We will always welcome you back. This is home. This will always be home."

"Leaving the valley was always a dream. But it was just a dream," Edil said.

"You have lots to learn before you leave- you and Gregor. It's a whole different world out there. They are not exactly tolerant. But you are tough. You can handle it."

Edil nodded. His heart was beating fast as he tried to comprehend what his father was telling him. They spent the rest of the night looking at the stars and planning the trip. Edil felt mixed with excitement and sadness as they discussed the outside world. He had so many questions that his father could not keep up with him.

In the morning, they headed back down. They told Gregor, Amelia, and Karina their plan. After they wiped away tears, it was decided. Edil and Gregor were to venture beyond the tunnel after the harvest.

The First Goodbye

There was never a need for the sled or troika in the valley, so Johan had left it in the tunnel all those years. With his sons, he entered the tunnel to clean them up and fix the areas worn away from time. Overall, because they kept them out of the elements, the old sled and troika were in good shape.

Johan also redesigned the large, planked door he thought would seal off the tunnel's entrance forever. He needed to keep the door strong and locked from inside the tunnel to keep the wolves out, but he also needed a simple way for his sons to open it from the outside when they returned.

They spent most of the warm season building furniture. Small tables and chairs. Ornate benches with floral designs carved into them. A couple of headboards and footboards for beds. Some stools.

Amelia and Karina also put their talents to work. They plucked goat hair from the meadow, cleaned, pulled, and spun it into yarn using a drop spindle. Together they knitted caps and shawls with yarn.

The crop fields grew plentiful as usual. They filled crates with their root vegetables. Amelia dried many herbs from the meadow by hanging bunches of plants upside down from the cabin's rafters. The home became overwhelmed with the floral and herbal smells.

Johan and Amelia held lessons about the outside world to teach the boys everything they might need to know. They uncovered a small sack of coins from the bottom of Johan's chest. It had not seen the light of day since Johan had no use for it. He sat with Edil and Gregor and taught them the value of the coins and how they could purchase a night at an inn or a meal in a tavern.

There was a small stack of writing paper that Amelia had to keep in touch with her family after she married. It had yellowed over the years from not being used since the children learned their ABCs and 123s by scratching it in the dirt. She spent the evening by firelight writing letters to her family so Edil and Gregor could forward them if they happened upon chance.

In the evenings, Johan took his sons up to the ice. Together, they studied how the sun would set and how it would rise. They took notice of all the details of twilight and dawn. They memorized the stars and noted the position of the moon throughout the night. When the warm valley's air became chilly and the nights were growing longer, Edil and Gregor were confident in stargazing skills.

When the harvest was done, it was time. The night before they were to leave, they had a feast. They fought back the tears and bravely smiled and laughed as they gorged themselves with everything the valley and their fields offered. They celebrated their successful years and said prayers in thanks. With stuffed bellies and lumps in their throats, they went to bed. As much as they tried, they tossed and turned throughout the night.

When dawn came, Edil went to fetch the reindeer. They decided that Buck and Junior would pull them to Bluster. Mimi was still nursing the twins. Baby, as big as he was growing, was still too young for the journey. Onyx would stay behind with Johan, where he belonged.

Edil put the bridles on the reindeer and waited for the family to exit the cabin. Together, they walked to the tunnel, Edil leading Buck and Junior by the reins. Johan, Amelia, Gregor, and Karina followed, heads down.

They spoke little as they traveled through the dark tunnel with lit lanterns. The flickering shadows on the black, cratered walls looked gloomy, matching their feelings. Finally, with heavy hearts and knotted stomachs, they reached the sled and troika, which were piled high and tied down with everything they would bring to the outside world. Furniture, garments, produce, blankets, and small carvings were under the large covering to keep them dry throughout the trip. They put long spears by the seat upfront to help fend off any possibilities of wolves attacking them.

"Remember everything you've learned," Johan reminded his sons as he hugged Gregor. Edil was keeping himself busy and focused on hitching Buck and Junior to the sled.

"You boys play smart," Amelia said, her voice catching as tears rolled down her cheeks. She thought it was a bad idea. Her heart hurt so much at the thought of her sons never returning that Amelia did not think she could bear it. She could not see how she would survive without them.

"It'll be fine, Mama," Gregor promised as he reached over to her and wiped her tears away. This only made her cry more. "We'll be back."

Karina clung to Amelia's skirts, her eyes huge and filled with tears. Her mouth was turned down, her bottom lip pouting out, and her chin quivering. Gregor picked her up and hugged her.

"You be good for Mama and Papa," Gregor told her. "You are going to have to help more. Fill in for us while we are gone."

"I want to go with you!" she cried. "I want to see the Land of the Giants too!"

"Oooh," he laughed. "Perhaps when you are older, you can come with us."

"What if you don't come back?" she asked innocently.

"Oh, hush now!" Edil called out, walking over to them. "All of you, blubbering over here. We are coming back."

As brave as he sounded, they could see he was fighting hard to keep his sobs down. He cleared his throat and blinked hard to keep the tears and cries from coming forward.

"We'll bring you back something- a surprise," Edil promised Karina as he ruffled her hair.

"Yes. We will bring back lots of stuff," Gregor nodded as he put Karina back down. "What would you like, Papa?"

"Sugar. Flour. Coffee. Bread! Real cheese from a cow! Butter! Sweets!" Johan ticked off as they laughed. "Oh! And Ale! Don't forget the Ale! That dandelion wine just doesn't cut it!"

"And you, Mama?" Edil asked, turning to his mother. "What does Mama want me to bring back?"

"Whatever your heart wants," she smiled. She just wanted them to come back soon and come back safe.

Edil nodded and leaned in to give her a quick peck on the cheek, then turned to climb into the sled before he cried. He just wanted to get away before he changed his mind.

Gregor climbed in next to him, wiping his tears on the back of his mitten. They stared straight ahead as Johan pulled the big, heavy, wooden door open. Sunlight and cold rushed into the tunnel. Edil had to take a minute to let his eyes adjust, but the reindeer were pulling on the reins, eager to get out. They were excited to get out in the cold air of the open tundra. Finally, he gave the reins slack, and with his heavy heart jumping with excitement, they jolted forward and out of the tunnel.

He was on the other side. Edil was finally on the other side, the ridge getting smaller and smaller behind him. His frown turned into a wide grin.

Return to Bluster

Johan had warned them that the tundra was nothing to be excited about. For days Gregor and Edil rode, heading south to the village of Bluster, and the excitement wore off quickly. It was flat, white, grey, and bland with nothing to see. The brothers jokingly named it "The Great Nothing."

It was a relatively uneventful trip as they crossed The Great Nothing. The only wolves they spotted were far off in the distance. Edil could not tell if they were Old Shadow and his pack. They did not even see reindeer.

The trip went on for days. Edil was growing weary of it, and Gregor thought they were lost. After more days, Gregor was about to suggest turning around when they saw it. The first sign of other people.

There were tracks in the snow- runners from a sled or troika had left grooves. They spotted some large footprints of a man. There were paw prints and hoof prints too. The snow became more muddied as they neared the village.

From a distance, against the grey skies, the shacks and shanties of Bluster rose. It was a small village but seemed large to Gregor and Edil. Edil pulled the reins to stop Buck and Junior. He wanted to take a few minutes to compose the excitement growing inside of him. He wanted to treasure his first view of the Land of the Giants.

"Are we ready for this?" Gregor whispered.

"I don't believe we have a choice," Edil responded softly.

"We could turn around," Gregor said, half-joking.

"Ugh. And cross The Great Nothing again so soon?" Edil laughed. "No. We are here. Let's do Mama and Papa proud."

With that, he clicked his tongue and gave the reins a light snap. Buck and Junior picked up the pace and trotted towards Bluster as Gregor's stomach formed a knot. Edil could feel his heart racing.

Whatever people were doing as the brothers rode down the one lone road into Bluster stopped. A woman churning butter ceased her pumping. A blacksmith hammering horseshoes did a double-take and stopped with his hammer in midair; his eyes focused on Edil and Gregor. Doors opened, and people stepped out and stared. Children stopped running about in the game of the chase. The entire village seemed to come to a standstill as they rode in.

"Hello," Edil called out nervously and nodded his head in a polite greeting.

"How do you do?" Gregor said, following his brother's lead.

Some people just instinctively nodded back or raised their hand in an unsure wave. They did not know how to respond to the little strangers.

"Can someone point us to the tavern?" Edil called out. His father had told them they should head straight to the tavern. A tavern was an excellent place to purchase a meal and drink. They could also get a feel for people and find out where they could make trades and deals.

"'Tis that way, sir," a little boy who appeared to be the same height as the brothers pointed down the road.

"Thank you," Edil said with a smile.

They continued to ride slowly and take in everything. They saw horses of different colors, large and small, that seemed so foreign to them compared to Onyx. Dogs wandered the street, making them nervous because they resembled wolves so much. But it was the people that fascinated them- the giants, who were not as large as Edil imagined. Some were very tall, and some were short. Some were plump, and others were scrawny. There were blondes and redheads- a hair color the brothers had never seen. They saw freckled faces and darker faces. Edil was more intrigued by the diversity of people than the size.

They stopped in front of the tavern and climbed down. Edil went to wrap the reins around a post when a huge spotted dog bounded towards him, causing him to jump back.

"He won't bite," a man called out. "He just wants a pet."

Edil nodded and gingerly reached out to touch his first dog ever. He had never seen an animal with such an excited tail. He smiled and laughed until the dog leaned in and gave him a big lick before bounding away. Edil's face fell in disgust as he wiped the slobber with his sleeve.

"You might want to put the deer with the others," the same man suggested to them.

"The others?" Edil asked.

"Aye. Right outside town. All the reindeer are penned up."

Edil looked over at Gregor in confusion.

"Reckon you two are here for the Reindeer Games, no?" the man said.

"Reindeer Games?" Edil repeated, looking at Gregor. He was trying to remember if their father had mentioned any such thing. Gregor just shrugged his shoulders.

"No. Just passing through," Gregor said. "Reindeer Games, is it? No reindeer game for us."

"Too bad. Them two are the finest deer I've seen in a while," the man said before walking off.

Confused but not wanting to appear naive, Edil and Gregor continued to tie the reindeer to the hitch and hang makeshift feed bags from their antlers. The feed bags were filled with moss and were another one of Johan's inventions.

They left the reindeer at the post and walked into the same tavern their father had walked into over two decades before. Not much had changed. It was more crowded than usual, making it loud and hot. The crowd became quiet, though, as all eyes went straight to Gregor and Edil. The brothers stood there, feeling uncomfortable being on display.

"What can we do for you, little fellas?" a large man asked from behind a counter. He was wearing an apron stained from spills and cooking.

"Um, might we sit anywhere?" Gregor asked nervously.

"Wherever it's empty," he said, pointing to some tables, benches, and chairs. "What can I bring you?"

"Two ales," Edil grinned while Gregor shot him a look. "And two of whatever is cooking over there in that pot will do. Thank you."

"Ales?" Gregor whispered as they maneuvered in between people towards an empty table.

"I want to see what Papa has been raving about all these years."

It was overwhelming, walking so close to people. They were used to being face to face with their parents. Here, they mostly came up to the hips of men and embarrassingly up to the chests of some women. By the time they made it to their table by the window, they were flushed and sweaty from nerves. It quickly passed as Edil noticed the window made of cuts of circular glass. He instantly became curious, and he touched and tapped on it.

"What are you doing?" Gregor hissed.

"Glass! It's glass! We should bring some back for the cabin."

The tavern keeper brought their steins of ale and bowls of stew. He stood above them as the brothers said their thanks and then took a spoonful of stew. It differed from the stew their mother would make. The meat was different- heartier and richer- with no grassy undertones to it.

"Delicious!" Edil said. "May I ask what kind of meat is this?"

"Cattle. Beef," he replied.

"Well, it's excellent," Edil said as Gregor nodded in agreement. He reached for the stein and gulped the brown, dark liquid. Immediately, Edil's face tightened up in disgust. The keeper burst out laughing.

"What's the matter, mate? Never had ale before?"

Edil shook his head frantically and swallowed hard.

"Bitter," he coughed. "No good."

"It's an acquired taste. I'll bring you some water," the keeper laughed.

"Thank you," Edil said sincerely, then turned to Gregor. "I think Papa is crazy. That is awful!"

People grew bored of Edil and Gregor and went back to their private conversations. Edil and Gregor felt more at ease and continued to eat their stew in peace and talk among themselves about what the next step would be in their visit to Bluster.

People came and went in the tavern, so they paid no mind to the door opening and closing. They did not even notice a tall, older man standing next to their table, looking down at them until he cleared his throat.

"Pardon me," he said when they looked up. "Do you mind?"

He grabbed an empty chair and sat down at the table. Edil and Gregor glanced at each other quizzically.

"Someone came to my home, telling me of two small men that had come to town. I had to see this for myself," he said.

It took Edil back. Was this what his parents warned him about? Was the teasing and taunting about to start?

"Excuse me, sir," Edil began with a defensive tone, but the man put his hand up.

"Hear me out," he said. "There has not been a small person in Bluster for many years. My sister, she was small, like you two. She left to live with her husband in his village, but we never heard from her again."

"Your sister?" Gregor repeated.

"Yes. She was a wonderful sister too. We waited for years to hear from her. Eventually, we came to terms with the fact that she and her husband most likely perished on their journey," he explained. "So, I never saw another small person again. I did not know there were more. I just wanted to see you and welcome you two. I'm Henrick."

He put his large hand out, extended for a friendly shake.

"Henrick? Your sister has not perished," Edil blurted out. "She's very much alive."

"I don't understand."

"Her name is Amelia, is it not?"

Henrick's eyes flew wide open. He was speechless, so he just nodded.

"And she married Johan, did she not?" Edil continued with a smile. "That's our parents. Johan and Amelia are our Papa and Mama."

Henrick sat back in his chair, looking back and forth at the young men. He could see it. He could see his own mother's eyes on one brother and his father's smile on the other.

"As a matter of fact, we have letters from our Mama for you and your family," Edil said proudly.

"Well, I'll be—" Henrick finally spoke. "After all these years."

He stood up suddenly and slapped both brothers on the back, letting out a loud laugh.

"Ale!" he called out. "We need a round of ale! These are my nephews! These are Amelia's boys!"

"No. No ale needed," Edil pleaded. "Not really our thing."

"Wine then!" Henrick laughed and slapped them again before sitting down with them. "Tell me, nephews, what can your old Uncle Henrick do for you? What do you need?"

"Well, we need to secure a room at the inn," Gregor said. "Can you help us with that?"

"Nonsense! You'll come back to the house. I have the old house now that my parents are gone, and my brothers have moved. There is plenty of room. You'll love it. It's where Amelia grew up."

His face softened.

"Your mother," he continued. "Tell me, how is my dear Amelia doing? Where is she? Is she happy?"

The keeper put down a stein of ale for Henrick and goblets of wine in front of the brothers. Edil noticed the wine looked nothing like the one his mother would occasionally make. It was dark and red. He took a small sip, bracing himself for an unpleasant taste like the ale, but he liked it.

"Our mother is quite well," Gregor said. "She and Papa are very happy and healthy. They found a nice place to settle down, away from people."

They agreed that under no circumstances were they ever to reveal details or whereabouts of the valley. This was something Johan made the boys promise before they left. He warned them that men were greedy creatures and would destroy everything the valley offered. The valley was theirs and only theirs.

"We have a sister as well," Edil joined in. "Karina. Just a wee little sprite."

"A niece," Henrick sighed. "And she's happy. Johan treats Amelia well?"

"She's the queen," Edil said. "And is very well provided for. Our father is quite the farmer and craftsman. He built a lovely home for her. For all of us."

"You must tell me more. You must stay with me," Henrick insisted.

Edil and Gregor looked at each other. They had not planned on meeting a family member. Amelia was not sure if they were still alive or even still in the town. She was almost right since he claimed to be the last one living in Bluster.

"I suppose we can stay with you. We are only here for just a short while," Edil said. "We have lots of goods we would like to trade."

"I can purchase them from you," Henrick said.

"No. Coin is not useful where we are from," Gregor said. "We would like to trade them for items we could use."

"Alright then," Henrick nodded before taking a big gulp from his stein. "Tomorrow, I'll introduce you to Nick. He'll know where to send you. Nick knows everyone."

"Who's Nick?"

"Tomorrow," he laughed. "Tomorrow, we set up business for you. Today, we celebrate! To family!"

He held up his stein in the gesture of a toast. Edil and Gregor joined him with their goblets and tapped them together. They could not believe their good fortune. The trip across The Great Nothing was worth it. Their adventure was beginning, and it was off to a good start.

Nick

Gregor and Edil spent the night in a room made of stone, warmed by an immense fireplace. They slept in big, ornate beds, and their mattresses were filled with downy feathers instead of straw. Their blankets were thick and soft, and they had more pillows in one bed than in their entire cabin back home in the valley.

As lush and wealthy as Henrick's home was, the brothers missed the comforts of their rooms and beds. They were simple men with simple needs. They found that years on the hard straw tick mattress and one flat pillow made the fluffy beds uncomfortable and tough on their hips and backs. If it was not for the wine that they drank to lull them to sleep, they might not have had any sleep at all.

They woke in the morning to the smells and sounds of breakfast cooking by Henrick's servants. They found Henrick himself sitting at the same dining table their parents had when they celebrated their wedding years ago. Edil's eyes widened at the sight of the breakfast spread: eggs and biscuits, bacon and gravy. Edil and Gregor never had any bread or eggs from chickens. The delicious, smoked, crispy bacon made them wonder about the two pigs back at home. Everything was just simply divine. They could not get enough.

Gregor was making a mental note of what needed to be taken back. Definitely a sack or two of flour to bake bread. Chickens to give them eggs. The valley supplied them with so much, but there were also so many items they were missing out on.

The subject of Nick came up. Henrick told them he would bring them to Nick later in the day.

"After he gives his Sunday sermon," Henrick said between bites of biscuits that he drenched in egg yolk.

"Sunday sermon? What's that?" Gregor asked.

"Nick has a little church just outside of town," Henrick continued. "He's a preacher. Preaches the Good Word. Don't you observe the Lord's Day back home?"

"Well, yes. We read from the Bible, give prayers and thanks. Mama makes a nice supper," Edil said.

"No house of worship? No church for townsfolk to gather at?"

Edil and Gregor eyed each other. It was clear to them that Henrick did not know just how isolated they were. They shook their heads and continued to eat their breakfast in silence.

"Well then. I'll take you to Nick's sermon. And then introduce you afterward. Maybe you'll get some business in before the Reindeer Games begin."

"Just what is this Reindeer Games we keep hearing about?"

"Oh, it's just this annual day of races and betting," Henrick explained. "People come from villages all over with their reindeer and race them. It's good business for the town. We've been doing it for about five years now."

The rest of the breakfast went quickly. The brothers ate until they felt like they would bust. Even then, with his belly full, Edil still forced a couple of more bites of biscuit and warm butter down. He never knew bread could be so good.

They left the large house that made them feel lost and hitched Buck and Junior to their sled and troika. They rode to the church with Henrick, something they had never seen or heard of before. The brothers were quite curious about people coming together in prayer.

The church was simple, on top of a hill, made of nothing more than wooden planks. There was a plain cross above the door. A small bell hung next to the door that a woman was pulling on to ring it, letting people know that church was about to begin.

Henrick led the way. He motioned quietly for Edil and Gregor to remove their knitted winter caps before entering the building. The building was just one room. Rows and rows of benches lined the room. Up at the front of the room was a tall, wooden stand. There was a young man behind it, and a book opened on the podium.

They took a seat on a bench, looking around. The man up front was smiling and nodding politely to people as they entered. His eyes landed on Edil and Gregor. They twinkled as he nodded an acknowledgment to them.

After a few minutes, the bustling of men, women, and children settled down, and silence fell over the room. All eyes were on the man upfront, waiting for him to speak. Even Edil and Gregor felt caught up in the anticipation, not knowing what to expect.

What happened next was unlike anything the brothers could have ever imagined. The man spoke, his voice deep and passionate, yet calm and soothing. He read a passage from the Bible aloud, encouraging his audience to imagine and believe in the story. When he was through reading, he closed the book and walked to the front of the stand, explaining the passage he had just read and how to incorporate its meaning into everyday life. His voice, choice of words, stance, and demeanor were all very captivating.

It was very different from the simple Bible readings Edil and Gregor had done with their family on Sundays. There was something powerful being with a large group of people. When everyone stood up to pray out loud at the end of service, the brothers recognized the prayer and stood to join in. The sound of all these voices, young and old, praying together filled Edil's heart with pride and joy.

Then, it was over. The people of the church waited for Nick to leave first before following him out the door. Henrick turned to his nephews as they waited for the small crowd to file out of the building.

"So, what do you think?"

"That was lovely," Edil admitted. "We've never experienced anything like that before."

"Come. Nick will be happy to hear that you enjoyed his sermon."

Nick was outside the door, shaking hands and laughing, saying goodbye to his congregation. He turned to see the last of his guests walking out and smiled.

Edil noticed he had a gentle smile. Nick was a young man, tall and thin, with a thick head of black hair. It was his eyes and smile that stood out, though. His blue eyes twinkled, and his smile was welcoming and warm.

"Who have we here, Henrick?" Nick asked as he pumped Henrick's hand.

"My nephews. Gregor and Edil. They very much enjoyed your sermon," Henrick said, introducing them.

"Here for the Reindeer Games?"

"No," Edil said. "We just came to visit. And to trade."

"They have quite some items," Henrick continued pointing to where the reindeer were waiting with the sleds. "Thought you might be interested in them."

Nick looked at the sled and troika. He could not make out what was under the large bundles that were roped down. A look of curiosity came over his face.

"All right," he nodded. "Come down to my post. We'll look at what you have."

He gave each brother a friendly pat on the shoulders before walking back into the church to provide it with a quick clean-up. The brothers followed their uncle.

"Post?" Gregor asked.

"Nick has a trading post," Henrick explained.

"And the church?"

"Nick is everywhere," he chuckled. "He's a good man to know. He may be young, but he's special. Nick is a friend. He's every man's friend."

Once again, the brothers followed their uncle's directions and led the reindeer to another small, simple building. This one was in town. They waited a bit until Nick arrived. He beckoned them to untie the ropes that held the bundles down. Henrick left his nephews with Nick to do their trading privately. He also wanted to check out the reindeer pen and see who he should bet on.

Nick poked and prodded around. He pulled out a carving of a bear and smiled at the craftsmanship. He admired a scarf that Amelia had knitted. He frowned at a small ornate bench Johan had made. He sniffed the satchels of herbs.

Edil and Gregor stood there, uncomfortable as they watched this stranger judge their hard work. They tried to distract themselves from Nick's scrutiny by watching the people out and about Bluster. The tavern was just down the road, attracting the largest crowd. Many loud men were entering and exiting it, excited for the Reindeer Games. There was one man, tall and broad, with the wild orange hair that stood out. He was loud and boisterous, surrounded by men listening to his tales. His coat was unlike anything Edil and Gregor had seen. It was long to the ground, made of shiny, thick, bright blue material, and the cuffs and collar were lush with black fur.

Even Nick seemed distracted by this man and his crowd as the laughter traveled down the street. Nick tucked the items back into the sled and covered it, tying it back down again.

"Come inside," he smiled. "I'll put up a pot of tea."

They followed him into the small building. Nick quickly lit some lanterns and opened some shutters to let light in. The sunlight revealed rows and rows of shelves and tables covered with odds and ends of items.

"Welcome to my post," he said as he moved to the back of the store where a small stove was. He put some kindling into the oven and lit it. "Walk around. Browse. We'll talk when the tea is ready."

Edil and Gregor walked around. They perused through things they had never seen before. There were bolts of fabric in all different colors, patterns, and materials. There were clothing and hats of all shapes and sizes. Nick had sacks of flour and wheat lining the walls and piles of books in corners. There were tools and pots and pans and plates and drinking glasses. The shelves were piled high and cluttered with so many things.

It was a figure of a little girl that stared at Edil with glass eyes that gave him a start. She had real hair and painted pink lips, and rosy cheeks.

"What is this?" he asked.

"That? Well, that's just a doll," Nick responded.

"A doll?"

"Yes. For a little girl. A plaything. A toy."

Edil carefully lifted it from the shelf. Her dress was elaborate for just a toy, green and shiny, trimmed with white lace. Her hair was golden and styled into tight curls with a big green bow. Her face was smooth and fragile.

"Karina would love this," he said, holding it up to show Gregor.

"Karina?" Nick asked.

"Our little sister," Gregor said, barely looking up from the pile of books. He never knew there were other books out there. The only book he had ever seen was the Bible.

"Dolls and toys are very popular here for the children," Nick nodded. "Take her for your sister before someone else does."

"Oh, I couldn't…."

"Why not? I'm sure you have something to trade for it. That's what I do. I trade and deal in items. Odds and ends that people don't need, but others might. No bargaining with coins here," Nick explained. "Tea is ready."

He set up a tray with cups of tea and a small plate of cookies and carried it to a table that he had available to trade. He set up three chairs around it and called them over.

"So, where did all the things in your sled come from?" he asked when they settled.

"We made them. Well, our whole family did," Gregor said.

"And where are you from?"

Edil and Gregor looked at each other. How do they explain the valley? How do they explain something without giving it away? Finally, Edil just pointed in the direction of north.

"Home," he replied.

Nick took the hint. They did not want to divulge details of their home life. He was sure they had their reasons, and he would not push for answers. Instead, he just smiled and nodded. The brothers appreciated his unspoken understanding.

"Well, it looks like you have many interesting things people will want. The herbs and spices will be very much in demand. The blankets and scarves and hats are of great workmanship. We can always use the crates of vegetables. I have several homes that need food. Their crops did not come in that well this harvest season, so they will be grateful," Nick preached. "But the furniture…."

"What of it? Our father is an excellent craftsman," Gregor said.

"Oh, no doubt. It is beautiful work," Nick nodded. "Just small."

"Oh," Gregor said, his face falling.

Edil frowned as he ate his cookie. Crumbs fell onto the doll he was still holding. He brushed the crumbs off her dress carefully when an idea came to him. He thought of Karina and her little tree stumps that she used as furniture to play tea.

"Toys," he mumbled with a mouthful of cookies. "Can you use the furniture for children?"

Nick broke out with a huge grin.

"What a marvelous idea! I don't see why not. The children will love the carvings too. I can most definitely give them away to deserving little boys and girls. Toys are, well, they just love them! You should see the children's faces and how they light up when they receive a new toy to play with."

"And I saw nothing in your shop like what we have," Edil reminded him.

"No. No figurines of bears or wolves. No furniture that they can call their own," Nick agreed. "I do believe you are on to a brilliant idea."

"So, we have a trade?" Gregor asked.

"Only if you tell me what you want in return."

"The doll," Edil said. "Definitely the doll."

"And this book," Gregor said, holding up a book.

"Fabric. We can use fabric, flour, and sugar. Have you any of that smoked, cured bacon?" Edil asked.

"Oh, and ale! Can't forget Papa wants ale," Gregor said excitedly as Nick let out a roaring laugh.

"Slow down," he chuckled. "We will make a list. You will look around some more. I will procure everything you need."

The brothers went back to browsing the store. Gregor found more books that piqued his interest. Edil found a slate board, and Nick showed him chalk pencils and how they worked. Edil smiled at the thought of Karina doing her lessons on the slate instead of the dirt in the ground.

They continued to look and come up with ideas of what they needed to bring back home. Nick followed them with a quill and paper, keeping track of what they shouted out in excitement. He could not help but bond with the two overly excited brothers.

"Let me ask you," he said as he jotted down coffee on the ever-growing list. "Are you and your family happy? Is it peaceful at home?"
"Very," Edil called out, trying on a cap.

"No problems? No pressure from anyone?"

"Not one."

"Well, then, I do have a favor to ask of you two if you don't mind," Nick said. He put down the quill and paper and leaned back on his counter, his arms folded in seriousness. Edil and Gregor stopped looking around. They noticed Nick had suddenly become very somber. The whimsical fun in the air had ceased.

"There's a village just a three-night ride from here to the Southeast," Nick began with a sigh. "It's called Katts Bog."

Edil nodded, letting Nick know they were listening.

"There is a family of bakers there. They make the most wonderful sweets," he smiled. "Anyway, the Baker's son is like the two of you."

"Like us?" Gregor asked suspiciously. "What is like us?"

"Well," Nick said cautiously. He wanted to handle this gently and not offend his new friends that he liked very much. "He's like you and Edil. You know, Northern."

Edil understood. Words did not need to be spoken. He understood that this baker's son was a small, little person in a land of giants.

"Northern. I understand," Gregor said, his guard lowering.

"The baker's son is a married man. His wife is Northern too. They are lovely people with amazing baking talents. But whenever we meet, I feel they are not…." Nick trailed off, not knowing the right words.

"Happy?" Edil asked.

"Yes. Not as happy as they could be. They work hard for his father, but they don't seem to be appreciated. It's almost as if the father feels they lack something because they are…."

"Northerners. Like us," Edil smiled as Nick nodded sadly. "What's the favor?"

"If you can, could you ride to Katts Bog and meet them? If they want, maybe they can ride back North with you? Start a new life?" Nick explained. "Someplace where they will feel appreciated and live happily?"

Edil looked at Gregor, who was shaking his head. They had a promise to keep. They needed to keep the valley unknown. They promised to keep it private and not let anyone else know about it. They did not want the giants coming and destroying it.

The baker's son and his wife were not giants, though. Edil realized his parents never said what to do if they should ever meet one of their kind. Edil nodded as Gregor looked surprised.

"Edil, no. We can't. We promised," Gregor insisted.

"It can't hurt to meet them," Edil said. "Aren't you a wee bit curious to at least meet other northerners?"

Gregor sighed and shook his head. He knew there was no convincing Edil otherwise. When Edil decided something, there was no changing it.

"This is good!" Nick said with a clap of his hands. "Now. Come! Let's watch the Reindeer Games. I'm not much of a betting man myself, but I enjoy witnessing the sport."

They walked out of the store to see a small crowd around Buck and Junior. Edil noticed the man he spotted earlier with the flamboyant blue coat and wild orange hair. He was running his hands along Buck's hind legs. Edil frowned as Buck was showing signs of annoyance at the stranger touching him.

"Quite the animal you have here, Nick," the man called out.

"Not mine, Ronan. They belong to my friends here," Nick said sternly.

Ronan looked down at Edil and Gregor and let out a laugh that seemed false and mocking.

"You two? You two own this magnificent beast?" he roared. "How do you handle him?"

"Handle him?" Edil asked, confused. He walked over to Buck and placed himself between the rude man and the deer.

"Yes. Handle him. You seem a bit tiny to show master over such a powerful animal," Ronan teased.

"Look here, sir," Gregor yelled. "We don't take kindly to such talk!"

Again, Ronan roared with laughter as his friends joined in.

"I reckon the little man is mad," he laughed. Ronan turned back to Edil and saw him staring at the fabric of his long, shiny coat.

"You like it?" he asked as he lifted it and showed it off. "It's silk. Won it in a bet. It was made in the Orient."

"Where's the Orient?" Edil asked as Ronan guffawed.

"Where's the Orient?" Ronan repeated. "Oh, this is too much! The little man doesn't know where the Orient is. I take it you haven't traveled much, have you, boy?"

Edil felt his ears turn red with embarrassment. These were the moments his parents warned them about- men like Ronan.

"Enough!" Nick yelled as he stepped forward. "Don't you have your own reindeer to tend to? Don't you have a race to prepare for?"

"My reindeer are always ready," Ronan smirked, but he backed away. He knew Nick well enough to let things be.

They watched as Ronan and his cronies walked away, heading along with many others towards the reindeer pen and the start of the games. Nick looked down at his friends and smiled apologetically.

"That was Ronan," he explained. "He's not from Bluster. He's a traveler and gambler. Not a nice man, really. Mostly a drunkard and braggart. He comes in every year for the Reindeer Games. Wins most years too."

He took Edil and Gregor up to a hill, where Henrick joined them. From their view, they could watch the games in the distance, away from the crowds. Edil watched with narrowed eyes as Ronan raced his sleigh with four reindeer pulling fast and his icy blue coat billowing out from behind him. Edil felt something in his stomach turn. Something was growing inside him, and it confused him at first. He had never felt this emotion before. It was not anger or fear. He realized it was disgust towards the man. He had never known it was possible not to like another person.

Bread and Sweets
For Sale

THE BAKER'S SON

The Reindeer Games excited Edil and Gregor as they cheered and celebrated with the rest of the people gathered in Bluster. Feeding off the good spirits of the people exhilarated them. After the races, they stuck with Nick and Henrick, who introduced them around town to people, food, and drinks. As the day gave way to the long night, the celebrations continued, and Edil and Gregor felt their bond with Nick strengthening. Their uncle was right about Nick. He was a friend to all, including them.

The day after the games, many people packed up and left Bluster to head back to their daily lives in their ordinary towns and villages. Edil and Gregor spent the day unloading their sled and troika into Nick's shop. It surprised them to see Nick already giving some of their stuff away- mostly little things to be used as toys for the children. They observed the way the children's faces lit up when taking off down the street, clutching a carved bird or deer to their chest with their tiny hands- just like Nick said they would. The children were not the only ones who lit up. Every time a child smiled with thanks, Nick's face was nothing but pure joy. Edil and Gregor could see how much he just loved giving to people because it made them happy— especially the children.

The following morning, the brothers headed to Katts Bog in search of the baker's son. They packed enough for the trip in the troika, leaving the big sled behind. They planned on coming back to Bluster one last time before heading home to the valley. They needed to pick up all the goods and wares they received from trading with Nick.

Light snow fell as they traveled southeast. Nick told them to stick by the side of a river, and eventually, they would hit Katts Bog. This trip differed from The Great Nothing. The tundra slowly gave way and eased into muddied, dirty snow with old brown grass peeking. The river was a source of wildlife as animals gathered to drink. Snow-capped mountain ranges with waterfalls were not far into the distance. The brothers rather enjoyed traveling to Katts Bog. It was not as cold and dreary. It reminded them somewhat of home.

Edil could tell that it displeased Gregor to travel and meet this man and wife. He was not sure what the point of it all was.

"It's an adventure!" Edil said gleefully. "Another village to explore. More land to travel!"

"And we meet the baker's son...and then what?"

"I don't know, really," Edil admitted. "But isn't that what an adventure is? The unknown? Whatever will be will be?"

They arrived at Katts Bog after their third night of camping riverside, just like Nick had promised them. The first building they encountered was an interesting one. It was built of lumber and stone right on the river with a large wheel attached to the side. The rushing waters of the river were turning the wheel. The brothers looked at each other and shrugged with quizzical expressions on their faces.

Nick told them to follow their noses to find the baker. He said it would be the sweetest smell in the air, from bread and cakes and all kinds of treats baking in the big ovens. Once again, Nick was right. They could smell the sweet air.

They rode through the small town, and just like when they arrived at Bluster, people stopped what they were doing and stared. People came to their doors and windows to watch them, two small men in a small troika, pulled by two reindeer.

The baker's building was also made of stone and lumber. Great plumes of smoke came from several chimneys. A large covered porch was in the front where a woman stood watch over tables with baskets of bread and sweet doughs. She was in the middle of pocketing a coin from a little boy when Edil and Gregor pulled to a stop. The woman's eyes widened as if she recognized them but felt confused by them at the same time.

They climbed out of the troika and approached her, caps in hands to show proper etiquette. She backed away from them before turning around and going inside the building without saying a word. Edil and Gregor frowned. That was not the reaction they were expecting.

A man came out, dressed with a yellowed apron down his front. His hands were covered in flour and specks of dough. Some flour was dusted on his face too, where he might have scratched an itch. He looked at the brothers, confused.

"Can I help you?" he finally spoke, wiping his hands on his apron.

"Are you the baker?" Edil asked.

"Aye."

"Oh, well, how do you do? I'm Edil, and here is my brother, Gregor. We are friends of Nick from Bluster. He sent us."

"Nick? Why?"

Edil looked over at his brother for help.

"Well, sir," Gregor said after clearing his voice. "Nick thought this would be a good opportunity for us to meet your son, perhaps?"

"Me son? Byron? Why?"

"Nick tells us he's one of us. He thought it might be nice if Byron knew there was more like him out in the world," Edil tried to explain.

The woman came back out, a stern scowl on her face. Her hands were on her hips as she looked down at Edil and Gregor.

"Now you look here," she began in a demanding voice. "Byron's busy with work, you see! He ain't no time to be socializing with the likes of you two."

Edil and Gregor were shocked by her rude scolding. They looked at the baker, waiting for him to correct her. Sadly, he shook his head and looked away as if he could not bear to look them in the face.

"Finish this off, Darvis. Then back to work," she demanded before returning to the shop.

The man looked back at the brothers.

"She's right, don't you know. You can't go interrupt a man's work," he said. "I'm sorry, lads, but the wife does run a tight ship."

"Oh, well, so sorry to disturb—" Edil began, but Gregor cut him off.

"We traveled three nights just to meet your son and give him support!" he yelled angrily, surprising both Edil and Darvis. "From what I gather, he is a grown man with a wife of his own! I would like to think he can decide whether or not he wants to meet the likes of us!"

"You don't understand," Darvis said softly. "It hasn't been easy for me wife. I'm sorry. I must go. Please, forgive me."

He walked back into the shop, his shoulders slumped and his head hanging. Edil could feel the shame coming from him.

"What do we do now?" Edil whispered. Gregor still looked angry.

"We wait. They can't keep him in there forever."

Gregor walked back to the troika and grabbed the feed bags for Buck and Junior. He had no intentions of moving from the front of the shop. People took notice as the two brothers settled into the troika and prepared to wait. Eventually, the woman came out again.

"Shoo! Go on with you two! There is nothing here for you!" she yelled from the porch.

"Just resting a bit," Gregor called back. "Ain't no rule that says we can't, now is there?"

She let out a frustrated grunt and stomped back into the shop. People watched to see what would happen next. Finally, the door opened timidly. Edil and Gregor sat up to see Byron shyly step out.

Byron was small, like them. He was round from his cheeks to his belly to the round, tight golden curls that circled his head. Even his eyes were round and bright blue with a mixture of fear and uncertainty.

Edil understood what Nick meant by Byron not being happy. He could see it written on Byron's face and in the way he held his posture. As Byron walked towards them, Edil could see the years of sadness etched into his frown. He walked like a man with a massive weight on his shoulders.

"Hello," Edil greeted him as he approached them. "Byron, is it?"

"Please," Bryon said, his voice begging. "You must leave. You mustn't stay. Me stepmother won't tolerate this. She says you are halting people from buying goods. We are losing money today, and she will take it out of me pay."

"Well, she's a wretched witch, isn't she?" Gregor grumbled. Edil thought he saw a small smile try to break from Byron's lips.

"'Tis just... I owe her so much, you know. I can't afford for her to take away me earnings. I just can't."

"Can we meet later then?" Gregor asked. "Get to know each other. We traveled a long way."

Byron shifted nervously and looked over his shoulder back at the shop. They could see the woman peering out the window, watching them.

"All right. I reckon it wouldn't hurt if we supper together," Byron sighed with a whisper under his breath. "There's a small cabin not far from here. 'Tis mine and me wife's."

He gave them directions to his cabin and instructed them to wait there until they relieved him and his wife of their duties for the day. He did not say how long he would be, but Edil and Gregor agreed to wait for him.

They arrived at Byron's cabin. It was indeed small and simple, reminding them of their own back in the valley. Trees sheltered it, and a small creek ran behind it. They brought the reindeer to the stream to drink and then unrolled their bedding to sit on and relax while they waited.

"He is sad," Gregor commented.

"Reminds me of a trapped rabbit," Edil said. "No place to go."

"Do you think he will come back with us? How do we explain that to Papa?"

"I don't know. We can't just expect someone to give up their entire life and follow strangers, can we?"

"What was Nick thinking?" Gregor said.

"Nick was thinking of how unhappy this Byron fellow is and how happy we are," Edil sighed. "I gather Nick likes to make people happy."

The sun was setting by the time they saw Byron coming down the little mud trail. A woman walked next to him, shorter than Byron, with one hand on her back and another on her swollen belly. She was careful with each step she took, making sure not to trip and fall.

"His wife is with child," Gregor said with a surprised voice.

"So sorry!" Byron called out to them with a wave. "So very sorry about me stepmother. Please, come in."

They all shuffled into the small, one-room cabin. Byron introduced his wife, Lorelai, who was timid but offered them a smile before getting supper ready. They lit a fire to warm the room, and the men took seats around the table.

They reintroduced themselves and awkwardly tried to get to know one another, making small talk. They told Byron how they lived but left out specifics.

"And where exactly are you from?" Byron had asked.

"Home," Edil responded, pointing towards the north.

"And you have no needs there?" Byron questioned.

"We are very well provided for," Gregor told him.

"And very happy," Edil said. "And free. We are free."

Edil and Gregor listened to Byron talk over a small meal of roasted vegetables and dark bread. Byron's mother had died giving birth to him. He was a weak child, and his father had remarried rather quickly, mostly so he would have someone to share the burden of caring for the child. Unfortunately, Byron's stepmother had grown to resent her life as a baker's wife and caretaker of his small, sickly child.

When he grew into good health, but not into the average height, she felt he needed to be put to work and pay back for all the sleepless nights he had caused, the purchased medicines, the meals, and the clothes.

"I owe them that," Byron said sadly.

"I don't think anyone owes anyone," Gregor told him.

"But, she saw to it that I have me own home. She even heard of Lorelai from travelers of villages over. Arranged our marriage, she did," Byron told them.

"And she won't let us forget that, will she?" Lorelai suddenly spoke from her corner. "Now I earn me keep too by cleaning her house, laundering her clothes, and whatnot. Nothing but chores for me."

"Lorelai, don't."

"And when our child is born?" Lorelai continued, ignoring her husband. "You best believe she will own him too."

She was bitter with her words, giving Edil chills and making Gregor angry and sad for her.

"Our child will be responsible and hardworking, aye?" Byron said. "There is nothing wrong with that, is there?"

"But are you happy?" Gregor asked him.

"I have food on me plate, a roof over me head, a lovely wife, clothes on me back, a child on the way…."

"But are you happy?" Gregor asked again.

"Is anybody, now? Isn't that life?"

"I was happy once," Lorelai said. "I was a happy little girl. I was a happy girl until I moved here and met her."

Silence came over the room. The gloom of the cabin was almost too much for Edil to bear. The sadness was almost suffocating.

"You know," Gregor said, "You can come back with us. There is plenty of room. No one will tell you what to do or how to do it. You won't need to earn your keep. You just need to do for yourself."

Byron let out a little laugh.

"Thank you, but I've been here me whole life. Can't just up and leave like that, don't you know?"

"Byron, maybe we should think about it," Lorelai suggested.

"No. No need to."

"But Byron—"

"I'm sorry, gentlemen," Byron said, shaking his head. "I believe Nick's sent you on a fool's errand. Your ideas are exciting me wife, and she's in a delicate situation, don't you see. I can't have her being all excited. Not good for the baby."

"No need to apologize," Edil said, raising from his chair. "We will be going. We'll just camp up the river for the night and leave in the morning."

"But if you change your mind, we will be in Bluster for a few days before heading home," Gregor told him just before leaving and shutting the sadness behind him.

They spent the night, as they said, camping by the river. In the morning, they rode back north and west. They had hoped Byron and Lorelai would come running behind them, calling their names. They had hoped Byron would reconsider and join them on the journey back to the valley. As much as they were not supposed to bring anyone back or tell anyone about the valley, they could not help but feel excitement at the possibility that maybe Byron would change his mind.

They rode through the town without a glimpse of Byron or his wife. Not even the stepmother was out, harking the bread and sweets. Just Darvis, Byron's father, was on the porch, sweeping crumbs away. He paused and watched as Edil and Gregor rode by. He lifted his hand in a sad, half-hearted farewell. Politely, Edil and Gregor nodded back. As they continued down the road, they could feel Darvis' eyes watching them.

The trip back to Bluster was the same as the trip away from Bluster-uneventful. The muddied snow turned over to ice under the runners of the troika. Nick greeted them, his smile as friendly as ever. He felt sad when they told him about their brief visit with Byron.

They spent another two days visiting with Nick and their uncle. They took in everything they loved about the village, making their visit a holiday of sorts. They packed up the sled and troika with so many items to bring back. They knew they had to leave soon, for the days were getting shorter and the nights longer. It would not be long before the brutal winter would arrive and stay for months, making The Great Nothing inhospitable.

They promised to be back the following year with more goods and wares to trade. They truly felt that Bluster had become a home away from home and was already looking forward to their next trip. With sacks of coffee and sugar and wheat, bolts of fabrics, jugs of ale, some cured and salted pork belly, some books, a doll, and a slate board with pencils, the brothers headed up the road out of Bluster. People gathered once again, but this time instead of staring, they waved goodbye and wished them safe travels. Children called out their hopes of seeing them the following year and their excitement of what toys they might bring for Nick to give out.

Edil and Gregor felt at peace with their trip. Their only regret was Byron, the baker's son. They almost wished they never met him at all. They carried Byron's weight of sorrow on their shoulders. They had never known such sadness could exist.

Across the Great Nothing

Edil felt good about his trip. It was the adventure he was longing for. He met other people and tasted unique foods that he had only heard about. They were only miles outside of Bluster when he was already plotting another trip. He needed more to trade. He liked the idea of the toys for children. He enjoyed seeing their faces and Nick's face beaming with joy.

He was lost in his quiet thoughts, no sound but the wind on the tundra and the plodding of Buck and Junior's hooves. Already, The Great Nothing that lay ahead of them was setting him into a trance.

"Someone is following us," Gregor spoke, breaking the silence.

Edil frowned and looked back over his shoulder. Indeed, there was a wagon in the distance, coming from Bluster. From what he could make of it, it was being pulled by two small horses.

"Can you make it out?" Gregor asked.

"No. I do not know who it is," Edil admitted, squinting to see it better.

"Do we wait?"

"Let's see. Maybe they are just going in the same direction and will turn off somewhere," Edil suggested. He clicked his tongue, letting the reindeer know to pick up the speed a bit. He wanted to put some more distance between them and whoever seemed to follow them.

They nervously kept looking back over their shoulders as they rode on. They just wanted to get their trip home going, but they could not risk having the valley discovered. The wagon with the two ponies continued to keep up with their pace. After several more miles, Edil gave up. He pulled the reins to stop.

"What are you doing?" Gregor asked.

"They don't seem to be going anywhere. There is nowhere else for them to go but back to Bluster. Might as well see who they are and what they want."

"Convince them to turn around?"

Edil nodded. He hoped he could convince them to turn around and quit following them. Otherwise, he and Gregor were not going home as soon as they thought they would.

The wagon approached, closing the distance between them. As it came closer, they could see two figures in the seat. Both of them were waving with excitement, and they could hear shouts of "Oi!" calling out to them. It was not a panicked wave or shout. It was rather a friendly, cheery wave that said they were glad to see Edil and Gregor.

"I don't believe it," Gregor smiled as they came even closer. "It's Byron and Lorelai."

Edil waved back with the same enthusiasm. It was indeed Byron and Lorelai sitting at the head of the large wagon. Two small but muscular ponies, grey and mottled in color, pulled it. The wagon's back was like Edil and Gregor's sled, covered with waterproof hide and tied down to protect the bundles of goods underneath.

When they pulled up next to the brothers, their smiles were broad, their eyes happy. Edil leaned back to see a large milking cow tied to the back of their wagon.

"We thought we missed you and missed our chance," Byron said breathlessly. One would have thought he had pulled the wagon all those miles to catch up; he was so out of breath. "If the offer still stands, we would very much like to go with you. We want to go home with you."

"We have lots to offer, don't you know," Lorelai said, pointing to the large bundle on the back of their wagon. "Darvis gave us everything. 'Tis all we need to set up home and perhaps a small bakery of our own. There's a proper oven back there, sacks and sacks of wheat, flour, seeds, sugar."

"Darvis? Your Papa?" Gregor asked. "He gave you all that?"

"Aye," Byron said, nodding enthusiastically.

"And the ponies, the wagon, the cow," Lorelai continued.

"Well, that sounds like there is a story behind that," Edil said. "If you don't mind sharing it, we would love to hear it when we camp for the night."

They continued to ride as the days were getting shorter and the nights were getting longer. They wanted to get as many miles as they could under them while the silver sun still shone. They rode, side by side, making small talk but saving Byron's story for later. The ponies were skittish around Buck and Junior, but the reindeer were calm. They were used to being around Onyx, so the ponies seemed familiar.

As the sun disappeared into the horizon, they stopped for the night and built a small fire. They set up the animals with feed and wrapped them in blankets to keep them warm for the night. They cooked a small, simple meal of dried meats and porridge over the fire. They broke a loaf of bread from Byron's bakery to share. They listened to

Byron explain how he ended up catching up with them.

It was Darvis that said they should go. He approached Byron the night Edil and Gregor had left town. Byron could tell something was bothering his father all day, and was worried.

Darvis pulled his son to the side, away from his wife's prying ears, and asked him about the visit with the strangers. Byron told him they offered a great opportunity. They spoke of promise for him and Lorelai to settle somewhere far but with a great and bountiful life. Byron also told his father how he turned down the opportunity because he knew his place was in Katts Bog. He knew he had to continue to pay back his father and stepmother for all they ever did for him. He knew the bakery needed him, and his stepmother needed Lorelai.

With those sad words, he parted ways with his father and headed home for the evening. It was a usual evening of supper with Lorelai and then to bed. It startled them to hear pounding on their door early in the morning before the sun even rose. Darvis was calling out his name, an urgent note in his voice. Byron and Lorelai leaped from their bed, scared of what could be wrong.

Darvis was a mess. He had not slept all night. He was unkempt, and his eyes were red. He told them they must go. Darvis said the life they lived in Katts Bog was no life at all. He told them this was their chance to live a normal and happy life, and they must seize it.

Byron felt confused at first. His stepmother had instilled that he must earn his keep all these years, and he reminded his father of that. Darvis then explained he had stood his ground with his wife, Byron's stepmother. He told her that Byron and Lorelai were grown people, and enough was enough. Byron had more than earned his keep and then some with all the years of hard work he put in.

With that, Darvis told them he would prepare them for their journey and their life beyond Katts Bog. There was no discussion to be had. Byron and Lorelai needed to pack up and get moving to catch up with Edil and Gregor.

They spent the next two days in a flurry packing up the cabin. Darvis ordered a trade for the wagon and ponies. He filled up sack after sack of everything from flour to sugar. He arranged for wheat, barley, rye, and spelt for Byron to plant so his supply of baking goods would never run out. Darvis crated chickens, strapped them to the wagon, and handed over their very best milking cow to his son, to his wife's dismay.

It was never said, but Byron knew his father gave all the items to him out of guilt. Darvis felt guilty for all the years that Byron was treated more like a servant than a son. He felt guilty for resenting Byron for surviving childbirth when his mother did not.

When Byron and Lorelai finally rode out of Katts Bog, they spoke very few words between father and son. Darvis just wished him well and asked that, if possible, he could contact him and let him know he was living a good life.

"And here I am," Byron said. "In a place where I never dreamed I would be."

"Stepmother did not even say her farewells. Naught a word 'twas spoken," Lorelai said.

"That's sad," Edil commented.

"Aye," Byron agreed. "We're better off, though, are we not? Least I hope so."

Byron looked out into the darkness. Just one day of riding, and he could see how bleak it was.

"'Tis gets better than this, no?" he asked.

"Yes. Just takes time to get there. Have patience," Gregor promised.

They settled in for the night, Edil and Gregor in their sled and Byron and Lorelai in their wagon. Eager to get going, they were all up before the sun and started again.

They rode side by side, passing the time with talks, jokes, stories, and songs. Edil and Gregor were glad to have the company. They just wished they knew how their parents would feel about them bringing back others to live in their valley. They wondered how their parents would be around strangers since they had no contact with the outside world for over twenty years.

The days turned into nights quickly, and the nights took longer to turn back to day. Byron was becoming discouraged by The Great Nothing, but Edil and Gregor kept promising him that good things were ahead. Lorelai, with her ever-growing belly, was becoming more and more uncomfortable. Byron felt the urgency to get the traveling over and done. He worried for the safety and health of Lorelai and their unborn child.

However, on what Edil promised to be the final day of traveling, Byron had to stop. He pulled the ponies to a halt. Edil and Gregor looked over to see Lorelai sweating, despite the cold air. Her face twisted in a grimace of discomfort, and a low moan escaped her throat. She hugged her belly as she looked up at the brothers.

"Apologies," she could barely whisper.

"No. No. One more day won't matter," Gregor assured her.

They helped Byron get her comfortable in the back of his wagon and set up camp, even though there were still hours of sunlight left. At times, Lorelai would get up and leave the wagon to walk through the pain. It was just too uncomfortable to lie down. Both she and Byron tried to talk through the aches and keep it light-hearted, but their eyes gave away the fear of something going wrong in the middle of nowhere.

Lorelai tried laying down for the umpteenth time, asking for time alone. The three men sat around the fire, not saying much. It was Gregor that sat up when he spotted it in the distance. He recognized it immediately.

"Old Shadow," Gregor said to Edil. Edil quickly stood up and looked in the direction Gregor was staring.

"What's an old shadow?" Byron asked.

"Not what. Who," Edil responded, pointing to the horizon.

There was a line of them, sitting there, watching the men, the wagon, the sled, and the animals. The wolves watched quietly, with Old Shadow sitting the tallest and darkest of them all.

"W-wolves?" Byron sputtered nervously. "They are not going to hurt us, are they?"

"Not if we can help it," Edil said, walking to his sled. He grabbed one of the many spears they made just for this reason and handed it to Byron. "Pack up. We have to keep moving."

"But- but, me wife!"

"Sorry. She is just going to do the best she can while we move. How fast can that cow run?"

"Cow? Run?" Byron screeched. It was becoming too much for him. Things were simpler in Katts Bog. He was beginning to think his father made a huge mistake sending him away.

Byron just stood there, flabbergasted, the spear in his hand. He watched as Edil and Gregor moved quickly, throwing their odds and ends back into the sled and harnessing up the reindeer again. The wolves were still in the distance, sitting still but watching their every move. Everything was happening too fast for Byron.

"Oi!" he finally yelled. "Stop!"

"Byron. There is no time to stop," Gregor said. "See the big one? The black one? That's Old Shadow. He's as mean as they come."

"I fought him. He's tough, and he's scary. Smart as a whip too. He's always watching. Always calculating," Edil joined in as he hitched up Byron's ponies.

"Our father fought him before we were born. It was the wolves that chased our parents into the valley," Gregor continued.

"Your father? The same wolf? That's not possible. Wolves don't live that long," Byron told them.

"Same one. We don't question it. We just know to avoid it if we can," Edil said.

"And if we can't?"

"We fight it," Gregor responded. "Now, go tell Lorelai we have to move. Do everything you can to make her comfortable for now."

Edil and Gregor climbed into their seats on the sled. They heard Byron mumble some frantic words to his wife, and she responded with a pain-filled grunt. Once Byron settled in his seat, they snapped the reins, and they moved.

They kept the reindeer and the ponies at a slow trot, not wanting to encourage the wolves to hunt them. They also wanted the animals to reserve their energy in case they were chased-- especially the cow. Edil and Gregor did not know how fast a cow could travel since they had never seen one before their trip. It did not appear to be a fast animal to them, so they had their doubts.

Lorelai let out a long wail from the back of Byron's wagon. This caused the wolves to howl in response. Edil looked back and saw they were moving. They headed towards them but not running.

"We have a feast for them this time," Gregor said in a low voice. "Cow, ponies, chickens, reindeer…."

"Stop," Edil whispered. "We'll get through this. We just need to keep calm."

The wolves picked up speed, their sauntering turning into a fast trot. As always, Old Shadow was in the lead. Byron looked over at them nervously. He looked as if he was going to be sick. Edil held up his hand as if to tell Byron to keep steady so no sudden movements would excite the wolves.

Another cry emerged from the wagon. Edil felt sorry for Lorelai, who had to go through a dramatic time in The Great Nothing. He truly hoped that if they could keep up with their pace, they just might arrive at the tunnel before the baby came, but he felt unsure from the sounds that she was making.

The wolves were getting closer. It was time to pick up speed. As soon as Edil snapped his reins and Byron followed with his ponies, the chase was on. Wolves broke out into a flat run as they closed the gap. They barked and yelped excitedly, calling to one another as they surrounded the sled and wagon. The cow let out an odd sound and kicked out, causing a young wolf to cry and fall behind.

Old Shadow came up alongside Edil; one gleaming yellow eye focused on him. The other eye was gone. Nothing but a scar ran alongside his face from when Edil had hit him with the shovel. He could not help but smirk at the sight of the wolf's old injury.

Edil handed the reins to Gregor and grabbed his spear. He jabbed it in Old Shadow's direction.

"Hah! Hah!" Edil hollered as the wolf jumped to the side to avoid being stabbed. This slowed Old Shadow down, his pack following him.

Edil could see that the cow was faltering. This animal was just not built for speed. She would never survive the chase. Lorelai let out another long cry as Edil tried to think fast.

He remembered the cured, smoked pork belly that Nick had given them. There were several pounds of it wrapped and packed away in the back of the sled.

"The bacon," Edil said to Gregor as he lifted the covering. "I must find the bacon and throw it to the wolves."

"Aw. Not the bacon," Gregor groaned, disappointed, but he knew Edil was right.

Edil climbed under the covering and dug through sacks and bundles and crates. He bounced around, back and forth, unsteady on his feet as Gregor continued to urge the reindeer forward. Finally, he found the slabs of meat. He lifted the side of the covering and began unwrapping the meat. He could see the wolves were once again running alongside the sled.

He hoisted the meat up high then flung it directly at the wolf. He was glad when he heard it thunk and saw it bounce off the wolf's head. Edil looked out to see the wolf stop and shake his head in confusion. Other wolves stopped to investigate what they threw at them. They growled and tore into the meat, tugging it back and forth.

"It's working!" Gregor shouted. "Throw more!"

Edil continued to unwrap the meat and untie the covering so he could throw the meat from all different sides of the sled. Wolves were stopping to grab their share, some fighting with each other. Eventually, even Old Shadow gave up the chase to make the others back away from what he felt was rightfully his. Edil watched as Old Shadow growled and snapped at some of the younger wolves, reminding them he was the leader, and the meat was his until he said they could have their share. As the sled continued to race across the frozen, hard ground, the wolves became smaller and smaller in the distance.

"Well," Edil beamed, climbing back up to the front and looking over at Byron. "That was an adventure, wasn't it?"

Byron nodded, speechless. The fear slowly turned to rushed adrenaline and excitement. He was about to say something, a grin creeping up on his face when Lorelai once again pierced the air with a scream.

"Hold up," Edil said, bringing the reindeer to a stop. "I'll take your wagon. You stay with your wife."

Edil climbed down quickly to take Byron's place. Byron thanked him before disappearing under his covering. With Gregor in the sled and Edil in the wagon, they continued to move, furthering their distance between Old Shadow's pack. They had to keep moving. The slabs of meat would not last forever, and if their calculations were correct, they would approach the valley in due time. There was no time to even stop to camp for the evening.

They could hear Lorelai's discomfort and Byron trying to soothe her with calm words. The brothers just rode quietly, not wanting to disrupt them. There was more hushed talking from the back of the wagon. Occasionally, the cow mooed, displeased with the constant traveling. A chicken let out a squawk, upset from being crated for so long.

And then, the sweetest sound rang out, causing the brothers to bring the animals to a halt. It was an innocent cry of a healthy newborn, followed by the laughter of the baby's parents.

Edil and Gregor smiled at each other and nodded with satisfaction. Once again, they urged the animals on. After some time, Byron finally came out from under the covering.

"'Tis a girl," he beamed. "Just a wee little thing, but she's got the fight in her, she does. We are going to call her Dana."

"And all is well?" Edil asked.

"All is well with mother and baby."

"Good," Edil said, then nodded ahead of him. "Almost there."

Byron looked out and saw that far into the distance, The Great Nothing ended, and a great wall climbed up towards the sky.

"We'll keep moving," Edil said. "And we should be home by morning light."

"Home," Byron grinned, his eyes filling with grateful tears and his chin quivering. "Taking me baby girl home."

It was then that he knew it was all worth it. The long trek across the cold, drab tundra. The chase from the wolves. The bitter nights and short, grey days. All of it was worth it because Dana was going to live a life where she would never have to worry about earning her keep.

Home Again

Johan spotted dark, bulky figures moving in the distance across the meadow. He squinted against the light and shaded his brow with his hand. *There were too many shadows moving to be just his sons*, he thought. Onyx distracted him by suddenly whinnying and frolicking in his pen. The horse kept calling out to the figures. A gentle breeze carried the sound of an answering nicker back.

It was Onyx's anxious sounds that bought Amelia and Karina out from the cabin. A smile broke out on their faces as they went to stand beside Johan.

"It's them!" Karina whooped as Amelia's heart skipped a beat in excitement.

"Too many," Johan said with a frown.

As the figures grew closer, two of them waved with enthusiasm. Johan could make them out. It was indeed his sons. Though he was curious about the two traveling with them, he felt great relief to know his sons were home and safe. A smile grew bigger and bigger as they walked closer and closer.

A sudden outburst of hooves pounded on the earth as Mimi bolted past them, followed by Baby, Dunder, and Blixem. They ran towards Buck and Junior, then pranced around each other excitedly. Onyx continued to grunt and call out, the two strange ponies answering back.

"Who are they?" Karina asked, her eyes large as she watched the strange couple follow her brothers.

Byron and Lorelai had wide eyes themselves. They felt amazed and shocked at the wonders and beauty of the valley. He led his ponies, and she carried their infant as they waded through the wildflowers, following Edil and Gregor. Edil kept looking back at them, grinning with pride at the place he called home.

"How is this possible?" Byron asked him, his neck constantly stretching and craning to see and take in everything around him.

"Does it matter?" Edil responded.

Byron shook his head. Any doubts that he had as they traveled across The Great Nothing washed away. As they had followed the brothers through the dark tunnel, any qualms that grew in his heart and mind had melted once they stepped into the sunlight of the valley.

"'Tis glorious," was the first thing Byron had said after taking it all in.

Edil and Gregor shouted to their family, their feet picking up the pace.

"What is that?!" Karina exclaimed, pointing to the creature that Gregor was leading. It was large and bulky, looking unsure on its small hooves, but had the kindest eyes and longest lashes Karina had ever seen on an animal.

"A cow," Johan laughed. "They bought back a cow!"

Johan and his family finally reunited. Tight hugs strengthened with love were all around. Byron and Lorelai stood aside, letting the family have their moment.

Once they settled down from the excitement of seeing each other again, they made the introductions. Amelia immediately swooped in to take baby Dana from Lorelai's tired arms and fussed over the newborn. Johan extended his hand in a warm, welcoming handshake to Byron as Edil gave a quick review of how, when, and where Byron and Lorelai, and baby Dana fit into their adventure.

The brothers put their fear of their father's possible anger to rest. Johan showed no signs of irritation or annoyance. Just relief and thankfulness that they were home and they were safe.

They relieved the ponies of the bundles they carried and put in the corral with Onyx, who seemed overly excited to see his kind, though he towered over them. They tied the cow to the side of the stable and gave it water. Once the animals were cared for, they all gathered around the table in the cabin. They had tales to tell, jokes to laugh at, and plans had to be made.

They placed a bountiful feast on the table, and the chatter was constant. Johan and Amelia glowed with excitement. It had been so long without the noise of other people. They had forgotten how good entertaining company felt.

After dinner, they took gifts out from the ponies' bundles. Amelia giggled at the sack of sugar, and Johan let out a whooping laugh at the jug of ale. Karina was bright-eyed and speechless when Edil presented her with the fragile doll, slate board, and chalk.

It delighted Johan to hear that Byron had come with goods of his own that would greatly contribute to their everyday life in the valley. Byron not only had baking knowledge and came with sacks of flour and sugar and tubs of yeast, but he also had some knowledge of growing wheat and oats and other grains. He had seeds that could start fields of grain. The two families would always have a source for bread and biscuits and any other dough they wanted to bake.

They made a small nest of blankets and pillows for Byron and Lorelai on the floor in front of the fire. They took out and dusted off the same cradle that Gregor, Edil, and Karina once used and gave it to Dana. They spent their first few weeks like that, the cabin cramped but happy.

Everyone seemed to fit in, and it was almost as if Byron and Lorelai were always there. Amelia and Lorelai bonded together; cooking, gathering, doing daily chores. Karina took pride in being elected to keep a watchful eye on Dana. Byron was always with the men as they found a perfect spot to build a cabin close to Johan's family.

The men spent their days clearing the land and building a cozy one-room cabin. They built a stable for the cow and the two grey ponies. Byron drew up a small, stone structure design that would serve as a "baking room." Together, with stones from the river and clay from the banks, they built a suitable place for Byron and Lorelai to continue their baking skills. It contained two ovens, tubs for yeast to grow, a smooth rock table for kneading, and a wall with shelves filled with flour, sugar, and whatever else Byron would need.

On their first night in their cabin, they invited Johan's family for supper. Byron presented them with an elaborate cake as his way of saying thank you. As they ate, they planned some more.

They talked about clearing fields for planting and building a small mill. They discussed creating a small church to put together their own Sunday services, similar to what Nick had done in Bluster.

"And we have to get ready for our next trip," Edil had said. The conversation died down when he spoke those words.

"Next trip?" Amelia asked.

"Oh, sure. We have so much to offer. I wouldn't mind seeing Nick and Uncle Henrick again," Edil responded. "Nick liked our furniture and small carvings. It amazed me how the kids loved getting these playthings. *Toys*, they call them. We could make some things for the kids and bring them to Nick."

"I didn't know you wanted to leave again so soon," Johan said with disappointment.

"Well, not right away," Edil said. "I was thinking in time for the Reindeer Games again. Lots of people travel for that. We'll be more prepared and maybe make some great trades. We'll need items again like coffee and sugar. I thought maybe we could make it a yearly tradition."

"Can I go?" Karina asked, looking up from playing with her doll. "I want to see the Reindeer Games."

"One day," Edil promised with a smile.

As they settled into their daily routines, Edil approached his mother about an idea he had for making dolls that were not as fragile as Karina's. Amelia came up with a simple doll with fabric and yarn she received from Nick and goat hair gathered from the meadows. It had a cloth face and body, scraps for a dress, and yarn for hair. Eventually, she was making several of them a week.

Gregor made small, carved reindeer with tiny wheels lodged into the hooves that would roll and bob when pushed along the floor. Johan and Edil continued to make furniture, the perfect size for them and the children.

Byron and Lorelai wanted to do their share in making gifts for children, so they began experimenting with sugar, water, and the different flavors from the wildflowers and herbs. They found they could crystalize some flowers and berries with sugar, making them pretty and sweet at the same time. A pan of nuts roasted then cooled with a sugary syrup made a great snack once it hardened. Their favorite was a thick, sugary syrup infused with mint spread over the cool rock table. It dried and hardened, looking like glass, but it was sweet and refreshing to suck on when it broke into pieces.

As the year went on, they tended the animals and cared for the fields they planted. Dana went through her milestones of cooing, sitting up, clapping her chubby little hands, crawling, and pulling herself up onto her chubby little legs. The two families saw each other daily, sharing chores and goods.

In the fall, Edil and Johan stood over their pile of wares. Ragdolls in different colored dresses with dark or light-colored yarn hair stared at them. Crates of wooden animals waited patiently for a child to love them. Carefully packed boxes of sweets from Byron lined against the wall.

Johan sighed and patted Edil on his back.

"You did real good, son," he smiled. "Real good."

"Are you sure you don't want to come this time?" Edil asked him.

"No. This is your thing."

They decided that once again, Johan and Amelia would stay behind in the valley with Karina. With Dana so little, Lorelai thought it would be best if she stayed behind too. Only the brothers and Byron would make the trip to Bluster.

In the morning, they all paraded towards the tunnel. To get the goods to the sleds waiting where they left them, they piled bundles on the backs of all five reindeer, the two ponies, and their backs. Onyx pulled a wagon loaded with the remaining bulkier items. They built the wagon precisely to fit through the tunnel.

On the other end of the tunnel, they transferred everything to the sleds. Byron sat in one with Dunder, and Blixem hitched to it. Gregor and Edil took the other, led by Buck and Junior.

"What can I bring back for you, Mama?" Edil called out. He was grinning with excitement. He could not wait to be back in the hustle and bustle of Bluster and felt better leaving this time. He knew it was not a simple trip but a doable one.

"Whatever your heart desires," Amelia smiled as she waved.

Edil nodded as he waved goodbye and turned the reindeer south. They began their journey to Bluster again, leaving Johan, Amelia, Karina, Lorelai, Dana, and the ponies, Onyx, Mimi, and Baby. Edil could not help but wonder what treasure he would bring back from this trip.

The Bet

It thrilled Nick to see his friends riding back into Bluster with their sleds piled high. Over a big pot of coffee, they caught up with one another and went over the items Edil had bought for him. Henrick had caught word that his nephews were back and joined them.

They impressed Nick and Henrick with the skills behind the toys and sweets. Nick thought the floppy, soft dolls with yarn hair were ingenious, and little girls everywhere would love them. He knew the children would love the treats that Byron concocted. Gregor's toy reindeer with little wheels for hooves were sure to be hit, especially with the Reindeer Games.

Without even realizing it, they discussed what toys they could design for the following year. There was no question about it. There was no doubt. Edil was already determined to return with another sled full of imaginative playthings that children had never seen before.

The town of Bluster was hectic with people getting ready for the Annual Reindeer Games. People were boisterous with good spirits. Familiar faces from the year before shouted out greetings to the little men as they traveled through the road to the tavern for supper with Nick and their uncle.

One familiar face smirked at them and laughed. The red-headed man from the year before, Ronan, sneered at them with a grin that turned Edil's stomach. Ronan turned back to the men that he always seemed to be surrounded by and continued his conversation.

"Got me one of them," Edil could overhear as they walked by. "They make dutiful pets. Almost as dutiful as my reindeer."

Ronan's crowd erupted with laughter as Edil looked over to Nick with a puzzled face. Nick just shook his head sadly and continued to lead the way to the tavern.

At the tavern, Edil felt better as they ate bowls of stew and crusty, doughy bread. All conversations around them were about the Reindeer Games that were to occur after Nick's church services the following day. Nick seemed more focused on the toys.

"They are truly spectacular," Nick complimented. "The children are going to be thrilled."

"We enjoyed making them," Gregor admitted with a smile.

"I think I'll save some this year," Nick said. "Give some out here, but put some away for later to give out to some towns going south. Christmastime is coming soon. I think I'll give toys out around then. It's our Lord's birthday, and he loved the little children. I think it's a good way to celebrate that."

"Very noble idea," Edil smiled, raising his goblet of wine and nodding in respect to his friend, Nick.

The sun was long gone by the time they walked out of the tavern. They bid Nick farewell with promises to be at his Sunday Service in the morning. They unhitched their reindeer from the post to head back to Henrick's house for the night when they heard the unmistakable laugh from Ronan.

"Well, I must say, Gentlemen," Ronan began as he approached them, followed by the usual crowd of cronies, "Those are some fine, fit reindeer. They would do very well on my team."

"They are not for sale," Gregor mumbled, trying his best to ignore him.

"Everything is for sale," Ronan laughed. "For the right price or bet. Oh, I do love a good bet."

"Bet?" Edil asked.

"Yes. Bet? Gamble? Game for coin? Do you not have games like that where you are from?"

Edil shook his head.

"Just where are you from anyway?" Ronan asked.

Edil raised his arm and pointed north.

"Home," was all he said.

"Hmmm..." Ronan responded, confused by Edil's answer. He was unsure if Edil was being clever and insulting him or if he was too stupid to know where he came from.

"Anyway, as I was saying. A bet," Ronan continued. "I love a good gamble. I think your reindeer are worth a gamble. How about if I win the race, I get your reindeer. And if you win, you get mine?"

"I don't need yours," Edil said.

"It's not about the reindeer!" Ronan shouted. "It's about the win!"

Henrick stepped between his nephews and Ronan. He could see that Ronan was getting hot under the collar and fired up.

"This is a wasted discussion, Ronan," Henrick said. "My nephews and their friend are not here to race. They merely came to visit family and trade."

"Nonsense," Ronan chuckled, calming down. "Everyone wants to race. How can they not with those beautiful creatures? Look at the structure on them. Those legs. The backs. The muscles. Tell me, what do you feed them?"

"Um...we let them feed themselves mostly," Edil told him.

Ronan gave him a quizzical look, his eyebrow raised. He let out a huff and shook his head.

"I don't know what to make of you, little man," Ronan said with a low voice. "You are a curious creature. Smart. Smarter than my Lottie, that's for sure."

It was Edil's turn to look confused. He just shook his head and climbed up into his sled. He wanted to get as far away from Ronan as possible. He was tired and cold and just wanted to climb into one of his uncle's warm, cozy beds and drift away for the night.

"Have you seen my Lottie?" Ronan continued, calling out after them as they started the reindeer down the road. "The dumbest thing, but does my bidding quite well. I would introduce her, but she is busy tending to my deer as I ordered her to do."

"What on earth is that buffoon rambling about?" Gregor asked Henrick as they put distance between them and Ronan.

"Does anyone ever know what Ronan is talking about?" Henrick laughed.

"Tomorrow!" Ronan shouted. "You'll see her tomorrow! Best prize I ever won!"

They continued to ignore Ronan's taunts as they rode away and headed to Henrick's house. Once settled, Edil did just what he wanted to do: sleep. He slept deeply and worry-free.

In the morning, Ronan was nothing but a distant, silly memory. Edil, Gregor, and Byron were excited to watch the games and be in town among the hustle and bustle. They loved the quietness of the valley but were enjoying their holiday in Bluster. It was nice to take in the sounds, smells, and flavors. It was a chance to have a conversation with others from different parts of the world and learn what went on around them.

Nick's church was packed wall to wall with people. They had to stand near the back; their necks craned as they listened to Nick's sermon and readings from the Bible. Edil spotted Ronan sitting towards the front. It was hard not to miss him with his fire-colored hair and blue silk coat. Next to Ronan was a small blonde girl, her hair a matted mess.

When Nick finished his sermons, he invited the racers to gather their reindeer and bring them outside the church. He wanted to bless them and wish them a healthy race.

The men who were racing filed out. Ronan leaned down to the little girl and whispered in her ear. She stood up and turned, giving Edil a perfect view. She was not a little girl but a grown young woman.

She was shorter than Edil with big blue eyes that looked sad. Her hair appeared tangled and matted, framing her dirty face. As she walked to the back of the church, Edil could see she wore rags. Two small sheets were sewn together to make a shapeless dress with a rope around her waist, acting as a belt. For a coat, it was a man's tattered, old dress jacket. Her feet and legs were wrapped in rags, looking like dirty bundles.

She kept her head down, not even noticing Edil, Gregor, or Byron. She walked as if she carried the shame of the world on her shoulders. She followed others out of the church and disappeared.

Edil looked back at Ronan, surprised to see that he watched him, a smile on his face. Edil hated Ronan's evil smile, filled with pride for all the wrong reasons. Ronan rose from his pew and approached them.

"I see you spotted my Lottie. I ordered her to fetch my reindeer for me," he said. "She's quite the specimen of your kind, is she not?"

"Who- who is she?" Edil demanded.

"Not who. What. And what she is, is mine. Won her in a bet about, oh, I don't know, seven, eight months ago."

"Won her?" Gregor questioned as Edil felt his blood boil. "How does one win a person?"

"You never heard of servants?" Ronan asked. "Oh, dear! Where do you people come from? Yes! I won her in a card game. Her father had no use for her. I had a hankering for one of you little people ever since I saw you last year. So, we gambled. I won. I always do."

"Do you, now?" Edil snarled, causing both Gregor and Byron to look at him with surprise. They had never seen Edil angry before. Not like this. Byron even reached out and placed his hand on Edil's shoulder to calm him down, but Edil shrugged it off almost violently.

"She's been a great little pet," Ronan continued, taking delight in Edil's anger. "Does my cooking, my cleaning, my laundering. Tends to the deer. Quite the servant, even if she is a bit daft. Best thing I ever won. Well, after this coat."

Ronan chuckled as he brushed the sleeves of his prized, blue coat that he was never without.

"Why, you—"

"Edil!" his uncle warned. "Not in our Lord's house! Let's join Nick outside for the blessing of the herd, shall we?"

Henrick almost had to shove Edil out the doors. He had to get Edil away from Ronan. Ronan was not a man for Edil to fight.

Nick was outside, watching people bring their reindeer up the hill from the town's pen. He was smiling, oblivious to what had transpired in his church. When he saw the anger on Edil's face, he knew something was wrong.

"What is it?" he asked, concerned.

"That girl! Who is that girl with Ronan?" Edil asked, his tone filled with disgust.

"What girl? I didn't notice a girl with Ronan."

Edil looked up, scanning the crowd. He finally spotted her. She was all alone, leading a team of six scrawny reindeer that looked just as pathetic as she did. He pointed her out to Nick.

"There! There she is. She's with Ronan. He said he won her in a game of cards!" Edil said.

Nick shook his head, not knowing what to say. Ronan appeared beside them, his ever-present sneer on his face.

"I see you are admiring my deer," Ronan said.

"You call those scrappy things reindeer?" Edil shot back with a sneer of his own. "They are nothing compared to mine."

A gleam lit up in Ronan's eyes. Edil could see the wheels turning in his head and could only imagine what Ronan was coming up with.

"Why don't you prove it?" Ronan asked.

"Prove what? I have nothing to prove to you."

"Your reindeer. Your team. Your four against my six *scrappy* things," he baited.

"We told you, we don't race," Henrick reminded him.

"This is between me and the mouthy little man," Ronan snarled.

"Come now, Ronan," Nick said calmly. "No need to taunt and tease like children."

"Not children. Men. Grown men," Ronan said. "Grown men that

play the game of chance. My offer still stands. Your deer if I win. Mine if you win."

"No," Edil shook his head. "Your reindeer are not worth a gamble. They are not worth spit."

"Ah. But there must be something you will bet. Every man has a price. Every man wants something someone else has."

Edil looked away, almost ashamed of what he was thinking. He looked out into the distance and felt surprised to see the girl staring at him, her eyes wide with wonderment and curiosity but still filled with sadness.

"What else you got? Make it worth my time and effort. Make it worth my deer's time and effort," Edil said as Ronan laughed.

"Edil—" Gregor began, but Edil's glare cut him off.

"All right. I've been trading and gambling. I have lots of goods lined up to come home with me. What would you like?" "Everything," Edil said coldly.

"Everything? You don't even know what I have."

"Everything," Edil repeated. "The goods. The sled. The reindeer. Everything you own and have with you right here, right now, in Bluster."

Ronan laughed.

"And what do you have, little man? What can you offer in this bet?"

"Everything," Edil said. His brother shook his head in disappointment. "Everything I own against everything you own."

"Your deer and sleds and goods for mine?"

"And the girl," Edil smiled.

"Wait. What?" Ronan asked, his face falling.

"What's her name? The girl who is with you?"

"Lottie? You want me to gamble Lottie?"

"Is that not how you came upon her? Is that not the bet? Everything you own? Do you not *own* her?" Edil asked, his voice getting stronger and his brow furrowing with a fury.

Ronan did not have an answer. He realized Edil was more intelligent than he thought. He did not want to risk his pride by losing everything to Edil. At the same time, he could only think of how great it would be to win all of Edil's belongings, especially his reindeer. He could feel the satisfaction and gratification if he won.

"Wait," Byron interrupted. "What if neither of you wins?"

Edil looked over to Nick for an answer. He had not thought of the consequences if neither won the race. All he cared about was the girl. He needed to free the girl from Ronan's clutches and felt concerned for Ronan's reindeer as they did not look healthy. They were skinny and tired-looking. He could tell Ronan did not care about them. He only cared about the money they bought in.

"I suppose we can talk to the Gamekeeper," Nick suggested. "Perhaps do a separate race with just you two."

"There. Do we have a bet?" Edil asked. It was his turn to sneer at Ronan.

Ronan let out another chuckle. He shook his head in disbelief. He felt the bet was humorous and yet slightly ridiculous.

"Yes, little man. We have a bet," he sneered back before walking away towards Lottie and his deer.

"I hope you know what you are doing," Henrick said to his nephew.

"So do I, Uncle. So do I."

Edil looked back at the girl. Lottie was her name. She was still staring at him, her eyes calling out to him, begging him. It was as if she knew he could save her. He could never get her out of his head again. Lottie

The Race

Edil ignored the cheers, hooting, and hollering that continuously erupted from the crowds. He spent his time in a quiet state, murmuring to his reindeer as he hitched them to his empty sled. He needed his sled as light as possible if he had any chance of beating Ronan. He petted his reindeer, apologized for putting them at the risk of being owned by Ronan, placed his head on Buck's- forehead to forehead- and prayed that he was not making a mistake. The more he thought about what had transpired between Ronan and himself, the more he felt sick. The reindeer were family. The idea of losing them turned his stomach.

Then he would think of Lottie. Poor, little Lottie with her sad, defeated eyes and rags for clothes that looked like she never had her own identity. The young girl would be worth it.

"We have to win," Edil whispered to Buck. "We have to fly."

Buck stuck his tongue out and gently licked Edil's face. If Edil did not know any better, he would swear the reindeer could understand his words.

"Edil! 'Tis almost time," Byron called out as he approached him. "Henrick, Gregor, and Nick be keeping a close eye on that fool. Making sure he best not be fixin' the race."

"I wouldn't put it past him," Edil agreed with a nod.

"He's won two races already, the dirty idjit. Good news, though. His reindeer be knackered out. Your reindeer are well rested and full of energy."

"That is true, Byron," Edil said, a smile forming on his face.

"Aye. And you're lighter too. Less weight to pull."

"And yet another good point. Maybe I can win this one after all."

Edil grabbed Buck's bridle to lead his team to the starting line. The crowds of people parted to make room for him to walk. They called out praise and commented on the body build of his reindeer. They smiled, cheered, and clapped.

"We are rooting for you, fella!" a man shouted.

"Best of luck, my good man! It will be nice to see someone beat Ronan," another called out.

Edil's smile and confidence grew as people reached out to clap him on the back and get a quick pet of the reindeer's fur. Some even tapped the sled for good luck. Edil could see the people wanted this. They wanted to see the underdog win. Ronan was old news. Edil was new and exciting. Word had escaped, and people knew what was at stake. Not just goods and reindeer, but Ronan's little servant. This was the most dramatic thing to happen in Bluster in a long time. This race was going to go down in history, regardless of who won. People would talk about it for generations to come.

Edil saw Gregor approaching him from the starting line. Nick and their uncle were waiting with Ronan and his team. Edil could see Ronan's sneer, even in the distance. Gregor fell in step with Edil.

"One more race, and then you and Ronan have at it," Gregor told him. "The course is twenty miles. You follow the path out of town, keep going until you see a green flag. At the flag, turn left. It will take you to a large lake. Go right and ride around the lake, then head back. They say the north shore is tricky, so be careful."

Edil just kept his head down, nodding at everything Gregor was telling him.

"This is the race of all races," Gregor said.

"Seems that way, doesn't it?" Edil smiled nervously.

As they approached the starting line, Edil could see Ronan's team already looked defeated. They were still panting from their last race. Their heads hung low as if the weight of their antlers were too much to carry. Their eyes held very little life in them--dull and blank.

Edil could see Ronan had instructed Lottie with the care of the reindeer. She was going from reindeer to reindeer, rubbing their skinny legs and haunches with her tiny hands, trying to massage any tightness in the muscles out. She glanced up at Edil, and her face turned red for a second. Then she smiled, but only briefly as if she feared it would displease Ronan.

Edil's heart skipped, and he, too, felt a burst of redness in his face. He turned away from her, closing his eyes for a moment and shaking his head. This was a new feeling he had never felt before. Like anger, Bluster seemed to bring out many undiscovered feelings that the valley did not.

The last race was already underway. Edil could hear the crowds cheering and jeering. He opened his eyes and could see a puff of smoke in the distance. This was a signal sent when racers had made it to the first point of the race. It let the people know how far the race had gone.

On a tall, rickety, wooden platform, a man stood with a telescope.

He would often yell to the crowd details about who was ahead or even who became injured. The crowd always seemed to quiet down with tension as the race's last leg went into action. Edil knew the race was ending. Cheers rose in the distance, traveling closer and louder because the racers and their teams headed close to town again.

Edil noticed his hands were shaking. Whatever little confidence he had left him. The sickness in the pit of his stomach was back. He looked at his brother and shook his head.

"I think I made a mistake," Edil said.

"No, brother. You have this," Gregor insisted. "It's too late now. They cannot know us as the little men who backed out on their word."

"But—"

"Look at him," Gregor demanded, nodding to Ronan. "Look at him standing there, thinking he has you beat already."

Edil looked over. Indeed, Ronan was standing there with his friends, his arms crossed, and a big leering grin on his face. He stared at Edil, taking joy that he looked sick and scared.

Nick noticed Edil looking ill also. He walked over to him and took the reins from Edil's hand. He walked them to the line.

"Come on," Nick smiled down at him. "You race to win."

Edil could not move.

"Edil. Do it for the girl," Nick reminded him.

Edil nodded but still did not move. Gregor nudged him.

"Hey. It's an adventure, is it not?" Gregor grinned.

Edil let out a small chuckle and rolled his eyes.

"Yes. It is."

"Now, go on then," Gregor said. "Get that look off your face and look proud. Don't let him see you look like that. Look like you have no worries."

Edil took a deep breath and put on a bigger smile. He hoped Ronan could not see the truth in his eyes as he approached him.

Nick had pulled Edil's team and sled next to Ronan's. It helped Edil feel better. With his reindeer standing proud and strong and muscular next to Ronan's tired ones, the realization of winning the race was more vital than ever. Even with Ronan having six reindeer to Edil's four.

The other race ended. Many cheers and some hissing burst out but quieted quickly as all eyes became focused on Edil and Ronan.

"You gentlemen ready?" the Gamekeeper called out from his stand next to the starting line.

"I'm always ready," Ronan laughed as he climbed into his sled.

Edil walked to each of his four reindeer and gave them a loving stroke on their head, between their velvety antlers. The spectators watched quietly as he paid tribute to his team.

"Fly," he whispered to them. His team let out a triumphant bellow as if on command, causing the crowd to gasp in amazement. Even Edil took a step back in disbelief. Again, he had to wonder if they understood him.

Edil climbed into his sled. He looked over at Ronan.

"Best of luck to you, sir," he said respectfully. Ronan just rolled his eyes and focused on his team.

"Ready, Sir Gamekeeper," Edil called out.

The air in Bluster was thick with anticipation as the crowd became still. Gregor, Byron, and Henrick barely breathed. Nick's lips moved in silent prayer. Edil grabbed the reins and held on tight, his feet braced on the floorboard. It was a scary thing, knowing there was no turning back. He glanced at Ronan to see the sneer was gone. He furrowed his brows in determination as he hunched forward, ready to whip his reindeer into a frenzied speed.

"And...you...are..." the Gamekeeper said loudly and slowly. "OFF!"

And with that command, Edil snapped his reins, and his team took off. The people waved their arms, clapped, and cheered as he rode by. Already, he was neck to neck with Ronan as they raced on the path that led out of Bluster.

Once the town ended and the crowd out of sight, Ronan looked over at Edil and grinned again. He winked as he began whipping his team to pick up speed and open up on the barren land ahead of them. His reindeer yelped as they sprinted forward, ahead of Edil and his team.

Edil was about to snap his reins to get Buck and the rest of his team to pick up speed in frustration, but then he had a quick thought. Ronan's team was visibly tired. They had to run out of steam eventually. Edil just needed to stay a bit behind Ronan. He needed to keep in sight and seem threatening enough for Ronan's poor animals to remain at top speed. Eventually, exhaustion would have to win, and Edil could urge his team to take the win.

In time they approached the green flag, as Gregor said they would. There was a small team of spotters tending a covered fire. When they saw Ronan and then Edil, they pulled the damp hide off the fire, letting the smoke rise to signal back to Bluster that they had arrived at the flag. They let out their cheers and whistles as they raced by.

They turned left sharply. Edil thought his sled was going to tip over as he braced himself for the end of his time in the race, but it righted itself as they continued to speed over the snow. Occasionally, Ronan's team would slow down, and Edil would urge his team on, but then Ronan would go into a fit of screams and whip them, and they would return to the top-notch speed they were known for. Edil's heart would sink, more out of pity for the poor creatures than out of fear of losing.

There was a second set of spotters as they neared the lake. They released their smoke as Ronan raced around the lake's shore. Edil followed, doubting his plan. Ronan's brutality kept the reindeer at full speed. His reindeer had no choice.

Edil urged his team forward. He snapped his reins and loosened his grip on them, letting Buck and the others know they were now in charge. They picked up speed as they came close to Ronan's sled. They bounded around the lake when suddenly, Ronan's reindeer lost footing.

They were at the tricky part that Gregor had warned him about. Edil watched as Ronan hit pure, sleek ice ahead of him. His reindeer slid and ceased to be the unanimous team they were. Instead, they were forced in different directions from the unsure footing on the ice. Ronan's sled sped to the right, then back to the left towards the lake's icy waters.

Edil watched as he pulled his reindeer to a halting stop before they hit the ice. While Ronan tried to control his team, Edil slowly let his team walk forward. He let Buck and the other reindeer walk carefully onto the ice, so they could see they were no longer walking on snow, and they must balance their footing differently. Once they knew what they were dealing with, Edil snapped the reins again.

Carefully, surely, and together as a team, they picked up speed and raced past Ronan and his disorganized team. This time it was Edil's turn to smile and wink at Ronan, teasing him. He heard him scream in rage behind him.

Edil continued, grinning at his smarts with racing on the ice. His pride was short-lived, though, as he heard Ronan yelling and getting closer. He looked over his shoulder to see that Ronan had gained control of his team again. He felt enraged that Edil had gained the lead. He could see that if Ronan became ahead of him again, he would not let Edil win. Edil had to keep the lead.

They were still on the ice, and he did not want to endanger his reindeer, but he knew he could not let Ronan keep up. He snapped his reins.

"Fly!" he yelled. "Fly!"

Suddenly, Buck looked like he lost his footing on the ice. Edil's eyes grew wide, and he gasped in terror as the other reindeer seemed to follow suit, and their hooves slipped and slid off the ice. Edil grabbed the reins tight, planted his feet on the footboard before him, and braced himself for them to come slamming down. His heart sank lower than ever.

His team lingered above the ground, their hooves pumped in the air, dragging the sled even faster. They suspended for several yards of the race before coming down gracefully, only to slip up and off the ice again. Edil's mouth dropped open with bewilderment. His brows knitted in confusion and shock as he looked behind him to see if Ronan saw what he saw.

Instead, Ronan seemed more involved in commanding his team as he fell further and further behind Edil. He went back to watching his team, making sure he did not imagine it. He watched as the team once again landed, ran a couple of more feet, then appeared to slip. Instead of falling, they rose, only a couple of feet off the ice, and continued to run on air. It was as if they were leaping, and with each leap, they went faster and carried on for several more feet before landing again.

They continued this until the ice turned back to snow. It baffled

Edil as they rounded the lake and headed back to Bluster, causing spotters to send the last puff of smoke. Once again, he looked behind him. Ronan was so far in the distance that it would be impossible for him to catch up. Without even approaching the finish line, Edil knew. He had won the race. He and his amazing reindeer that somehow did indeed understand him and miraculously flew had won.

"We got this now, friends," he yelled to them with a laugh. "I do not know what happened back there, but thank you!"

As they approached Bluster, the crowd went crazy. Edil could even hear a band start up a joyful tune. They raced towards the finish line, and Ronan was nowhere in sight. People chanted Edil's name and waved their scarves like flags. He felt like he would burst with amazement and pride when he saw his brother, uncle, Byron, and Nick. The were crazed with joy as they clapped, hollered, and jumped.

And then he saw her. Lottie, free of Ronan's demeaning cruelty, was smiling and waiting for him. Her eyes were bright. Her cheeks flushed. He no longer heard the cheers of his name or saw his family and friends waiting for him. Edil saw Lottie, and again that strange feeling snuck up on him, causing his heart to skip a beat and his cheeks to turn red. He liked this feeling so much better than the anger and hate he felt for Ronan.

Lottie

"You are not getting my coat," was the last thing Ronan growled to Edil after handing over his team, his goods, and Lottie.

Edil sniffed at the air then replied with a smirk, "No one wants your stinking coat anyway, Ronan."

This caused Lottie to giggle, but Gregor nudged him and shot him a look to remind him not to gloat. He was a better man than that.

They watched as Ronan climbed into a wagon he was hitching a ride from, with nothing but his prized blue coat on his back. The wagon driver snapped the reins, and the horses trotted down the road, out of Bluster. Everyone noticed how Ronan looked back at them, focused on Edil, his eyes blazing and determined. They knew he was not a man to move on and forget. They knew that if Edil ever ran into him again, there would be trouble.

For the time being, their troubles were over. Gregor and Byron took a quick inventory of Ronan's items and felt pleased to find pretty trinkets, bolts of fabric, and unique items of foodstuffs and drinks they could bring back to the valley. Edil only cared about the reindeer and Lottie.

He looked at Lottie and her matted hair, dirty face, and rags that were not fit to be called clothing. Despite that, he saw she smiled gently, and her eyes were large and inquisitive, wondering what was next for her. Anything had to be better than her time with Ronan. Growing up with her uncaring father, who was nothing but ashamed of her, was better than being with Ronan.

"Well," Edil smiled, "I think we should get you a proper meal, a proper bath, and a proper bed for some rest. Then we can talk about what you would like to do."

"Do?" she asked.

"Tomorrow, we shall talk. Uncle?"

Henrick stepped forward to lead Lottie to his wagon, talking about all the good food he had back at his house. She looked over her shoulder, back at Edil, and smiled again. His cheeks flushed as he smiled and giggled before looking away with embarrassment.

At Henrick's house, a maid prepared a hot meal of soup and bread with tea for Lottie before drawing her a hot bath. With some patience and a stiff hairbrush, the maid worked through the tangles of Lottie's blonde hair. The strong but floral-smelling soap washed away weeks of grime and dirt. Henrick located a trunk in the attic filled with some old clothes of his sister's that she left behind. He left the chest in her bedroom to explore and pick out what she would like to wear.

By the time Edil arrived home with Gregor and Byron, a different girl greeted them. The ragged, dirty waif became a golden-haired little lady. She sat at the dinner table, wearing a stylish pink dress with green ribbons and a high, lacy collar.

"How did you get clothes made so fast, Uncle?" Gregor asked.

"Your mother," he responded. "She left behind some things when she married your father. It's nice to see them go to good use."

"Indeed," Edil smiled as he took his place across from her at the table. He could not believe it was the same girl. It was not just the clothes and bath that made her different, but she sat with her head high, her smile bright. Her posture no longer slumped in shame.

"So," she said as she helped herself to some potatoes and glanced at Edil. "Talk."

"I beg your pardon?"

"Talk. You said we would talk. I know you said we would talk tomorrow, but we are all here now, so shall we talk about what I am to do?"

He could hear the confidence in her voice and see in her mannerism there was nothing meek about her. He realized that she never walked in shame of herself but the shame of Ronan. Once Ronan left her life, her true self could come out.

"Right. Yes," Edil nodded. "Um...talk. You will need a place to stay. You have options."

"Options? Well, that's a first for me," she joked. "And what are my options?"

"You are welcome to stay on here in exchange for work," Henrick said. "You will be treated fairly."

"And Nick mentioned to us he could also take you in, so that's another option," Gregor told her.

She nodded, never taking her eyes off of Edil. "Those are some good options."

"Or..." Edil began, trailing off, glancing at Gregor and Byron. "I'm sorry, we barely know you. We don't know your story."

"My story?" she laughed. "Ok. Once upon a time, my mother gave birth to the world's tiniest baby. She died when I was three. My father felt ashamed of me and my size. He gambled me. Ronan won me. Then you won me. And now, here I am. That's my story, in a nutshell."

"I didn't win you," Edil stammered, his cheeks turning red.

"Did you not win a bet?"

"Well, yes, but—"

"And yet, here I am. Eating fine food with you, fine gentlemen. Now, options…"

"Freedom!" Edil blurted out. She was making his head spin. No one ever made him flabbergasted before.

"I'm sorry?"

"Freedom," he repeated with a softer tone. "I didn't win you. I won your freedom."

She sat there for a minute, taking in what he had said, and then she grinned. Raising her glass of wine, she said, "And that you did. And to you, I thank you. To Freedom."

"Here, here!" Henrick cheered, joining her toast.

"And with that freedom comes another option," Edil said, looking at Gregor and Byron. They nodded, telling him silently to offer the third option.

"Oh, I can't imagine a better option than what Mr. Nick and Mr. Henrick have already offered. They have been so kind and generous," she said gracefully.

"Oi! You wait, lassie," Byron giggled.

"You can come back with us," Edil said.

"And where is that?"

"Home," he replied, pointing north with his fork. She raised an eyebrow quizzically.

"We have lots of land," Gregor told her. "And our families are there. We live a peaceful life. No one bothers us."

"No one stares," Byron joined in.

"We are truly free there," Edil told her.

They did not have to say anything else. She could see it written on their faces. Wherever they were from, it had a hold over them in a tranquil sense. She could see the love and respect they had for their home as if it was a living being.

She sighed and nodded with a small smile. She knew she wanted to see it for herself, even though she knew nothing about it. She wanted to have that peaceful, knowing look they had.

"Ok. Home it is," Lottie finally spoke, nodding and smiling, her eyes never leaving Edil. He did not just smile. He beamed.

Time Stands Still

The ride home across the bleak nothingness with Lottie was fairly uneventful. Shadow made his appearance with his pack, but Edil, Gregor, and Byron were ready for it. They would take no more chances on their trips. They were stocked with scraps of meat and bone to throw to the wolves. All the reindeer knew to pick up their speed when the wolves gave chase.

Edil wanted to test the "fly" command with his reindeer to see if they really could lift their hooves off the ground or if it was just a figment of his imagination during the race. The reindeer proved again that they could indeed suspend themselves in the air and run gracefully and quickly without touching the ground for long seconds at a time. This time the others were there to witness it, their mouths open in disbelief.

"'Tis magic," Byron had whispered. Eventually, even Ronan's reindeer followed suit and ran on a cushion of air only a couple of feet off the ground.

When the wolves were not following them or the reindeer were not magically floating, they took their time trekking across the flatness of the land. They talked and learned about Lottie.

She was strong and forward, nothing like the meek girl they first encountered in Nick's church. She voiced her opinions and quipped jokes. She was exceptionally bright, learning how to handle the team of reindeer, and did her share of driving. She could set up camp quicker than the rest of them and was not afraid of hard, dirty work.

She talked about her father, a man who showed no interest in his only daughter, so it left her to fend for herself most of the time. She spoke briefly of the embarrassment of being gambled away, like an unwanted animal or a little trinket that had no value. She spoke of Ronan with a sneer and told them he was a man of brutal words but little action.

"Quite a weakling, actually," she told them with a chuckle.

Edil liked her more and more as they traveled closer and closer to home. Her toughness, her honesty, and her sense of humor were what he loved about her. He found they were forming a pleasant friendship, and he looked forward to talking with her and hearing her opinions and stories.

They finally reached the wall, which piqued Lottie's interest about what was beyond it. They traveled through the dark tunnel, and Edil made sure his eyes focused on Lottie's face so he could see her immediate reaction to the valley. He was not disappointed as her eyes grew huge, taking in the warm sunlight, the butterflies and hummingbirds bouncing from wildflower to wildflower, the occasional rabbit scurrying away.

"This...this..." she trailed off, speechless.

"I know," Edil smiled.

It was Lorelai who first noticed the tiny caravan of humans and reindeer in the distance. She was hanging Dana's little washed diapers to dry on a line when she saw them. She immediately saw more reindeer than what they had left with, but it took her a moment to notice Lottie.

She shouted excitedly towards Johan and Amelia's cabin. Karina came from behind the cabin where she had been reading to baby Dana from a storybook. Amelia and Johan came out, curiously scanning the horizon. Amelia immediately noticed the strange girl and her son smiling. She recognized how they looked at each other because it was the same way she and Johan looked. She smiled knowingly as they approached the cabin.

Byron and Lorelai greeted each other enthusiastically. Johan's family passed around warm hugs. They made introductions for Lottie, and questions flew with excitement. For such a small group of people, the enthusiasm was immense. Gregor talked of the new reindeer, Byron told of the race- and Ronan- and Edil just wanted his family to get to know Lottie and like her as much as he did. Everyone's voices overlapped each other's. It was a flurry of words.

Finally, things calmed down. Amelia, Johan, and Lorelai were just all happy that their boys were home, safe and sound. Supper needed cooking, the reindeer required tending, and the wagons in the tunnel needed unloading. And, like the year before, they needed to make plans.

Where would Lottie live? Would she stay with Edil's family or with Byron's? Plus, they needed to get started on making toys and sweets. Edil wanted to expand their ideas and imagination beyond the soft cloth dolls and wooden reindeer. And Byron had discovered exotic spices that Ronan had in his stash that Edil won. Byron could not wait to experiment with them. He was particularly fond of a spice labeled *Ginger* and thought how well it might go with some molasses.

Over supper, their tales were told, including how it seems like the reindeer might fly, even for just a fraction of time. They brainstormed new ideas. Lottie fit right in as if she was there all along. Amelia was the only one who remained on the quiet side, frightened for her son's story of Ronan and the race but prideful as well. She watched over the candlelight how Edil and Lottie talked and seemed as if they had been friends for years. Best of friends.

They immediately fell back into a routine in the valley. Lottie stayed with Byron and Lorelai since she and Lorelai were close in age. She helped wherever she could: baking with Byron, caring for Dana, farming or gathering, even schooling Karina. When they came together with ideas for toys and sweets to give the children to the south, Lottie had appointed herself an organizer of some sort. She had found a ledger with blank pages to keep track of the ideas and to help keep inventory on what they had and what they would need from the next trip to Bluster.

She recruited Edil to help her build a small shack with shelves to organize the dolls and little wooden animals they made as the days and weeks went by. She dusted the toys, kept them clean and ready to be loved by some child. While looking at the dolls, an idea came to mind one day, and she excitedly ran out to share it with the first person she could think of.

"Boys need a doll too," she told Edil as she approached him. He was with Ronan's reindeer. They had put on weight over the weeks in Edil's care, and their fur was growing in thick and healthy.

"Dolls are a little girl's thing," Edil laughed. "Like a baby. Boys don't want to take care of a baby."

Lottie rolled her eyes and made a face. She watched as Edil called

Buck over and gently scratched Buck's furry neck. She glanced over to the next corral where Gregor was tending to the ponies and Onyx. Johan milked the cow.

"You know, not all girls want to take care of babies. Besides, what if the doll wasn't a baby?" she asked. "What if it was an animal?"

"An animal?"

"Boys and some girls take care of animals, don't they? Reindeer, horses, cows-"

Edil looked up from Buck, nodding at her idea.

"What if it was an animal you really can't tend to?" Edil suggested. "Like...hmm..."

"A wolf?"

"No! No wolves!" he frowned, shaking his head. "Maybe a fox or a wildcat?"

"Maybe something larger like a bear?"

"A bear! What a fun idea! I like that," he exclaimed, nodding his head. "Can we do that? A bear-doll type thing for the children to care for? Like a pet?"

"I'll ask your mother. I bet she comes up with something brilliant," Lottie said as she took off excitedly.

And Amelia did. With bolts of fur from Ronan's stash and button eyes, she created perfect little, soft bears stuffed with goat fur. And they joined Lottie's shelves, waiting with the dolls to be loved.

The year went by quickly with chores, farming, hunting, gathering, baking, and toy-making. Karina and Dana were another year older, and Byron and Lorelai were expecting their second child. It was time again to head back to Bluster, their wagons carrying even more toys and sweets than before.

For the third time, Edil and Gregor traveled to Bluster with Bryon and Lottie accompanying them. Nick waited for them eagerly, excited to see what he could give to the children. Henrick welcomed them, as usual, with open arms. Ronan was not around this time. They all enjoyed the Reindeer Games as spectators, though people still talked about Edil's race and remarked how healthy Ronan's reindeer looked in Edil's care.

Nick was pleased to see Lottie and how well she was thriving. He could see that the friendship between Edil and Lottie was blossoming. He loved the little stuffed bears and found Byron's creation of something he called "gingerbread men," both adorable and delicious.

"Never could turn down a good cookie," Nick joked as he ate his third one.

Nick even had suggestions of his own for toys.

"Some boys had requested little figurines that are soldiers. Some children have talked about hoops that you can roll down the street. I was thinking maybe some sort of bow and arrow, but with little cloth pillows as the tips, so they won't get hurt."

Lottie immediately bought a new ledger to keep track of Nick's ideas and any other ideas that might have come up.

As fast as their visit came, it was over, and they were back in the valley, and everything started all over again: farming, hunting, gathering, baking, toy making. Lorelai gave birth to a baby boy they named Pell. Dana was a happy toddler, and Karina was getting older and wiser. Johan and Amelia gave Edil and Lottie their blessing to be married and have their own home.

Again, the time came, and back to Bluster, they went. Nick waited with more ideas. He told them how the children waited patiently all year, and he overheard parents use him as a threat to keep their children in line.

"Be good, or else Nick won't give you a toy this Christmastime," he chuckled.

He showed them a small stack of letters that some children had written, wishing for a specific toy or treat. Lottie took them and carefully stored them away so they could read them when they returned home.

At home, they took the children's wishes seriously and did their best to create the toys they desired. More time passed, and more children wrote letters, so more toys were made. More reindeer were born. They made more trips. Sometimes Shadow would show up and chase them. They were always prepared. The reindeer seemed to master their talent of floating and flew more and longer with each trip. Karina stopped aging, just like the rest of the adults in the valley. Henrick showed more wrinkles with each visit. Nick was no longer a young man but an adult with slight grey at his temples.

Karina was no longer a child and joined them on their trips as her brothers had promised years before. They were up to five wagons and sleds loaded down, one for each of them to drive with their team of reindeer. Every year, the townspeople looked forward to their visits and lined the streets to cheer on the caravan as it paraded down the main street of Bluster, with Nick waiting at the end. Children would run along, ringing little bells, trying to get a peek inside the wagons.

One year, it surprised them to see Nick was beaming, a short, neat greying beard around his grin. Next to him was a pretty, dark-haired lady. He introduced his wife to them: Effie. Like Lottie, she had the organizational skills and had organized children's letters and names and wishes from the previous year. She and Lottie instantly took to each other and went to work on keeping track of Nick's hundreds of children.

Every year the story of Nick and his mysterious little friends spread further and further beyond the towns that surrounded Bluster. Children from all over were hearing about this generous man who gave children toys at Christmastime. They heard of his friends who made the toys and came with wagons pulled by reindeer. More and more of these children sent Nick letters asking for dolls, wooden soldiers, and candied sweets.

And it was not just the children who were hearing stories of Nick and the toys.

After years of it just being Edil, Lottie, Gregor, Byron, and Karina coming from the North, it surprised them to see Nick and Effie waiting for them with a small crowd of little people around them.

A Rumor

Edil climbed down from his wagon with a small group of children crowding him excitedly. He smiled and patted them on their heads. Nick could see the curiosity in not only Edil's eyes but on the faces of the rest of his troupe. Nick and Effie waited on the porch of their store patiently with the little strangers around them. Edil made his way through the children as he called out good-natured greetings with the citizens of Bluster.

Finally, Edil broke through the crowd and up Nick's steps. They exchanged a hug that old friends would share, slapping each other's backs. Edil looked around at the strange people. He quickly estimated just over a dozen- some taller than him, some shorter. There were men and women and two tiny boys, and an infant. They all stared at Edil with amazement and wonder, whispering among themselves. Edil shook his head and glanced at Gregor, who just shrugged his shoulder, looking confused too.

"Things change, eh Nick?" Edil finally said, tilting his head to the crowd.

"We need to talk," Nick said, nodding his head before turning to address the strangers. "Why don't we let them get settled. Give them a chance to unwind. We will meet again later today."

A small murmuring sound went through the people as they dispersed down the wooden steps. Nick opened the door to his shop, letting his friends in, removing their hats, mittens, and scarves and welcoming the warmth from the little stove in the corner.

"Tea?" Effie offered as they all settled down. Byron produced a small box of cookies he had baked, especially for Nick.

"My favorite!" Nick exclaimed, dunking a gingerbread man in his tea before taking a bite. Crumbs fell into his salt and pepper beard, which he had now grown down to his chest.

"Nick," Gregor said. "The people. Who are they?"

"Yes. Right," Nick nodded. "The people."

He sighed and sat back in his chair. They gave him a moment to collect his thoughts. Lottie and Karina waited patiently, but Edil, Gregor, and Byron were at the edge of their seats.

"Well," Nick began. "Word has spread far. Not only about the toys and the obedient children at Christmastime but about you."

"Us?" Edil asked.

"Yes," Nick continued. "After you left last year, I did my usual and packed up the toys and traveled throughout December and into January to distribute them. When I came home—"

"There were already three of them here," Effie continued as she stood behind Nick, her hand on his shoulder. "Two brothers and a cousin. They just showed up one snowy night, freezing and almost frostbitten. They traveled far by foot because they heard of all of you."

"Why?" Gregor asked.

"Well, because you are all thriving," Nick said.

"I don't understand," Edil said, shaking his head.

"People such as yourselves don't do well in the outside world," Nick explained. "They are mocked and sometimes treated like animals or worse, like a novelty."

Lottie looked down at the cup of tea in her hands, her eyes welling up. She quickly wiped the tears with the back of her hand.

"There are other Ronans in this world," she said sadly.

"Indeed," Nick nodded.

"So, the first three came in hopes of maybe joining you back to your home. They had heard stories and legends of this small group of little people that live somewhere up north," Effie continued. "They risked their lives traveling in such conditions. They said they traveled for months and months. They left during summer weather, but the journey was more than they imagined."

"I can't imagine," Karina said.

"They were nothing but skin and bones, dressed in bundles of rags. Their teeth were chattering so loudly, their noses and fingertips blue..." Effie trailed off.

"Effie did what she does best," Nick smiled with pride. "She took them in, and with soups and stews and teas and bread and lots and lots of blankets, she nursed them back to health. Imagine my surprise when I returned home to see these three gentlemen, bedded down by the fire, slowly getting better with hope on their chapped faces."

"As soon as they were well, we found places for them to hold them over until now," Effie said. "Henrick has one staying with him in exchange for work. The tavern took the brother for helping keep the rooms clean. And the cousin works for us."

"At the end of spring, the family came; mother, father, two little boys," Nick said. "They too were not living a good life."

"Far from it. Their stories are not ones I care to repeat."

"But, they too heard of what seemed like an impossible tale where maybe, just maybe, they can have a better life. Not only for them but their little boys," Nick told them.

"And we found work for the father while the mother could raise and tend to the boys."

"The others just started trickling in over time," Nick continued. "One here. One there. A young couple, pregnant with child…."

"And you found work and homes for them?" Gregor asked.

Nick sighed and smiled sadly. He leaned forward to put his teacup down, then stood up, brushing the cookie crumbs from his beard.

"Come," he instructed as he walked through the storefront and into the back room. They followed him with Effie behind them. He stopped and swept his arm to their back window, motioning them to look out.

They walked apprehensively to the window. Behind Nick and Effie's store and home was a crudely built village of tents. It was roughly put together around a communal fire pit. There was a small corral with a couple of ponies and a coop with some chickens.

The people they saw just a while ago were walking around or sitting and tending to chores. One woman was mending while a man milked a goat. Two young boys were chasing each other, laughing while another woman washed clothes and another hung them. Some men gathered by the fire to chat and take in the scents of that day's meal, simmering in an enormous pot.

It was a community like any other, small and poor, but the people seemed happy and hopeful.

"There were only so many places that could give them work for room and board," Nick explained. "People of Bluster have their own to care for. So, we are doing our best. We gave them our land to set up something. On frigid days, we welcome them in our home or church. They do their best with what is donated. Occasionally they exchange their time for goods. They appear grateful because they hope to get to a proper home with you good folks if you take them."

Edil turned away from the window and looked at Gregor and Lottie. He did not know what to do or what to say. For years they had it so well in the valley. He was not sure he wanted these strangers to disrupt it. Would they disrupt it? Would they be a benefit to the valley? Or a burden?

"I-I don't know," he finally admitted. "We know what we have back home. We don't know what we will get. That's a lot of people."

"True," said Gregor.

"How many are there now?" Byron asked.

"Fourteen, including the children," Effie replied.

"Fourteen good people," Nick said. "I've had the pleasure of getting to know each one of them well. I wouldn't put this on you if I thought there was a rotten apple in the bunch."

"Hmm," Edil said, nodding in agreement. He knew Nick took time and care to acquaint himself with them.

He looked back at the little tent village. It might have looked dreary to the average person, but the people looked content. They gave off an energy that Edil could not explain.

"They risked limb and life just to be with us, did they not?" Byron commented.

"Yes," Edil said, not taking his eyes off the people.

"They came based on just hearing a...a myth really," Karina said with amazement.

"A rumor," Effie said.

"Yes," Edil repeated.

Nick walked forward. He put his hand on Edil's shoulder and squeezed it gently, knowing that Edil was coming around. Edil's head drooped, and his shoulders slumped.

"The world is cruel as it is," Nick sighed. "You and your family have been fortunate. Luckier than the average person."

"There are other Ronans in this world," Lottie reminded him again, this time her voice strong and determined. Edil looked up at his wife and smiled.

"Perhaps you should meet them," Effie suggested. "Before making up your minds."

"Of course," Edil agreed. "It's always good to meet new friends, yes?"

Lottie threw her arms around him and hugged him. Nick threw his head back and let out a laugh that came from deep in his belly.

"I guess the valley is going to have a population boom," Gregor chuckled. "Can't wait to see Mama and Papa's face when we come back with this one."

New Friends

Nick took his old friends outside to introduce them to his new friends. Edil was a little overwhelmed by the clamor and excitement that came from them. He was not worthy of the praise and honor they gave him. He hoped they would see that he and his family were not the heroes that stories made them, but simple people who lived relatively normal lives. The toy-making and sweets were nothing more than a livelihood. It was nothing but a purpose in what would otherwise be a rather mundane life.

When the excitement settled down, the people invited them to sit at the community fire and share in the big pot of stew that had been simmering all day. They listened to the people's stories full of hardship yet determination and hope.

They told of where they were from; from the east, the west, and some from the south. One came from so far south that he claimed it was always warm, and he never saw snow until he headed to Bluster. They all came from destitute situations. Whether poor in money or poor in spirit, it was all the same to them. They were tired of being shamed or mocked as servants or entertainers. They just wanted a life like everyone else.

As the sun lay low on the distant horizon, they were still there. The stew pot was long empty, and they replaced it with small pots of coffee and tea. Byron had found, buried in his wagon, some sweet honey cakes he had baked and handed them out. They listened as stories became ideas.

"Little houses with tiny furniture for small doll families. Mothers, fathers, siblings, even grandparents perhaps," a young girl by the name of Susie said, her fingers and hands flying with excitement, showing just how small the dolls should be. "Tiny clothes and blankets and dishware—"

"I am, was, a metal smith's apprentice," a man named Xander said. "I can set up a nice shop and make toys of tin soldiers instead of wood, perhaps."

"Parlor games with wooden boards and pieces—"

"I'm quite the accomplished artist. Perhaps fun and silly card games."

"Other soft animal dolls—"

"Have you heard of chocolate yet? It would go great in sweets and candies."

Edil's head was spinning. So many enthusiastic ideas. Maybe too many. He looked over to see Lottie and Effie with their books, trying as hard as possible to keep notes. He thanked God for them. Bookkeeping was not his strong suit.

"Well," he said as the last of the sun slipped away. He stood up, pulling his scarf around him. "It has been quite an amazing day. You all have fine ideas. It will be a busy few days here in Bluster. The trip back north is long and not always an easy one. It is bleak, and there are wolves."

"We've survived worse just to get here," Susie reminded him.

"That is true," Edil nodded. "Nevertheless, we have to make sure all of us are protected as we journey back. If you don't have wagons or sleds, I suggest you acquire them. Build them if you have to. You cannot outrun Old Shadow and his pack on foot. We also need to make sure we have the means to bring food and goods back. The kind people of Bluster, Nick and Effie, always provide us with seeds, meats, bolts of fabric, tools, anything we need to survive another year and keep up with the ever-growing demand for the children's gifts."

"We could also use some help unpacking the wagons we brought down," Gregor suggested. "Since we didn't get to it today. And I am sure Lottie and Effie could use help organizing the gifts. They have quite the efficient system."

"The sooner we take care of that, the sooner we can concentrate on packing up your camp and moving you north," Nick said.

"Excuse me," Xander spoke up, his hand raised like a schoolboy. "But where exactly are we going? Does this town have a name?"

Edil pointed north and smiled. "Home. You are going home."

"And you are going to love it," Lottie beamed.

"Thank you for a lovely day," Edil told them as he walked away. "And for sharing your meal, your stories, and your ideas. We will be back tomorrow, but in the meantime, we have to visit our uncle."

The people who were no longer strangers rose and followed them, excitement once again in their voices. They waved goodbye and bid their farewells before turning back to their tents. Their low voices carried in the quiet night as they mulled over what had transpired. Edil could hear both their nervousness and their optimism as he rode away.

He and his own family had their discussions while riding to Henrick's house. As they approached the large house, it was well-lit with flickering lights from candles and fireplaces. They could smell the supper Henrick had his staff keeping warm. Their voices and the clip-clop of the reindeer's hooves brought Henrick to the front door. At first, they were excited to see him, but their faces quickly fell when he stepped out of the shadows.

He had aged terribly over the year since they last saw him. While he had been gradually aging for quite some time as the years went by, something had taken a toll on him. He stood hunched over, leaning on a cane. He had a large shawl draped around his shoulders, and he clutched it closed with a thin, bird-like hand. He was very thin, his skin sagging and wrinkled. His cheeks were sunken in, and large bags hung under his eyes.

Henrick smiled at his nephews, nieces, and Byron, who he also considered family. His smile was still warm and welcoming. His eyes were still filled with kindness and love for his family.

"I was getting worried," he said, gesturing for them to come into the house. "So good to see you all!"

He shuffled into the house and gave them all hugs. It surprised them at how frail he felt under the shawl. They tried to keep their smiles on their faces and not let on how shocked they were.

"Ah, my Karina," Henrick said, looking at his niece sadly. "You look more and more like your mother with every visit. I miss my sister something awful."

"The cane, Uncle," she said, the only one brave enough to point it out. "What happened?"

"Bah!" he grumbled. "A nasty fall a while back. That is all."

"Are you alright, Uncle?" Gregor asked.

"Oh, fine. Fine. Not getting any younger, that's for certain," he laughed. "But look at you kids, huh? Still the same. Nary a grey hair on your head. Remarkable."

They cast their eyes down from embarrassment. They knew they had not aged. They knew nothing in or around the valley aged; not them, not the animals, not even Old Shadow, which should have died of old age a long time ago. They knew, but they rarely talked about it.

"Enough about getting old," Henrick grinned. "Come! Come! Get comfortable and meet my new friend, Benedict. Benny! Come out!"

From the direction of the kitchen, a small man appeared. He was wearing an apron and wiping his hands on it. He looked similar to one of the other men with his curly brown hair and blue eyes.

"This is Benedict," Henrick introduced. "He is one of the originals that first came to Bluster."

"Oh, yes," Edil nodded, extending his hand. "One of the brothers."

"Yes," he replied politely, shaking his hand. "Perhaps you met my brother in town today. Christoph. Or our cousin, Robert."

"We did. I believe we met them all," Gregor said.

"Quite an amazing group of people," Edil told him.

"Benny here is quite the cook," Henrick told them as they walked into the dining room. "Come see what he has whipped up for you kids."

They walked into the dining room to see the table spread out with meats and vegetables. The stew they had eaten earlier was long forgotten as they smelled the spices and savories.

"This looks amazing," Lottie commented.

"Oh, it's just a little something," Benedict said sheepishly. "After going hungry for a while and eating nothing but roots and dead grass, one learns to appreciate the different flavors and techniques with food."

Dinner was quiet, not because they had nothing to say, but they were busy eating Benedict's good cooking. Their mouths were always full. After dinner, they all retired to their warm, comfortable beds that Henrick always had waiting for them. Edil and Lottie whispered to each other, talking of their uncle, new friends, and plans. Eventually, they drifted off into a deep sleep, making up for the restless nights when they traveled in the open, cold air.

In the morning, after a fantastic breakfast of Benedict's honey-sweetened waffles and sausages, they headed back to Nick's. It was a full day of unpacking the toys and sweets and organizing them for Nick's upcoming travels. The people of the little tent village helped in any way they could. Edil and Gregor agreed that working together was a great way to get to know them even more. They all did their parts and even seemed appreciative of the hard work.

Lottie and Effie were at a table surrounded by their books, quills, ink, and letters from the children. Karina kept their cups filled with coffee to keep them alert and their eyes from getting weary. Every year the little stack of letters grew and grew until it became piles.

"Don't know how we are going to get this little one his very own horse to ride," Effie said, putting a letter down after reading it. "Not sure the parents will appreciate that one."

Christoph, Benedict's brother, was walking by with Byron when he overheard her. He stopped and glanced at the letter.

"Hmmm...I might have ideas," he told them.

"Fantastic," Lottie said. "Mull on them, and we will work it out when we get home."

"And this one?" Effie asked, waving another letter with a sigh. "She wants a tree made of candy."

"Oi!" Byron exclaimed as he grabbed the letter from Effie. "Quite the little dreamer this lass is!! 'Tis a marvelous thought! A candy tree! Love it, I do!"

"Good," Lottie laughed. "Hope you love it enough to grow one by next year somehow."

"Aye, never underestimate the workings of a talented baker," he smiled.

By evening, everything was in its place. Toys filled large, red velvet sacks that Effie had made Nick over the years. They carefully placed sweets in Nick's wagon. The ledgers were closed, and the letters were filed for Lottie to bring back home. She could not wait to assign jobs to their new friends and see what toys they could craft. They seemed eager to get started as well.

The following day was the annual Reindeer Games. Even though Edil had not participated in another race since Ronan, they all still looked forward to the festivities. Even fragile Uncle Henrick ventured into town with the help of Benedict for the races.

As tradition called, they all attended Nick's church service in the morning. So many people had been coming to Bluster for the games that Nick had to do his sermon with the church windows and doors wide open so the extra crowds could hear him from the outside.

The blessing of the reindeer followed service, and then the hooting and hollering, the drinking and eating, and the dancing and gambling began. Edil used to search the crowds for Ronan and his blue silk coat, but not anymore. It had been too long. He eventually concluded that he might never see Ronan and his spiteful sneer again, and he was grateful for that.

Two days after the games, Edil announced it was time to get ready for the journey home. The people going back with them were eager to show off the wagons they had built or bartered for.

Seven wagons lined the back of Nick's house. Five were small, piled down with goods. Edil liked that they looked small enough to pull through the tunnel. Two turned into holding pens on wheels lined with chicken wire for their livestock, which impressed Edil. Now they could bring their chickens and the few goats and sheep they had. They had spears ready if they needed to fight off wolves, blankets and furs for warmth, food for meals, and firewood to cook. They were prepared.

On the morning of departure, people lined the streets again, waiting for their caravan to parade out of the little town. Similar to the Reindeer Games, the citizens of Bluster were in a joyous mood.

Henrick rode into town again with Benedict driving the carriage. Benedict helped the older man climb carefully and slowly down from the carriage.

"Benny!" Christoph called to his brother. "Hurry. We saved a space for your belongings."

Benedict glanced at Henrick, who gave him a gentle pat on the shoulder.

"Where are your belongings?" Christoph asked with a confused note in his voice. He did not see a satchel or trunk with his brother.

"Nephews!" Henrick called out, walking away from the brothers, giving them time to talk on their own. "Edil! Gregor!"

His nephews heard him calling and walked out of Nick's shop, where they were sharing their last cup of coffee with their friend.

"Uncle," Gregor called. "I thought we said our goodbyes this morning."

"We did, but I thought we should have one last chat before you are on your way."

He walked up into Nick's shop. Effie gave him a chair to settle in comfortably while Nick emptied the shop. Eventually, it was just Henrick, Edil, and Gregor.

"Is something wrong?" Edil asked.

"Well," Henrick began, nodding towards the window. They could see Benedict and Christoph having what appeared to be an intense conversation. "Benedict will not be joining you kids. Not on this trip anyway. He has decided to stay at the house. He has been quite helpful to me ever since my fall. And he is just not ready to make another long journey. Not after barely surviving getting this far."

"I see," Edil said.

"He will eventually join you on one of your other trips," Henrick continued. "When his services and friendship are no longer required."

"No longer required?" Gregor asked. "I don't understand."

"My dear boy, I am not long for this world. I am lucky if the good Lord gives me another year or two."

"Uncle, don't say that!" Edil scolded.

"Come now! So is life. Things live. Things die."

Edil and Gregor cast looks at each other, again ashamed. They have never known anyone to die. Henrick saw their glances and knew, but instead of asking about it, he smiled bravely.

"Besides, I am getting tired. The old bones rattle and ache," he told them. "But I plan to fight it and stick around a bit longer if I can. You see, with your next visit, can you bring something for me?"

"Of course. Anything," Edil agreed.

"My sister. Can you bring her back to me? I would like to see her one more time before I can't."

"Oh," was all Edil could say. He did not know how his mother would respond to such a request. She had never shown interest in returning to Bluster.

"We can ask her," Gregor promised.

"That's all I want," Henrick said. "Tell me, is she well? There are only a couple of years between us. Has time caught up with her as it did with me? Or is she as young as her children?"

Again, Gregor and Edil looked at each other.

"Ah," Henrick nodded, knowing. "Good. Good. She deserves it. Nothing but the best for my sister. She's a wonderful woman. Always was. And she raised kind children."

"We'll do our best to bring her back," Edil told him. "But you have to promise us you will still be here. Promise us!"

"I'll do my best. Besides, Benedict has become quite the companion. He cooks and cleans for me. He's a great conversationalist and a fantastic chess opponent. He cares for me well. He'll see to it I survive another year," he chuckled, rising from his chair.

"Til next year, Uncle," Gregor said, standing up with Edil.

"Yes. Yes, my good nephews. Til next year."

Neighbors

Edil left Bluster leading a line of a dozen wagons. Together, they all followed one another across the snowy tundra. They kept one another occupied with songs and stories, sharing meals and advice. After a few days of traveling by day and sleeping next to campfires in huddled bundles by night, their new friends had their first encounter with Shadow and his pack.

Edil's adrenaline always surged when his old nemesis surfaced. He knew Old Shadow was nothing more than a wolf, but he also knew that Old Shadow had been around for a long, long time. He was a wise and possibly timeless old wolf. Edil had gained respect for the wolf and even looked forward to the excitement that would break up the bleak travels.

Old Shadow and his pack had grown less intimidating over the years to Edil and his family. Through trial and error, the wolf had known that the travelers kept themselves armed with sharp and painful spears to fight off any wolf that dared to leap upon the wagons or reindeer. He had learned that the reindeer seemed to run faster and faster with each passing year and seemed to gain an ability even briefly to fly.

And he had learned that with patience and persistence, Edil and his people would eventually throw scraps of meat and bones to the pack to slow them down. In the end, there was always a prize for the pack, no matter what. It was an uneasy relationship between the wolves and the people. The wolves chased and howled and bared their teeth. The people rewarded them with a decent hearty meal, and the wolves would ease up and eventually disappear into the grey horizon.

It terrified the new travelers when the pack appeared, but they followed Edil and Gregor's orders shouted over the bellows of the reindeer and the howls and growls of the wolves. They questioned Edil's sanity when they saw him yelling, teasing, and taunting the wolves.

"Come on, you mangy cur!" Edil would holler with laughter. "You think you're so big and scary?"

After a while, they saw the chase as a game. Susie even became intrigued and let her hand out to pet one of the beautiful creatures that panted and lopped alongside her wagon. The wolf suddenly growled and jumped up, snapping viciously at her hand. Luckily, she had pulled it away in time, and all the wolf had was a mouthful of air as his teeth snapped loudly. Xander jabbed him with his spear, causing the wolf to yelp and run off.

"Never let your guard down!" Gregor yelled from his wagon. "They are still hungry, wild animals!"

Eventually, the wolves slowed down, left in the distance eating away at the scraps and bones tossed to them. Everyone could settle in again, waiting for their pounding hearts to calm.

"Til next year, Shadow," Edil said quietly, looking back at the large, black wolf. He could have sworn Old Shadow looked up at him, so much knowledge in his one eye, and then gave him a nod.

The rest of the trip was uneventful and tiresome from boredom. When the great wall of ice came into view, they picked up their bobbing, sleepy heads in amazement. They had arrived. On the other side, they knew it was a paradise that Edil had promised them. A home where they could live peacefully. And yet, they struggled to imagine it after being surrounded by nothing but flatlands, snow, and a silver sky.

Gregor and Karina jumped down from their wagon seats to unlock the great wooden door that opened to the long dark tunnel. They lit the torches that waited for them just inside the entrance and passed them out among the people.

"Are you ready?" Edil smiled. "You are home."

With that, he snapped his reins gently and led the caravan into the darkness. The goat and sheep wagon were too tall to fit, so Christoph and Xander quickly unhitched their ponies and let the animals out to herd them through. Without a word spoken among any of them, it was a silent trek with just the sounds of hooves and wagon wheels echoing on the hard, rock-like ground. Occasionally they heard the trickle of water. If they listened close enough, they could almost hear their heartbeats all pounding with anticipation. Eventually, the darkness became lighter as sunlight wafted in, eager to greet them.

Gone was the dark tunnel. Gone was the stark, treeless nothing that they had traveled across. They all gasped, wagon by wagon and foot by foot, as they entered the lush, colorful, sunlit, bright valley.

The newcomers stopped to take it all in. They climbed down from their seats to touch and smell the flowers. The tiny herd of goats and sheep immediately began grazing, not having had fresh greens in a long, long time.

"It's warm," Susie sighed happily, turning her face to the sun and closing her eyes. She removed her hat and mittens and unwrapped her scarf, and the others followed suit.

"This is fantastic," Christoph nodded with tears in his eyes.

"Aye, 'tis but just the beginning, me friend," Byron chuckled.

At the cabins by the stream, Amelia tended to Byron and Lorelai's children. She sat outside at a table with Dana and Pell, teaching them their letters and marks. Lorelai was in her cabin, making the day's supper while Johan tended to one of the many little vegetable gardens they had growing. All of them were unaware of the caravan headed their way.

They heard them first. Strange voices carried softly over the fields. Laughter and some banter among people. Though the voices sounded friendly, it caused Amelia to stand up suddenly and Johan and Lorelai to come outside, with looks of alarm. Lorelai hurried to the children and put her arms around them protectively. Johan clutched his garden hoe and walked up to Amelia. Silently and fearfully, they scanned the distance.

Over a small knoll, a wagon appeared led by reindeer. The driver waved enthusiastically to them.

"It's just Edil, Ama," Dana said with a giggle to Amelia. The adults all looked so tense but breathed with relief.

Behind Edil, Gregor followed. Then Lottie. Then Byron. Then Karina. And it did not end there. Two men came over next with staffs in hands, herding the small number of goats and sheep.

"Oh," Lorelai smiled. "New neighbors, I suppose."

And then six more wagons came, piled high and tied down with shapeless bundles. They were all driven by people just like them. Some wagons had two or three people in them. Reindeer led some, others by ponies and horses. One had a team of oxen. One had the sounds of loud, nervous chickens squawking from the back. All of them followed Edil and headed towards them.

"Goodness," Amelia whispered. "I guess we have a village now."

Smiles, hugs, and questions greeted them. Introductions were quick and a bit disorganized, but they knew they would get to know each other in time. It delighted Dana and Pell to see the two young brothers, Phineas and Tomas, for they never had playmates before. Women gathered around Amelia and Lorelai, who directed them to set up a cooking fire. The men immediately followed Johan's instructions on where to pen the animals and find firewood and fresh water.

Eventually, over the weeks, the tents came down. The people spread out throughout the valley and built their own homes, barns, and pens. Xander, a metalsmith, built a small shack to work. Susie settled by the stream and built a cozy home with a workshop to hone her skills as a potter and sculptor with clay. Christoph and Robert helped Lottie, Gregor, and Edil build a larger building for toy making and storage. Byron took on a young apprentice in his bakery and sweets shop.

Throughout the year, they held Sunday worship and Saturday picnics. They traded stories and recipes. There were a couple of weddings, including Gregor and Susie's. They worked together on ideas and made wishes from the children's letters come to reality.

Lottie felt pleased with Christoph's simple idea of a stick with a wheel on the bottom and a block of wood carved into the shape of a horse's head attached to the top to create a "riding horse" for a child. She told him to make as many as he could. She loved the dollhouses with the figurines made from Susie's crafty hand to live in them.

Lottie and Edil were on their way to speak to Amelia and Johan one morning about possibly taking the next trip with them back to Bluster when Byron burst out of his shop, waving his arms excitedly.

"Come! Come!" he called. "See what I have done!"

Curiously, they crossed the field. They followed him into the sweet and yeasty-smelling bakery. He turned to them, his hands on his hips and his chest thrust out with pride. His cheeks were round and rosy with excitement.

"What? What is it?" Edil asked.

"'Tis the tree!" Byron exclaimed, gesturing to the table he was standing next to.

A small, tiny pine tree, no taller than two feet, stood on the table, the bottom nailed to planks. From its branches hung delicate little gingerbread men with loops of shiny ribbon.

"A- a tree?" Edil asked, confused, but Lottie remembered.

"The tree of sweets!" she said, clapping her hands and stepping forward to inspect it closer.

"Aye, mate! Just like the little lassie's wish, is it not? And look! Look here!!"

Byron showed them a tray that had small cane-shaped candies on them. He picked one up carefully.

"Me apprentice is a smart one. He is," he smiled. "He took me peppermint candy sticks and bent them just so before they cooled. And look!!"

He gingerly hooked the cane around a branch. Then he stood back to admire it as it hung delicately and glistened in the light. Lottie and Edil followed suit, hanging the rest from different branches.

"He calls them Candy Canes," Byron said.

"Candy Canes," Edil nodded with a smile. "Excellent! I like that.

Make more candy canes for the children. Lots and lots more."

Edil plucked a candy cane from the tree, popped one end in his mouth, and began sucking. He winked at Byron good-naturedly, enjoying the sugary mint flavor. He walked out, Lottie beside him.

"Isn't that brilliant?" Lottie said, opening her ledger that she always seemed to carry. With her quill, she could mark off the little girl who wanted a candy tree from Nick.

They continued to walk to Edil's parents' home, the excitement of the candy tree and the newly invented candy cane dwindling from them. They needed to have a conversation about Henrick. They had long avoided this conversation with the hustle and bustle of their new community.

They found Amelia sitting outside in her rocking chair, weaving yarn into the soft cloth scalp of her latest rag doll. Johan was close by, pulling weeds from their garden.

"Mother," Edil greeted, taking the candy cane out of his mouth to give her a quick peck on the cheek.

"How are things going, son?" his father called out.

Edil nodded and spoke briefly of Byron's tree. Lottie read out some impressive numbers from her book.

"Sounds like you will have loads to bring back to Nick this year," Amelia smiled. "He will be happy."

"Yes. Speaking of Nick…" Lottie said, giving Edil a look, telling him silently to stop stalling.

"We think you should make the trip to Bluster this year," Edil finally said. "And Papa, too, if he wants to come."

"Oh, I don't think so," Amelia said, shaking her head. "We made that journey once. That is more than enough for me."

"Yes. I know, but Uncle Henrick…." Edil trailed off, trying to find the proper words.

"Uncle Henrick was not in the best of health," Lottie said gently.

"Henrick? My brother?"

"Yes, Mama. He is not aging well. And he took a great fall that he was not healing from," Edil admitted. "I'm sorry to be the one to tell you this."

"You should have told me sooner! You waited all this time?" Amelia scolded.

"I know. And I am sorry. We just didn't know how or when to tell you with all that has happened. The year went by so quickly," Edil explained. "I'm sorry."

"Henrick would very much like to see you," Lottie said. "Before it's too late."

Amelia sat there, no longer rocking. Edil and Lottie could see the hurt and anger in her eyes as she glared at them.

"I can't talk to you two right now," Amelia finally said. "Does your brother and sister know about this?"

Edil nodded guiltily.

"Unacceptable to keep these sorts of things from your mother," Johan scolded.

"We are sorry. We truly are. This could be a good thing, though. You and Papa get to visit Uncle and see Bluster again. You'll be in the wonderful parade they throw for us, and children ring bells and sing and dance, and you'll finally get to meet Nick and Effie—"

"Enough!" Amelia snapped, cutting him off. She rose from her chair, the unfinished doll clenched in her hand and stormed off into the cabin. Edil dropped his head down in shame.

"Give her time," his father finally spoke. "She needs to think things through."

"Of course," Lottie agreed. "Edil, let's go."

"Should have sent Gregor to tell her," he mumbled as they walked away.

Henrick's Last Wish

Amelia did not speak of their conversation about Henrick until the day came where they were to leave the valley to return to Bluster. Edil felt unsure and sad. He could not join in the excitement. There were new toys to show Nick and wagons to parade through the road in Bluster. Some people even took care to paint and decorate their wagons in festive colors, garlands of pine branches, and little jingling bells. They packed their wagons with care, making sure no toys or sweets would get damaged. They joked and sang songs.

Edil remained somber as he double-checked his wagon. He had pride and love for his people and their skills. They accomplished great things over their first year in the valley, but he just could not bring himself to join in the songs and the jubilations. He worried about his mother and her uncharacteristic quietness. He worried about his uncle and what might wait for him when he returned. Would he still be there?

At Lottie's approval, people climbed into their wagons, bidding farewell to the few staying behind. Soon, it was just Edil who was not yet in his wagon. He stood beside Buck, scratching between his antlers, feeling conflicted. Everyone waited patiently. It was Edil who would traditionally lead the procession of wagons out of the valley.

Lottie approached him, knowing he was not himself. She placed her hand on his. Edil smiled sadly and looked over to Gregor, who was sitting with his new bride, Susie. Gregor could only shrug his shoulders. He also did not know what Amelia's thoughts were or why she and Johan were not in the small group of people saying their goodbyes and wishing safe travels to all.

Suddenly, he could see a small carriage pulled by the great Onyx. It had been years since they had harnessed Onyx to pull something other than the occasional plow or logs for lumber. He had a delightful step in his trot as he pulled the carriage. Edil could not remember the last time his parents used a carriage. Everything and everyone was within a short hike away. The carriage and harnessed horse could only mean one thing.

"They are coming with us," he smiled as he waved.

Johan rode up alongside Edil and Lottie's wagon. Amelia looked apprehensive and sat with her hands folded in her lap, staring down at them.

"Thought Onyx should get out a bit. It's been years," Johan joked, trying to break the ice.

"All right," Edil nodded. "Mama?"

"Yes," Amelia nodded. "I need to see Henrick. This is the right thing to do."

"Don't feel saddened by this," Edil said. "It's good. It'll be nice for you to see your childhood home again."

Amelia nodded. Onyx pawed at the ground in frustration, blowing air noisily through his flared nostrils. He wanted to get out and go, remembering what it felt like to wear a harness again.

"Look at him," Johan laughed.

Edil and Lottie climbed into their wagon, and people cheered. He stood in his seat so everyone could see and hear him.

"My parents used to tell us it was Onyx, this great and mighty black horse- the biggest but most gentle of all of the valley's creatures- that led them here," Edil preached. "And today, I will not be leading us out. I give that honor back to Onyx."

People clapped as he sat down and settled into his seat. He grabbed the reins to his team of reindeer and looked over at his parents.

"Father," he nodded. "Lead the way."

Johan smiled and snapped his reins. People cheered when Onyx pulled the carriage to the front of the line and headed towards the tunnel. Excitement was in the air, and Edil was happy to welcome it finally. The journey to Bluster was a good one. It was enjoyable with more people. Of course, Shadow and his pack arrived, but the people were always the masters of the chase.

The townspeople spotted them in the distance and lined the street, anticipating their arrival. They waited with their bells to ring, and some even made colorful little pennants to wave. It surprised them to see the large black horse lead the parade, almost dancing with enthusiasm. They greeted the wagon with boisterous and joyful voices. They loved the wagons that were decorated and festive. They loved there were more wagons than the year before.

Amelia sat in awe, her eyes wide with wonderment. Her hometown, which at one time either ignored her or shamed her was so welcoming. The people were genuinely excited to see them. It was one big welcoming celebration. Her awe turned to pride because she realized it was her sons that did this. Her sons were the reason they celebrated.

As always, Nick and Effie waited at the end of the road. Like the year before, more people with short stature and hopeful faces surrounded them.

"Oh," Edil said, nodding to himself when he saw them. "Fine. This is fine."

Nick quickly filled him in when he could. They came in over the year again. The news was traveling further and further. Nick said he told them as much as he could and made sure they were ready for the trip North goods that might be useful to keep what appeared to be an ever-growing village thriving.

Nick was happy to see that the people from the year before looked healthy, well-fed, and content. It was almost immediately that all the people mingled as they unloaded the wagons.

"Wait until you see what Byron came up with," Lottie said, pulling her ledger from her bag. "And these adorable riding ponies and-"

"Soon," Effie said. "I think you should head to Henrick's."

Edil looked at Nick with a questioning look.

"He's fighting," Nick admitted. "I'm afraid it won't be much longer."

Edil nodded as he saw Amelia blink away her tears and take a quivering but brave breath.

Traveling to the house, Amelia could not believe how little it had changed and how much she had forgotten over the years. Edil noticed the air was still, no scents of a warm meal waiting for them. The atmosphere seemed dreary. No one opened the door, ready to greet them warmly. Something was amiss. He and the others knew it was not good.

They climbed the wooden steps up to the large porch, and after a few short raps on the big door, Benedict opened it. He exchanged quick, solemn hugs with his brother and cousin as they walked into the foyer. He was happy to see them so well, but the weight of Henrick weighed heavily on his shoulders.

"He rests in the parlor," he told Amelia as he took her shawl and coat. "He can no longer make it up and down the stairs to the bedrooms. The staff and I have made sure that he is comfortable the last couple of months. Nick, Effie, and other townspeople have been very kind and visit almost daily. He speaks of you often. He will be so pleased that you came."

Amelia nodded her thanks to Benedict and walked to the parlor. A large bed filled the center of the room, near the fireside. Henrick lay sleeping, propped up on several pillows, and buried under thick blankets. She walked quietly to him, not wanting to disturb him.

She felt shocked at how old he looked. When she left, he was a big, strapping, strong young man. Before her now lay a fragile, thin, brittle bird of an old man with paper-thin, wrinkled skin. His hair was mostly gone, only a few wisps of white. His hands were gnarled into claws. She did not recognize him and searched his face for something familiar. Tears rolled down her cheeks when she could not find it.

Carefully, she took his hand. It was cold and boney to the touch. Henrick's eyelids fluttered for a few seconds before opening. He stared at his sister, unsure if he was dreaming or not. Then, he smiled, and she saw it.

"There you are, brother," she said, choking back a sob as she remembered his good-natured smile. He still had it.

"Amelia! Amelia, is it you? Did you really come?" he cried, trying to pull himself up to get a better look. "Benny! Benny, my spectacles, please!"

Benedict rushed into the parlor and found his glasses sitting on his side table. Henrick fumbled to put them on with shaky hands. Once he did, his smile grew even larger. There she was, as clear and as young as the day she left when she was a young bride.

"Oh, my lord! What great blessings to see you!" he exclaimed as she threw herself on him, her arms wrapped gingerly around his shoulders.

"Henrick. I am so sorry. I should have come years ago," she told him.

"No, no, my dear sister. This is marvelous. Let me look at you," he insisted.

She pulled herself up, and he reached to her face, wiping her tears away.

"Remarkable. You have been untouched by the cruel hands of time," he said. He looked behind her to see Johan standing there. He, too, had no wrinkles on his face and nary a strand of grey hair on his head.

"Truly remarkable," he repeated.

"I'm sorry," Amelia said, embarrassed. She should be as old and as wrinkled and grey and frail as her brother. She felt shame in her unexplainable youth.

"No apologies," he scoffed. "I am so happy for you and Johan. What a family you raised. You truly blessed me with fine nephews and a wonderful niece. I have nothing but pride in my family. Their visits kept me going for many years."

Henrick motioned for Benedict to put on some tea. Edil and Gregor placed more pillows around their uncle to help him sit up more so he could enjoy his company. They sat around his bed as he listened to how their village grew and introduced him to Susie, the newest member of their family. They sipped their tea and listened to Amelia and Henrick share memories and laugh over childhood jokes. He told them all how good Benedict was to him and how he was more of a companion than a servant.

Eventually, they could see the excitement was taking its toll on Henrick. He was tiring out quickly. Every so often, his eyes would close, and his head would bob down. They called it a night to get some sleep.

As they tried to leave the room quietly, he woke up and called out to Edil and Gregor. They stayed behind to hear what he needed.

"Thank you," was all he needed to say. "Thank you for bringing her back. Thank you for making an old man's last wish come true. And thank you for being such good men."

"Of course, Uncle," they responded.

The following day, Henrick seemed to gain some strength and insisted on sitting at the dining table to join them for breakfast. After eating, everyone left for town. Amelia and Henrick stayed behind together to catch up and make up for all the lost years. While they organized and went over their hoard for Nick in town, Amelia and Henrick visited and talked. There was so much to say, a lifetime to cover. When Henrick felt tired and napped, Amelia wandered her childhood home. She looked at things and touched things she never thought she would ever see again.

Her room was untouched, with the same thick quilt on the bed. She found some odds and ends in a chest exactly where she left it in the back of her closet. The dinner and drinkware never changed, and the curtains had the same gold trim. Everything was the same, and it all brought back so many memories.

She went to her parents' graves, wishing that she and Johan had traveled back much sooner so she could have seen them before they departed this world. They were gone when Edil and Gregor made the first trip to Bluster.

By the evening, when everyone came back to the house, she was helping Henrick sit at the table again so he could enjoy a pleasant supper with his family. Enthusiasm filled the room with talk of the next day's annual Reindeer Games.

"I would like to join you," Henrick announced. "I would like to see the Reindeer Games one more time. Never missed it since you boys started coming to Bluster."

"Of course, Uncle," Gregor said. "It's tradition."

They immediately went to work to develop a plan on how to move Henrick and keep him comfortable. By morning, they transformed the back of Edil's wagon into a bed of sorts for Henrick to lounge. They took mattresses from their beds and lots of pillows and blankets and quilts to get it just right for him. Benedict had rigged up a canopy over him to help keep the sun and snowy glare out of Henrick's eyes. Henrick clapped like a child and declared the wagon was fit for a king. It took some time and effort to help him climb in, but he was determined. Once he settled in, Amelia joined him to keep him company.

As one big family, they rode into town. They listened to Nick's sermon from outside one of the church's windows and attended the blessing of the reindeer. Then found a quiet spot where Henrick could watch the races.

The fresh air seemed to do him wonders. His cheeks flushed with excitement. He ate the picnic Benedict packed for everyone with vigor and drank more than his share in ale. He cheered with the rest of the crowds and booed when his favorites lost. Not once did he tire or nod out into a catnap.

The ride back to his home was a happy one. It was indeed a holiday occasion for them. They struggled a bit to get him up and out of the wagon and then settled him back into his bed. He immediately closed his eyes, the fresh air, long hours, excitement, and ale catching up with him. A deep snore rose from his chest as they all left him to rest.

The night was content with no sounds except for the occasional snore or a crackle from a fire. They all drifted into slumber. Henrick dreamed of what a wonderful day he had with his sister and her husband and his nephews and nieces. Deeper and deeper, he spiraled into his dream. He smiled in his sleep, for he was just as young and agile as the rest of his family.

By morning, he was gone.

Amelia's Decision

Edil, Gregor, and Karina had never attended a funeral before. Their emotions jumbled with a mixture of feelings as they watched Henrick's simple wooden casket lowered into the ground. The sadness weighed heavily on them, but they also felt fear. They feared crying too much or not crying enough. They feared saying the wrong thing or perhaps saying too little. Mostly, they feared the lump in their throat that reached down to squeeze their heart before settling into a knot in a deep part of their stomach they never even knew existed. This grief was a sensation unlike anything they had ever felt before, and they did not know how to react. They had never had to say goodbye permanently.

Edil kept his composure, though one could see the heartbreak in his eyes as he bereaved his uncle's passing. He listened half-heartedly to the kind words and short and simple sermon Nick said over Henrick's grave. He shook hands and accepted the expressions of sympathy from the many townspeople who came out to pay their respects.

"I never want to go through this again," Edil had told Lottie as she nodded with agreement. They sat in Henrick's dining room, staring at the small plate of food somebody had given them. Everyone insisted they eat, yet no one seemed to be hungry.

"But it is life," Nick said, overhearing him. "We are born. We die. Birth and death go hand in hand. Both a miracle in its way."

"Not for us," Edil whispered. "Not yet, anyway."

Nick looked at him, his face both puzzling and accepting.

"Well, there are always bigger miracles," he said. "But know this: Henrick is in a good place now. He no longer has pain. He fought for a long time, uncomfortable and crippled in every way but his mind and heart. He fought so he could see his sister one last time. He died a fortunate man."

Edil nodded, but he still did not feel any better. He aimlessly pushed some food around on his plate with his fork.

"He was a good man," Lottie said. "So kind, always so very welcoming. We will just have to remember and learn to achieve to be the person Henrick was."

"True," Edil responded.

"Listen, I was going to wait to discuss something with you," Nick said, leaning in. "But since I have your ear now, and you seem to need something to take your mind off of the current situation at hand."

Edil looked up from his plate.

"I thought that maybe next year you can plan to go with me as I deliver the toys," Nick continued. "You work so hard that I thought it would be nice for you to see the outcome."

"Outcome?"

"The children's faces. The laughter and smiles. The little squeals of delight. There is nothing like it," Nick smiled. "I want you to see how you are a large part of the Christmastime spirit. Besides, I could use some help. Every year, more and more children write to me. More and more wishes to be delivered further and further away."

"Oh, I don't know…." Edil trailed off.

"Take the year to think about it. If you come, you come. If you don't, then you don't. I understand, but I could use the company too," he winked. "It would be nice to have a conversation to make the journey go by quicker."

He stood up, taking his cup of tea with him. Nick patted Edil on the back before walking away. Edil sat there, pondering what Nick just suggested. He had never thought about the other children Nick delivered to, the children who wrote all the letters Lottie and Effie would read and file. The children of Bluster and their adult counterparts were always enough fulfillment for him.

The idea intrigued him. To travel beyond Bluster was more than he could dream. He remembered back to his younger days where Gregor would find him sitting up high on the ridge, overlooking the barren nothing, wondering what lies beyond that. He would dream of traveling outside of the valley's icy walls. He accomplished that and yet never went beyond the grey, cold town of Bluster.

He shook his head to himself. He was a grown man now with a wife and responsibilities. He had the townspeople that looked to him for direction and support. He had his village to attend to. If he joined Nick, he would be gone for several more weeks than he usually was.

He knew Nick's schedule. Nick spoke of it many times. He would set out in time to have gifts delivered to the nearest towns by early December. He continued to travel further and further away throughout the Christmas season and then delivered the last gifts by early January. Then it was a long ride north back to Bluster.

Edil pushed Nick's idea to the back of his mind. He could not think about it. He just lost his uncle, and he still had to get ready for the ride back home. He needed to tend to the new migrants that built a larger tent village behind Nick and Effie's shop. He had to make sure everyone's affairs were in order, and they were ready for the long, tedious trek back to the valley. He had to make sure his mother was doing well after losing her brother. He had to see Gregor and Karina and make sure they, too, were well. It was too much to think about while planning a trip south with Nick. He feared leaving Lottie, his family, and the rest of his village. So, he pushed Nick's idea away. He would think about it another time, when things settled and when he was back home where he could think clearly.

Edil decided that the best way to move through his grief was to get back to work. He spent the next few days looking at the people's wagons and sleds, making sure they were sturdy enough for the journey. He took inventory of what people were bringing back to the village to contribute to what appeared to be an ever-growing population. He also made a note of items they would still need to keep the village flourishing. He took his time to listen to the new people and get to know them. Like the others before them, they searched for a better life without torment, mocking, and sometimes persecution. It made Edil feel good and take pride in his valley. It could provide them with the life they deserved to have.

They were nearing the end of their preparations and getting close to returning north when Johan announced they needed a private, family dinner to discuss things. Edil, Gregor, and Karina felt confused but thought a final dinner at Henrick's house would be nice.

They took notice with sadness that the parlor no longer held their uncle's bed as they walked to the dining room. They all sat around the large table that Benedict had set with a delicious meal of roasted chickens and vegetables. He quickly and quietly served them before leaving them alone. He had things he needed to pack. With Henrick gone, he was no longer needed. He was ready to join his cousin and brother back in the valley.

"Thank you for insisting I come back," Amelia finally spoke. "I am pleased that I could see Henrick before his passing."

"Of course, Mama," Edil said as everyone nodded.

"And I am so proud. Your father and I are both so very proud of all of you," she continued. "We knew you were doing good, but to see with our own eyes the laughing children, to hear the greetings shouted to us as we rode down the street is not the Bluster I grew up in. What you have accomplished is nothing short of amazing."

Edil and Gregor beamed as their cheeks turned red.

"And that makes things better for us," Johan spoke up. "It makes it easier for us because, well, we will not be returning to the valley."

"What now?" Edil gasped. He did not understand what his parents were saying.

"There are things that need to be taken care of," Amelia said. "With Henrick's passing, he leaves behind an enormous house—"

"An estate," Johan nodded.

"And I might have two other brothers that are still out there in the world somewhere," Amelia reminded them. "I need to take care of my home—"

"Your home is in the valley!" Gregor said angrily.

"This is my childhood home!" she reminded him, standing up, not liking his tone of voice. "And as of right now, I am Henrick's next of kin. Now, I know you lot have little experience with death, but some things need handling when someone dies. I can't just leave the staff, and I certainly can't just leave this house to crumble and rot!"

They sat quietly, eyes down on their dinner plates. Everyone lost their appetites. Amelia took a deep, shuddering breath before sitting down again. She could not remember a time where she had ever raised her voice before.

"Will you come back next year?" Edil asked quietly.

"Perhaps," she nodded. "I don't know what the year will bring. I have to find and contact Willem and Antoine if they are even still alive. If I can't, then I don't know. I will figure that out when I come to that. There are authorities I need to speak to and experts of the law in these sorts of affairs. I need to go through deeds and paperwork. There is a lot to do. We shall see how long it takes. But no matter because your father and I will be here when you arrive back."

"It will be ok," Johan smiled. "A little adventure of our own."

"Well, I don't like it," Gregor said.

"It must be done," Susie said to him softly.

"I could stay with you," Karina suggested. "I don't mind. Maybe help Effie and Nick out at the post. See how things run on this end. If more people come, I can help get them prepared for their lives in the valley."

"That's actually not a bad idea," Edil agreed.

"Then, it's settled," Amelia declared. "I won't hear any more about it. And no tears and drawn-out goodbyes either. We've been at this back and forth over The Great Nothing and making gifts for years. This is nothing new. Nothing different. Tomorrow you leave, and next year we will be here when you come back. Just business as always."

"Yes, Mama," Edil said. "Business as usual."

The table was quiet again. The air was heavy with sadness. Between Henrick's passing and Amelia and Johan's decision to stay behind, this was not a pleasant trip. Edil tried to remind himself that it was only for a year and that a year passed quickly. But as much as time stands still in the valley, he also knew that a lot could happen outside of the valley's icy walls in just one year. He saw what time did to his uncle. He was seeing what time was doing to Nick. He did not trust time anymore. Outside the valley walls, somewhere where The Great Nothing met the rest of the world, time was not their friend.

They Came in Droves

The year was a busy one and went by quickly in the valley, despite the absence of Amelia, Johan, and Karina. The valley grew with a bigger church and more workshops to create art and expand skills. Some people bought dogs to herd the growing flocks of sheep and goats. There were more cows and ponies. Onyx remained in Bluster, his large but gentle self missed by those who knew him.

Lottie ordered a warehouse to be built with long tables for people to work at and shelves all along the walls to organize and store the hundreds and hundreds of playthings they made. They made dolls from cloth and clay. They crafted soldiers of painted wood and tin. They made colorful rattles for the babies and designed games of boards, pieces, and cards for teens.

Every morning people filled the warehouse. They sat at the tables and were merry as they talked and sang, ate sweets, and drank coffee and tea as they worked. It was a lively place to spend the day and work. They could work at their own pace and create from their imaginations. Their results always amazed Lottie and Edil when they came in to check on their progress.

On Friday evenings, the people of the valley loved to unwind by gathering in a place that became a town square. There were posts with lanterns on top to give light. Benches where people could sit. A fire pit in the middle where people could gather and share in pots of coffee or tea. They passed the occasional jug of wine or ale around from time to time. One of their newest neighbors had introduced Byron to a sweet, sticky sap from a mallow plant. Byron created a gooey, sticky cloud of white sweetness that he would bring out for children. The children would put it on the end of sticks and dip them into the fire for only a few seconds, just to get them brown and slightly crackling on the outside before popping them in their mouths. The older citizens would indulge in chestnuts that they roasted on the open fire.

Those, who were forced into entertaining at one time, would perform for people in the town square. One would juggle, a former minstrel would recite poetry, and a small band was highly talented in their instrument playing.

Sometimes, Edil still liked to hike up to the top of the ridge, just to be by himself and collect his thoughts. He would find a spot just to sit and reflect on the years that passed. He would remember when it was just him, his siblings, his parents, and nothing else but flora and fauna of the valley. It seemed so much simpler back then. Then he remembered his lust to travel beyond the wall and his desire for adventure and to meet new people and see what the land of giants offered.

He would look down and see the tiny village alive with smoke from chimneys and children playing in the fields. He would see the pens of animals and people walking to or from a neighbor's home. He could hear a dog bark, and he could smell cakes from Byron's shop and meat smoking from someone's smokehouse. Edil would smile with contentment. It was not the giants that offered all that was below him. It was his very own people. They had created their tiny nation with their own culture and way of life, and it was a respectable one.

He would walk across the ridge and look out into The Great Nothing. There was never anything to see. It was the opposite of the valley. Nothing but white and grey. Nothing but complete silence and not a hint of any scent.

He thought over Nick's offer to join him on his travels south. It would be nice to go back to his initial desire to travel and see other places. It would be nice to have an adventure again. Maybe he would find more people like himself, and he could point them in the direction of Bluster and eventually take them home. He needed to discuss things with Lottie because the trip to Bluster would be different that year.

Many thoughts were racing through Edil's mind as he thought of traveling with Nick. He thought of the people who had been joining them, making the caravan larger. This meant a more considerable risk with Old Shadow. For the first time, Gregor would not be joining them. He and Susie were expecting their first child, who was due at the time of their travels. Gregor was not about to miss it, and they would not dream of risking her giving birth on their journey. They had been through that once with Lorelai and never wanted to experience that again.

Edil's mind continued to race and tried to process the upcoming trip if he did not return home with the rest of the people. Lottie would have to be in charge with Byron's help on the drive back north. If Edil himself was traveling back home at a much later date and on his own, it would be a very lonely and dangerous trip out there in The Great Nothing.

He sighed, walking away from the ridge back down to the valley with thoughts jumbled in his head. The "what ifs" and "maybes" danced around, but one thought became clear: he wanted to go with Nick

He discussed it over supper with Lottie, Gregor and Susie, Byron, Lorelai, and their family. Dana was old enough to join in on her first journey with her father, so she was excited to be part of the plans. Pell listened in on the conversation with a scowl on his youthful face. He was to be left in the valley again to help his mother run the bakery, a job he did not like and a skill he felt he lacked.

They agreed Edil would stay on in Bluster and continue traveling south with Nick. Lottie and Byron would lead their people back home to the valley after trading and visiting with the townspeople and the Reindeer Games. Lottie worried at the idea of her husband traveling on his own from Bluster to the valley. Edil insisted he would travel a lot faster, saddled atop Buck with no wagon, sled, or team to slow them down. Just him and his old faithful reindeer, Buck.

The day arrived for them to head south. Edil felt saddened by the idea of Gregor not joining them. It was just the two of them on their first trip, and Gregor was his brother and partner. Edil was also excited to see his parents and Karina again and see how the year outside the valley's walls treated them. It was nice knowing that even though Henrick passed, someone was still at the big house to greet them.

A combination of sixteen wagons, sleds, and carriages waited at the tunnel entrance. Both ponies and reindeer pulled them. They decorated most of the wagons and sleds with fun, festive colors and decor. They bundled some down with toys and games. They built others to carry Byron's sweets and cakes and pies. Some just carried tents, blankets, firewood, and other necessities they would need for traveling and camping. One was nothing but a platform with red curtains creating a mini, traveling stage for their entertainers to perform.

They traveled The Great Nothing with anticipation and had been practicing their entrance into town. The townspeople always waited for them eagerly and cheered them on. They knew the children were always excited. This time they wanted to give them a proper parade and put on a show for them. They wanted to provide them with a celebration as a thank you in return for all the years of warm, joyous welcomes. They wanted to start the Christmastime Season off with a wondrous celebration.

The townspeople of Bluster and the visitors that were there for the Reindeer Games could hear them coming from a distance with a fiddle, a mandolin, a hurdy-gurdy, and bells playing a tune. Voices joined in the music, singing along. They rushed out of their homes and shops, ran from their tents and chores, and lined the main road into Bluster.

With wide-open eyes and jaws slacked in amazement, they watched the jolly procession enter the town. Edil and Lottie led the parade waving with painted banners running alongside their wagon, saying "Happy Christmas" in bright red letters. Dana drove her father's wagon as he tossed candy canes and sweet, colorful suckers wrapped in waxed paper to the children. Other wagons followed with more banners that proclaimed such things as "Hurrah for Nick!" and "Let's Go Reindeer Games!" The final wagon was the small band on the stage, playing their tunes. The juggler sat on the back, his feet dangling over the edge as he carefully juggled many colorful little wooden blocks.

The people loved it. It was a clever way to begin a happy but cold and long season. They cheered and waved back. They pointed and clapped. Nick and Effie waited in their usual place on the porch of his shop. Nick himself laughed and smiled, his blue eyes twinkling like a child. They were alone. No small, hopeful crowd surrounded them. Edil was a little disappointed that he would not bring back new neighbors who needed a good life in the valley.

"You've outdone yourself, my friend," Nick shouted out to him. "Absolutely fantastic!!"

"Glad you are pleased," Edil smiled as he climbed down from his wagon. "But, no newcomers this year?"

"Oh, I think I'll let your parents fill you in on that subject."

Edil looked at him, confused.

"In the meantime," Nick continued. "Have you given thought to coming South with me?"

"I have. I have indeed," he beamed.

"Ah. By the looks of your face, I am going to assume you will join me?"

Edil nodded as he walked to the back of his wagon to unload.

"Excellent! We shall talk more!!" Nick chuckled, heading in his direction to oversee the stocking and storing of the toys.

Edil laughed to himself, climbing up into the back of his wagon. He smiled as he untied bundles and handed items down to Christoph and Robert. He was glad to be back in Bluster and felt extremely satisfied with how well their little parade was received.

He looked at the people of Bluster, the hustle and bustle as they continued to celebrate the return of the little people from the North and the upcoming Reindeer Games. Children ran and played, most of them with Byron's candies sticking out of their mouths. People were stopping each other for a quick, friendly chat. Laughter filled the air, handshakes and hugs exchanged. A quick flash of blue weaved in and out of the crowds before it disappeared.

Edil froze. His heart skipped a beat. He knew that color, that unmistakable deep, shiny blue unlike any other shade of blue he ever saw. It had been a long time since he saw that blue. It could not be.

"Nick," he called out, looking around him, but Nick was nowhere in sight. He had already gone back into his shop to help Effie and Lottie attend to things. Edil scanned the crowd, trying to find that glimpse of blue again, but it disappeared.

"You alright there, mate?" Byron called from his wagon, seeing Edil just standing there with a perplexed look on his face.

"Yes. Fine," Edil said, snapping out of his daze and smiling a little. He doubted he ever saw it. Nick would have told him. It had been so long. It could not be that after all these years, Ronan and his blue coat had returned to Bluster.

"Just thought I saw someone," Edil told Byron before returning to unloading his goods. He needed to get the chores done so he could be off to see his parents and Karina.

Edil, Lottie, Byron, and Dana all went in one sled when they completed the chores. Nick and Effie joined them in their carriage. Dana was excited to see her "Ama" and "Jo-jo." Amelia and Johan were the closest things to grandparents Dana ever had, and she had missed them terribly.

It surprised them to see that not only was Henrick's large house all lit up from top to bottom but so was the barn. They slowed their reindeer down, confused at the commotion of little people walking around, tending to chores, entering and exiting the house and barn. There were wagons and sleds, horses, ponies, and livestock. Dogs ran about, and cats lounged on the porch. So many people. More than they had in their village. Henrick's property had become a small village of its own.

"Oi!" Byron exclaimed. "Whatever on God's snowy earth happened here?"

Edil was speechless.

"No wonder Nick and Effie had no one. They are all here!" Lottie realized. "Edil, they still came!"

Edil shot Nick a look that made him laugh.

"My property was too small," Nick explained. "Johan and Amelia came up with a wonderful solution." "They used to come far away by foot," Effie said. "But now they are coming by sea from around the world."

Edil could see faces unlike any he ever saw before. Skin tones of different shades. Hair is either tight and curled or stiff and dark or even long, straight, silky black like a raven. Eyes of different colors. No matter the color or hair, the eyes or features, they all had that same, familiar look of hope.

"Fine," Edil smiled. "This is fine."

Karina was the first to notice her family riding towards the house. She waved with enthusiasm as she called for her parents. They came out of the house as fast as their legs could carry them to greet them.

"Where's Gregor?" Amelia asked in a worried voice that only a mother would have. "Why is he not here with you?"

"It's fine, Mama," Edil told her. "Susie is expecting any day. She might have even had the baby by now."

Amelia screeched and clapped her hands and then hugged Lottie and Dana. Johan threw his arm around his son and turned him to look at the crowd forming around them.

"Isn't this something, son?" Johan beamed with pride. "The house and barn are now boarding houses. It keeps the people out of the cold.

They've been coming in droves all year from all over!!"

"Australia, the Americas, Asia, even an entire tribe from Africa," Amelia told them, pointing to different people.

"You don't say," Edil said, feeling overwhelmed.

"Oh, yes. It's been quite an accomplished year. And everyone is just wonderful. We are all learning from each other. We have all been pitching in and helping one another."

"The house has been perfect for giving these people a place to stay," Karina said. "It's such a large house, and we are such small people. It took little to build bunks and fill the emptiness."

"I think Henrick would be pleased with what we have done with the house," Amelia said.

"Mother, don't you plan on returning with us?" Edil asked.

"Oh, son. Not yet. People need us. They need this house. We will come back when the people stop coming," she said. "The house is indeed mine. I never found my other brothers, so It was signed over to do what I please. It pleases me to have this boarding house and give our people from all over the world a safe place to stay until you can bring them home."

"I'll be returning, though," Karina said excitedly. "I made a friend."

She motioned for a young man to step forward. He had long black hair with a single feather dangling from the side. His tan face lit up with dark, intelligent eyes and a bright, friendly smile.

"This is Chayton," she introduced. "He came from America."

Edil could see the look on his sister's face and glanced at his parents knowingly. It was the same look he gave Lottie and the same look Gregor had for Susie. He knew it was only a matter of time before Chayton would be a member of their family.

“How many are there?” Lottie asked, her eyes scanning the people. There were men, women, and children all around them.

“One hundred and thirty-six,” Johan answered.

Edil frowned. He relished the idea of the village growing with new people, new skills, new culture, but it scared him that it meant the valley was going to get smaller. He turned his frown into a smile. They would have to come up with something to make everything and everyone works in harmony. They always did.

A Familiar Face

They spent the night celebrating at the old house, meeting new people. Gone was the parlor and dining room furniture. Instead, Amelia saw that every room had bunk beds lining the walls with curtains for privacy. More bunks were in the many bedrooms and even the attic. Every room had tables for people to eat at or read or just come together to sit and talk. The kitchen was a constant bustle, baking hundreds of loaves of bread and cooking enormous pots of grub. They would turn cuts of meat on spits over the fires in hearths throughout the house.

Those that came later in the year who could no longer fit in the house found a place to sleep in the barn. Even more people slept in tents. On freezing days, Johan said they lined the floors of the hallways in the house. Everyone did their part, taking care of each other. Karina had set up a small school for the children on the front porch, where Nick had supplied her with books, slates, and chalks for children. Edil was very impressed by his mother, father, and sister's ideas to keep the people safe, fed, and occupied.

In the morning, Edil headed into town to spend time with Nick to discuss and plan their travels. Effie had put out a nice little spread for coffee, warm toasted rolls, and cookies. There were always cookies for Nick. They ate and peered over a map Nick had drawn up. He trailed his fingertip along the fine line of ink that represented his path to several different towns. Katts Bog, Byron's hometown, was the first stop, followed by several more small villages and towns that went south and west before crossing back to the east and looping back up north. Edil was excited to see that the furthest town west was actually on the seaside. He was going to see ships and the sea itself for the first time. It was more than his adventure-seeking imagination had ever dreamed.

He noticed the sun was high in the sky when he left Nick in his shop to check on the chores he left the people to do the day before. They bagged and stacked toys and sweets onto Nick's oversized wagon, inspecting and cleaning it before the long, tedious journey. It was an impressive wagon that Nick designed over the years. He hired the best wainwright he could find to build it. A comfortable, padded bench was upfront for Nick with several compartments, covered chests, and drawers throughout the long and deep back to keep the treasures safe and dry. They designed the wheels to cut through both snow and mud, the two things that Nick always encountered on the roads south.

When Edil felt satisfied that everything looked ready for Nick, he headed to Nick's pen to see to tend to the reindeer. He halted and gasped. One lone man was standing at the pen, staring at the animals. Some of the reindeer pranced and bellowed nervously. Like Edil, they knew and remembered who he was.

His blue coat was still as bright as the first day Edil had seen him. His head was down when Edil first saw him, his back to him. When he lifted his head, Edil could see he no longer had that fiery orange hair. Instead, his head was covered with wispy white hair, his pink scalp peeking in the light.

Ronan turned from the pen, about to walk away, when he saw Edil standing before him, frozen with his fist clenched at his sides. The years were not kind to Ronan. He was no longer thin and young. He was broad, his brow wrinkled and thick, permanently knitted together. His shoulders slumped with a slight hump on his back which caused him to lean forward. Gone was the tall and boastful man. The only thing young about Ronan was his coat. He had somehow kept that coat looking brand new as all the years went by. He truly treasured the coat, the only thing Edil let him keep from the bet many years ago.

Ronan was just as shocked to see Edil. He knew the little people were in town. He saw many of them walking around and patronizing the shops of Bluster. He had caught a quick glimpse of the parade but preferred to walk away and have a drink in the tavern. He knew from overheard town gossip that the people were from the same place his reindeer and belongings went, but he doubted he would see Edil again. He had doubted Edil was even still alive.

There they were, just staring at each other, not sure they believed what they were seeing. Edil knew people had aged. He had seen it with his uncle. He saw it every year he returned to Nick and Effie. It was still surprising to see Ronan looking aged. Ronan was in shock that Edil looked the same with his mop of dark, shaggy hair and his face with barely a line on it. It did not seem fair that the man who once humiliated him and kept him from coming back to Bluster for years was still so full of youth. Time was everyone's punishment for living. Why was it not Edil's?

Ronan looked back over his shoulder at the reindeer. He had seen them earlier, and they had seemed so familiar, it puzzled him. He thought he was losing his mind as he questioned whether some of those reindeer were the same ones that cost him the race and eventually ownership of them.

"Those are my reindeer, are they not?" he finally spoke, pointing to the animals.

"They haven't been your deer for a long, long time," Edil spoke, finding his voice.

"How long?"

"I-I don't know. I have lost track of the years," Edil admitted as Ronan chuckled and shook his head.

"Those reindeer can't be. It shouldn't be!" he snarled. "And yet, here they are. They should be long dead. Reindeer don't live this long!"

"Properly cared for ones do," Edil smirked, even though he knew Ronan was correct about the lifespan of reindeer.

"Properly cared for..." Ronan repeated and laughed. It was too much to take in. He looked up at the sky and shook his head to clear his thoughts as he let out a big, angry huff of a sigh and looked back down at Edil. Edil could see the confusion and madness in Ronan's eyes. He looked like a trapped wild animal.

"This isn't over yet, little man," he growled as he shoved past Edil, almost knocking him to the ground.

Edil watched as he stomped towards the center of town, his blue coat billowing behind him. Edil let out a sigh of relief as he realized he was shaking. He walked to the reindeer to calm them and himself down. He had to think. Lottie. He had to warn Lottie.

It was the first thing he did when he rode back to the house. She was just as shocked as he was, though she kept her composure. She could see how worried her husband was for her, and she smiled sweetly, taking his hand.

"Since when do old men scare us," she winked, trying to make light of the situation.

They remained at the house for the rest of the day, keeping themselves busy, not thinking of what another encounter with Ronan might bring. Edil and his family and all the boarders traveled to town for the Reindeer Games and celebrations in the morning. They went by wagon and carriage, sled and horseback. Many of them walked. They were all excited, but Edil and Lottie were nervous. They knew how Ronan felt about them and their kind. They knew he would never forget and never let go of the fact that a man who thought was beneath him had beaten him.

They spotted him in church. Lottie whispered that if it were not for the coat, she would never have recognized him. Byron had nodded in agreement. Edil just frowned, wondering how a man who lived a life of jealous, evil deeds and thoughts could sit in the house of God and listen to Nick's sermons on living a kind and Godly life. Edil had to suppress a giggle as he pictured a lightning bolt coming through the church window and striking Ronan, burning his precious blue coat.

When service was over, the congregation stood up to follow Nick's lead to the Blessing of the Herd. Ronan was once again stopped in his tracks as he spotted Lottie. The last time he saw her, she was filthy with tangled knots of hair. He sneered as he saw her fresh, smiling face, her hair a neat, golden braid that draped over her shoulder, and her clothes finely tailored by someone of skill. And young. She was as young as the day he won her. He also recognized the little, round man with curls from the day of his last race. He, too, had never aged.

He quietly walked outside and scanned the crowds. He could not believe the number of little people that mingled in the mob of excited spectators. There were so many more than what first appeared just two days before.

He walked towards Edil and his family, calmly but seething. It made no sense. It defied all logic that they seemed to be immortal. He did not understand how it could be or how the people of Bluster did not talk about it or question it.

"Hello, Little Lottie," he taunted, a slight growl in his voice. She turned, shielding her eyes from the sun as she looked up at him.

"Ronan," she finally said calmly.

"Well, don't you look fine. The years have been very generous towards you."

"Wish I could say the same to you," she taunted back.

His fake, plastered grin fell from his face as he took a quick, threatening step towards her. Nick jumped between them as Edil pulled her back protectively.

"There will not be a problem now, is there, Ronan?" Nick asked. "I can get the constable and take care of things."

"No need," Ronan said, backing away. He saw how Edil held onto Lottie's arm. He laughed as he realized.

"Really?" he continued. "You married my pet?"

"Ronan!" Nick warned. Edil had never heard Nick speak with that tone. "Let it be. Enjoy the games. Place some bets. Have a drink. Just let it be. Bygones are bygones. Too many years have passed us. Edil and his family are a big part of Bluster. They are very respected here. Unfortunately, I cannot speak the same of you."

Ronan scoffed. He rubbed his head angrily. Then he turned to Nick.

"That's just it, Nick," he hissed. "Too many years have gone by, and yet...."

He trailed off, thrusting his arm out to point to Edil, Lottie, and Byron. He looked at Nick as if to say, "Why are you not saying it?!" He turned back to Edil.

"Your Uncle is long dead and buried, from what I hear. Nick here is becoming an old man. I am an old man!" he continued. "But you. You and your horde of tiny freaks, is it sorcery of a sort? Is there something in the air or the water where you are from? Or are you all just born with some magical trait that makes you timeless?"

"Son, who is this rude man!?! I will not have him talk to you like this!" Johan spoke up.

"It's all good, Papa. He is nothing new to us," Edil said as Nick began pulling Ronan away by his arm.

"This is your father?!" Ronan screeched. "No one sees this? No one questions this?"

"Enough!" Nick bellowed. "Not now! Not today!"

Ronan looked around. People of all sizes, shapes, and colors were staring at him. They whispered behind their mitten-covered hands and pointed at him. He shrugged Nick's hand off his arm and brushed his coat as if Nick had somehow dirtied it.

"Enough," Nick repeatedly softly. "It is what it is."

"But it's so curious," Ronan said, almost sadly.

"Forget it, Ronan. Go off and forget it," Nick advised. "Remember what they say."

"What do they say, Nick? Tell me."

"Curiosity killed the cat," Nick told him.

Ronan grunted as he flipped up his black fur collar and tucked his chin into his coat. He stormed away from prying eyes, mumbling to himself, and headed to the tavern. Nick looked back at Edil, who nodded his thanks, but the two friends knew. Ronan was not the type of man to let things go.

Travels with Nick

Ronan disappeared with all the other visitors that come to Bluster every year for the Games. After a day, Edil said goodbye to Lottie and the large caravan of people she led back north to their new home in the valley. He fretted as he waved to them from the front porch of the big house. It was the first time he and Lottie would be apart for so long, which worried him. They were well prepared for Old Shadow and his pack and the cold and sometimes windy and snowy days and nights, but he still worried. He wondered if there would ever be a day where their luck when traveling would finally run out.

Amelia and Johan chose to once again stay behind at the house. Edil did not like that decision, but nothing he could do or say to change their minds.

"We are needed here," Amelia told him. "More people will come."

"Will you ever come back home?" Edil had asked.

"When the people stop coming," she replied.

That saddened Edil. He knew that day was not coming for a long time, if ever.

Edil also kept Buck behind. When he finished his trip with Nick, he planned to ride home on Buck's back. He figured the trip would be faster if they did not weigh Buck down with a wagon. Edil was keeping the journey as simple as possible. Just him, Buck, a saddlebag, and a rucksack on his back.

But first, he had his trip with Nick. Taking a final inventory and helping Nick load the wagon kept his mind off his worries and sorrows. The night before they ventured out, they had dinner with Effie and Edil's parents. They toasted to a safe journey. All night, Edil tossed and turned. He paced the floors of the house, which seemed so large and empty since everyone had left. In the morning, he practically ran out the door when he heard Nick's horses clip-clopping down the road to pick him up.

He barely said goodbye to his parents; he was so excited. He climbed up onto the wagon and took his seat on the comfortable, padded bench next to Nick. He waved a happy, enthusiastic wave to Amelia and Johan as Nick started the horses trotting away from the house.

"Be safe, my son!" Johan yelled out.

"See you in a few weeks!" he called back. He was finally getting the adventure of his dreams. The experience that he had forgotten about for so long.

Edil and Nick swapped stories and tales as they rode along. Sometimes one would nap while the other would take the reins. At night, they ate and slept by a small campfire. Eventually, they made it to Katts Bog.

Like his last trip he made many years before, Katts Bog was warmer than Bluster. Most of the ground was muddy with hard-packed dirt. Some trees had shed their leaves recently.

Edil and Nick's first stop was Byron's father's bakery. Byron had asked Edil if he could please check on his father and drop off a crate of gifts. Edil did not have the heart to tell him that his father may not be around, so he promised he would.

The bakery seemed to have seen better days. The roof over the porch was sagging. Dead leaves had collected in the corners. The bins that once held fresh rolls and loaves of bread for sale were all empty and filled with dirt and debris.

Nick held the door open for Edil, who carried Byron's carefully packed wooden crate. The store was empty as Edil walked in tenderly.

"Hello?" Edil called out.

"Oi! 'Tis but a moment," a voice responded from the back.

Edil heard some movement and shuffling before an elderly man came out, wiping his hands on his apron. He squinted in the poorly lit shop and then smiled with recognition.

"'Tis you!" he exclaimed. "Friend of me son!"

"Yes!" Edil nodded, so thrilled to see Darvis was alive and well. Elderly, but still well. "Happy Christmas! I come bearing gifts from Byron."

"Yer don't say! Oh, tell me he's good, is he not? And his wife?"

Edil placed the crate on a small table, nodding.

"Excellent, sir. They have a family and a wonderful bakery of their own."

"Grandchildren!" Darvis grinned, "I've some grandchildren?"

"A young lady by the name of Dana and a boy named Pell."

Darvis continued to smile, wiping tears from his eyes. He perused through Byron's crate to see candies, a pie, and a cake all carefully packed. Edil and Nick could see the love and admiration on Darvis's face.

"'Tis lovely," he said quietly. "Been alone all these years. Me dreadful wife left not long after I sent Byron your way. She didn't like the work. No, she did not, the grim witch."

"Darvis!" Nick said, trying to stifle a chuckle.

"Well, she was. 'Tis no matter. I am so happy to hear about me son. He has a good life, yes?"

"Yes," Edil promised. "Very good indeed. And he is very grateful for you sending him."

"Good. Good," Darvis nodded.

"He's a talented man," Nick continued. "All those sweets the children get? They are all his creations. I think you see he learned from the best."

"Yes. Yes. Thank you. Thank you for bringing me his wares and telling me of his health and happiness," Darvis smiled, his eyes still brimming with tears.

They left Darvis to try Byron's goods and reminisce. They continued to travel into the small town center of Katts Bog. Nick pulled out a stick covered with little tinkling bells and began ringing them. Everywhere, doors flew open, and children of all ages ran out as fast as they could. Adults followed, some carrying infants and toddlers to see the man who came bearing gifts.

"Nick! Nick!" the children yelled as they surrounded the wagon. Their faces were nothing but innocence and sheer joy as they looked up to Nick, who laughed a deep belly laugh.

Nick climbed down and ordered Edil to climb into the back of the wagon to help hand out gifts. Children clamored and pushed against one another as they crowded around Nick.

"One at a time, boys and girls," Nick ordered. "Everyone gets a turn. Have we all been good this year?"

"Yes!!" the children cheered.

"Any naughty boys or girls I should know about?"

"Nooooooo!" they laughed.

"Do the Mums and Papas agree?"

The adults laughed and nodded, just as excited to see what Nick had brought for the children.

Edil stood in the wagon and began unpacking toys and treats. He handed them out the back one by one as Nick called out a child's name. He spent a few minutes with each child, telling them how good they had been and asking simple questions about their chores, schoolwork, and home life. Then he gave them a brief hug and sent them on their way to play with their toy or eat the fantastic sweet made just for them. He would then move on to the next child. And then the next.

"Let's not forget to thank my good friend, Edil," Nick said after he gave out the last gift for the children of Katts Bog. "He is the one that makes the gifts in a little village up north."

"Thank you, Ediiiilllll," the chorus of children's voices sang out from all over the town center. Edil's heart filled with warmth and joy when he heard that.

"You are all very welcome!! Happy Christmas to all!!" he called back as he climbed back up front with Nick.

"And to all a good night!!" Nick bellowed as he snapped the reins. They waved as they pulled away. The children waved back with the happiest faces Edil had ever seen.

They continued to travel south and west. Every town was the same, and Edil never tired of it. Sometimes they stopped at an orphanage. Most of the time, it was a town center of sorts. All of the time, it was nothing but a joyous occasion. Edil could see why Nick loved doing this and why he sacrificed weeks on the road. There was something about the children's faces and voices that just filled him with a mysterious, wondrous, gleeful spirit.

They traveled on snow and mud. They crossed fields, streams and even had a ferry take them across the largest river Edil had ever seen. Eventually, they reached the furthest town. It was the last town before they would loop around and up back to Bluster. It was a seaport town.

It took Edil's breath away. The size of the ships with their great, white billowing sails towering up into the sky astonished Edil. He was in awe at the sandy beaches and the crashing, foamy waves of the sea. It was majestic and a bit terrifying at the same time. He never saw such power before.

"One day, I would like to take our gifts on one of those ships," Nick told him. "Continue my journey across the seas."

"Where do the ships go?" Edil asked.

"All over the world, my good friend. All over the world. What do you think?"

"Amazing," Edil nodded. "I also think we need to make small toy ships...little wooden ships with tiny sails that the children can sail on streams and in creeks and puddles...maybe even in their tubs when they take their baths."

"Always thinking of toys!" Nick laughed. "Indeed, that is a splendid idea. Toy ships will surely make the children happy."

The trip back north went just as well as the trip south. Edil planned more and more toys, getting inspiration from everywhere he looked. The ships and tiny figures go with the ships, such as sailors and pirates. He thought of toy wooden swords for the children to play fight. Then he thought of puppets. Big ones that go over the hands. Little ones for just the fingers. That was just the beginning of his imagination.

"Will you be joining me again next year?" Nick said as their weeks of traveling ended.

"If you don't mind."

"I would be delighted."

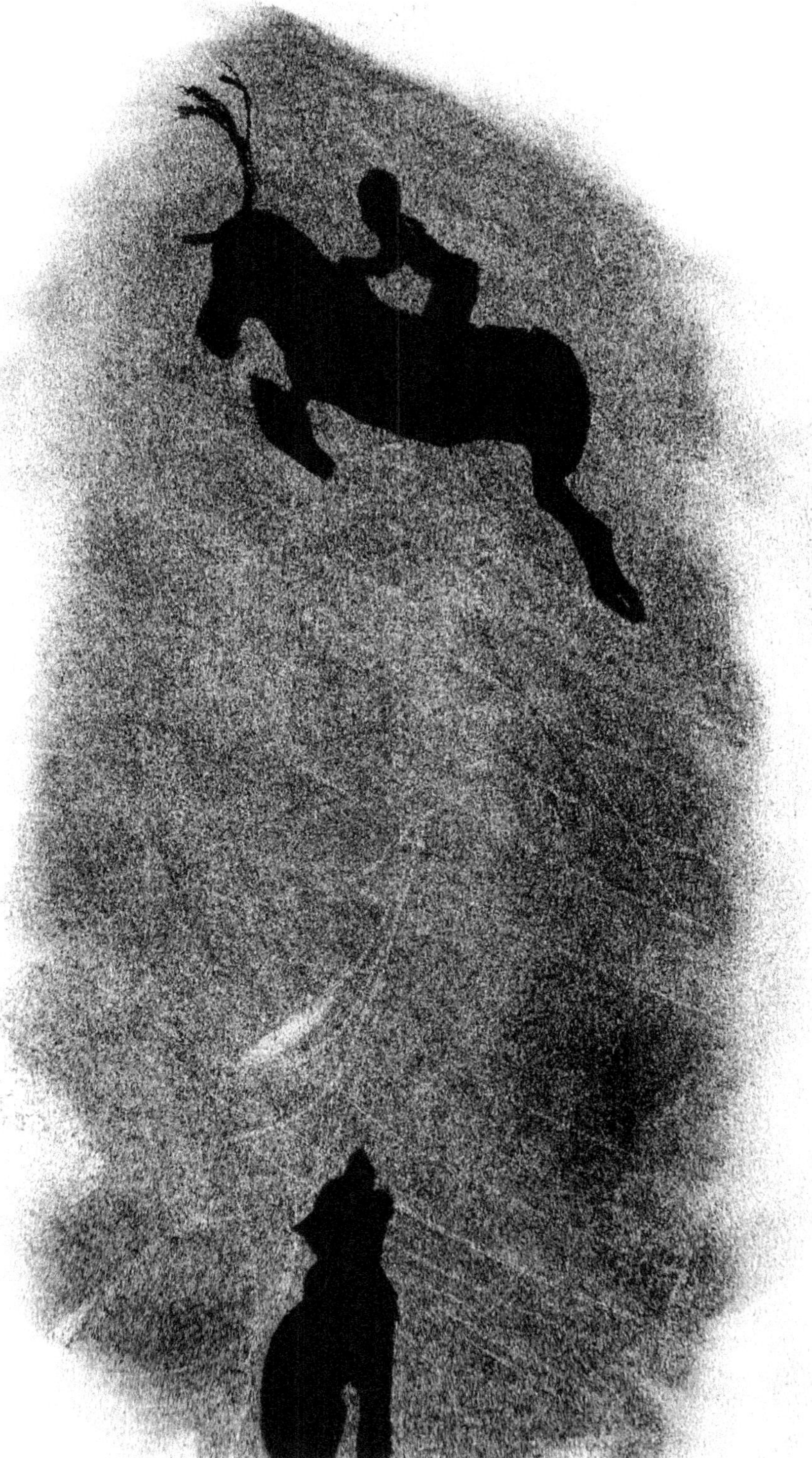

Taking Flight

Edil spent a couple of days with his parents, helping them clean up the bunkrooms of the big, old house and getting them ready for any possible weary but hopeful travelers that might arrive in the upcoming year. When it was time to leave, he mounted Buck's back, a warm blanket around his shoulders, a rucksack on his back, and a saddlebag across Buck's shoulders. There was no big farewell, no caravan, no wagons and sleds, no joyful voices singing and laughing to pass the time. It was just him and Buck waving goodbye to Amelia and Johan as they stood on the front porch. It was just Edil and Buck traveling across The Great Nothing.

To make the bleak hours and dark, frosty nights go by quicker, Edil would reminisce about his trip south. He missed Nick and the nights they spent by their campfire talking and debating as men do. But he missed Lottie and his village more and hoped everyone was home safe and sound.

It was not long before Edil noticed he had company in the distance. It was hard to miss Old Shadow and his large pack sitting and watching, dark against the silver horizon. Edil gulped. He dreaded encountering

Shadow more than the lonely, vast, empty days of traveling. There were only so many scraps and bones he could carry on Buck's back. With the caravan, every wagon would throw remnants of old meals eaten long ago. There was always enough to slow down, distract, and eventually satisfy the wolf pack. Edil knew he could slow them down on his own. He could keep them distracted for just a bit. He also knew there was no way he had enough to satisfy them.

He planned without a wagon to pull and other reindeer in his team, so Buck could hopefully run much quicker than usual. He prayed Buck could run fast enough and far enough to keep a great distance between them and the pack as the pack ate what dried meats and bits of fat and bones he tossed to them.

Edil kept a watchful eye on Shadow and the others. They, too, watched him with curiosity. It seemed to Edil that the pack found it odd that there was just one lone traveler. Edil felt Shadow was amused by his daring and maybe even foolish attempt of crossing The Great Nothing on his own.

Slowly, Shadow stood up, and the others followed suit. With their heads and tails low and their mighty paws padding on the icy ground, they moved steadily, cautiously, but threateningly. Edil breathed in and out, trying to keep himself calm and his head clear. Buck let out a huffing grunt, pulling on his reins a bit as if to say, "*Come now! Let's go!*"

After a few miles of pretending not to notice the wolves following them, Edil could see their pace was picking up. They were bored and wanted a game of chase. Edil unbuckled the straps of his saddlebag and reached in to grab some scraps of dried meat.

"All right, Buck," he said under his breath. "This is it. I am going to need you to give it all you have. More than that idiotic race with Ronan. Right?"

With that, he let the reins go slack, wrapping them around the horn of his saddle. Buck took that as a sign to take off as fast as he could go. The wolves yipped with delight and broke out into a flat run in unison, excited that their deadly game had begun. Edil began pitching the meats and bones as far as possible, gripping his saddle for balance with his legs.

Some wolves stopped to eat. Many stopped to fight with each other since there was not enough meat to go around. Not Old Shadow. His one eye remained focused on Edil, his tongue lolling out of the side of his grinning mouth, dripping with spittle. He was determined to reach Edil and finally win his prize after all these years.

Closer and closer, he sprinted. Buck bellowed nervously as the gap between them became too close for comfort. Edil's eyes widened with panic. He reached into the saddlebag only to find a measly little chicken bone was all that was left. He almost felt he was insulting Old Shadow as he threw the pathetic scrap at him. Shadow ignored it. It was not worth his time stopping for it. Not when he could make a very fulfilling meal out of Edil and his reindeer.

Shadow's pace picked up. He ran alongside Buck, looking up at Edil with his good eye, taunting him. Edil could see his large, yellowed teeth. The foam had gathered in the corners of Shadow's mouth, saliva drooling from his lethal fangs. Shadow snarled at him and teasingly snapped around Edil's ankle.

"Fly! Buck, Fly!" Edil screamed in terror, his heart pounding in his ears. He picked up the reins again and snapped them. He bought his little legs out only to bring them back in to kick and nudge Buck to go faster.

Buck's head went down, his neck flat with his back, as he leaped forward. He glided over the ice and continued to pump his hooves on the cold draft of air. He lifted his head back up, and his front legs went out and then under his body quickly as he climbed more than just a few inches of air.

Edil looked down to see they were several feet above the ground. They were several feet above Shadow, who continued to run with a perplexed look on his face.

"That's my boy!" Edil yelled with both fear and delight. He gripped his saddle tighter, afraid he would fall off, down into Shadows gaping jaws. "Keep going! Fly! Fly, my good boy!"

And to Edil's amazement, Buck flew. Without the weight of a carriage or sled to hold him down, Buck continued to pump his powerful legs from under his body and climbed higher. Not wanting to let his prey get away, Shadow leaped up, his jaws snapping down on nothing as Buck traveled far into the sky. Edil watched as Shadow crashed down, clumsily and dismayed, onto his back, left with nothing but the unbelievable sight of a reindeer carrying a man across the grey sky.

Once Old Shadow was in the distance, Edil looked around, assessing the miraculous predicament. Again, his ears roared with the pounding of his heart. The wind whistled and whipped around them. They were higher than Edil could ever imagine any man could ever achieve. He had a bird's eye view of the wolves left far in the distance behind him. They were nothing but specks on the snow and ice. He was frightened of how they would ever get down. He wondered how far Buck could keep up his flight. Would he tire suddenly, and they would just drop to their deaths? Can Buck land gracefully like a bird flitting to a tree branch?

Edil tried to remain calm as Buck continued to fly over the land. He did not want to distract Buck. He did not want to give Buck any reminder that reindeer are not supposed to fly.

Lightly feathered wisps of cloud surrounded them as Edil watched the movements Buck went through and tried to figure out how it was all possible. He watched Buck's heavy antlered head bob up and down in time to his legs folding under and then out pumping on the cold air. It made no sense to Edil, but it worked.

Edil realized they were covering so many miles in a quick and timely manner. What should have taken hours was going by in mere minutes. The dark silhouette of the valley's walls came into sight. They were approaching home.

"I think it's time to come down," Edil said to Buck. "Maybe carefully?"

Buck ignored him if he understood him. He continued to fly straight towards the ridge.

"Buck," Edil pleaded. "The tunnel is down there."

Buck flew over the outer edge of the ridge and suddenly stopped moving his legs. They outstretched in front and behind him as he glided down on the breeze. As fast as the flight began, it was over. When the ground was just a couple of feet from them, Buck pulled his legs in, his hooves gingerly touching the icy ridge. He broke out into a trot, Edil bouncing on his back, then came to a complete stop.

They were home, and they were safe, atop the ridge. They were safe from the cold and emptiness. Safe from the wolves. Safe from the height.

Edil realized he was shaking. He had to replay what had happened over and over in his mind. He wondered if he dreamt it, but how could he explain how they ended up on top of the wall rather than outside it?

Buck let out a calm snort and pawed at the ground, breaking up some of the ice and snow to find a patch of dried grass to nibble on. Edil knitted his brows together and wondered if Buck always knew he had the fantastic skill of flying. He wondered if the other reindeer knew it too, or was Buck just highly gifted.

Edil sighed and dismounted. He was going to have to mull over what had just happened. He wondered if Buck's ability to fly meant something. If it would change life as he knew it. He wondered if Buck could do it again or if this was maybe just a miracle of God saving them from demise at Old Shadow's teeth.

"That was quite an adventure," he told Buck, giving him a loving scratch between his antlers.

He took the reins and led him across the rest of the ridge to the valley. He smiled when he saw the lush, bountiful land below him. It looked so busy with more cabins and shops being built, more fields being plowed, and more pens for the growing livestock.

"That's a right proper village now, ain't it," he said to Buck as he walked down the path.

It surprised the people when someone spotted him walking down the ridge and pointed him out. By the time Edil reached the bottom, news had traveled fast. Lottie ran to him with open arms, so happy to see he had finally returned safe and sound. Gregor approached him, smiling but confused as he looked up at the ridge.

"How did you come from up there?" he asked.

Edil smiled, shaking his head and laughing. He looked at Buck, who stood proudly, looking back.

"That, brother, is a curious tale."

Santa and His Elf

It was a hectic year in the valley. Gregor's wife, Susie, had given birth while Edil was away. She had twin boys, one baby much larger than the other. Gregor had named them after ancient tales he had read about in books, Remus and Romulus, but because Romulus was always silent unless Remus cried or cooed or laughed first, they gave him the nickname "Echo." Eventually, everyone forgot his actual name.

Edil would tell tales of his travels with Nick and drew designs for different toys his trip inspired, including the ships with their great sails. To a select few, he let them in on Buck's secret. They did not believe him until early one morning; they took Buck up to the top of the ridge.

"We'll show you," Edil told them as he mounted Buck. Byron, Lottie, and Gregor looked on. Byron was curious. Lottie looked worried. Gregor stood there with his arms crossed and a tired look on his face. There were so many other chores that needed to be done, and he found Edil's tales of a flying reindeer hard to swallow. He believed that in Edil's panic state with the wolves chasing him and the loneliness of The Great Nothing, Edil had imagined the whole adventure.

Edil bought his heels to Buck's sides and snapped the reins, heading straight to the outside cliff of the wall. Faster and faster, Buck ran. When there was no more ground, and the ridge just dropped, Lottie screamed in terror. Buck, with Edil on his back, ran straight off the cliff, dropped out of sight.

Everyone gasped, their hands covering their mouths, their hearts slamming down into the pits of their stomachs. Suddenly, Buck and Edil came back into view, running on the air off into the distance at a quick speed unlike they had ever seen.

"Impossible," Gregor whispered as they faded away into the distance.

They came back out of the distant low clouds in a blink of an eye, heading back to the ridge. They grew larger and came closer. Just like that, they were back, walking casually on the ground beneath them. Edil was beaming; his cheeks flushed with exhilaration. Gregor, Lottie, and Byron stood there in shock.

"H-how?" Gregor stammered. "It's impossible!"

"Everything about this valley is impossible," Edil reminded him.

"'Tis true, innit?" Byron murmured, still in disbelief.

"Can they all fly?" Lottie wondered. They looked at each other, knowing they had to find out the answer to that question.

The following morning, along with Christoph, Benedict, and Robert, they brought the entire large herd of reindeer up to the top of the ridge. Once again, Edil mounted Buck and ran him to the edge. Once again, Buck flew off and out into the distance. One by one, almost all the other reindeer followed, leaving behind the babies of the herd.

They watched in disbelief as the herd gracefully danced across the sky at a remarkable speed, following Buck. They then turned to glide in and land with their babies and eat grass under the snow. Edil dismounted, and they all found a spot to sit and discuss the logistics of the flying reindeer.

"How can they do that? They have no wings or feathers," Christoph mused.

"I don't think we will ever be able to answer how," Gregor admitted. "But the question is why."

"I think they fly out of fear," Edil said. "When we were racing or when the wolves chased the caravan, they always showed signs of flying with their...gliding on air. We have witnessed that."

"But it was only for a few feet at a time and only a few inches off the ground," Lottie reminded him.

"True, but what if the wagons were holding them down," Gregor realized.

"Or...or they knew if they flew, the wagons would be all flip-floppy, and we would fall out," Byron mused.

"You think they fly out of fear? Why did they not fly the day we rescued the original deer?" Gregor wondered.

"The babies," Edil said. "They didn't want to leave their babies. The babies obviously cannot fly."

"Huh," Gregor nodded, thinking about it.

"They are so fast, ain't they?" Byron said. "Imagine the wagons could hold steady and fly with them."

"Now, there is an idea," Edil smiled. "Think of it. We would get to Bluster so much faster and be out of Old Shadow's reach."

"No one can know, though," Lottie said. "Outside of the valley, no one can know."

They agreed. Like the valley's other secrets, they accepted it but did not talk about it. Gradually, they let the entire valley in on the reindeer's miraculous talent.

People would take the reindeer up the ridge to ride them and experience the exhilarating speed and height. Xander, the metalsmith, worked with woodcarvers, tanners, and a naturalist to develop designs for wagons and carriages that would fly straight and balance behind a team of flying reindeer.

Xander crafted long metal poles that ran from the back of the wagon, along the sides of the wagon, and continued through the harness on the reindeer to help distribute the weight. The tanner and naturalist came up with long and narrow wings, modeled after bats and flying squirrels, to help balance and glide the wagons on air currents.

Edil and Gregor took a small team and wagon out for a flight. It was smooth, and Edil imagined it was like sailing on a boat at sea. They flew as fast and as far as they could toward Bluster. They turned around just outside of town before anyone could spot them and returned home. The trip all together took only a couple of hours as opposed to days on land.

When the people heard how fast they traveled to Bluster, they quickly went to work, building a road for more wagons to reach the top of the ridge. They created more wagons that could sail in the clouds.

Those who were not working on the road or the wagons continued working on the toys and treats. Lottie kept busy with her inventory notes. There were so many children and letters that her one ledger grew to several. After checking on the toy warehouse, she lugged a thick book to Byron's bakery to count and marvel over his creations. He and his apprentices had added color to the candy canes, making them red with white swirls. He did the same to suckers on sticks and peppermint drops that they individually wrapped in thin paper. He finally found chocolate, a marvelous ingredient that some of the more recent travelers had with them, and from them, he made the most amazing gooey cookies dotted with melted chips of chocolate. He could not wait to see if he could get more on his next trip to Bluster because he had many ideas.

Lottie marked her book as she heard the sounds of a crash coming from the candy room. Pell came out, his father chasing after him. There was a scowl on Pell's face.

"Look what you've done, boy! A whole tray of candy to waste!" Byron was yelling. "How many times I tell ya, don't touch 'til it cools! Do I not?"

Pell continued to sulk as he plopped down on a sack of flour, his arms folded across his chest.

"Oi! Troublemaker. That one is!" Byron told Lottie.

Lottie sighed, closing up her book. She felt terrible for Pell, who seemed to be more of a nuisance in the bakery than a help. He did not seem to have the passion or talent for baking and candy making like his sister.

"Come, Pell," Lottie said, waving him over. "Why don't you get out of your father's hair for a bit. I can use the help tallying up some numbers today and going through letters."

After that, Pell spent more and more time away from the bakery and assisting Lottie. He learned her system rather quickly and had a brilliant head for numbers. Eventually, they understood that he no longer worked for his father but Lottie instead.

When the day came, the entire village with their reindeer marched up the road to the top of the ridge. People climbed in their wagons, all of which were painted in red and white to match Byron's fun and festive peppermint candies. They trimmed the wagons in pine garland, decorated with pinecones and berries. They made sure everything was bundled down and tied tight so nothing could fly off. They had done many practice runs, so they were ready.

With just a few people to stay behind to tend to livestock, fields, and children too small to travel, they flew off the ridge one by one. There were too many wagons for Edil to count this time. They flew fast and elegantly. The flight was so smooth; it was almost natural. Edil looked down below and could spot Old Shadow and his pack looking up at them, trying to run along and keep up, but they were soon gone. There was nothing but a distant, lingering howl in the wind. Edil could hear the disappointment in Shadow's call and briefly felt bad for him.

They came down and landed a half day's ride from Bluster. They could risk no one seeing them fly in. They also needed a spot to fold in the wings against the body of the wagons. They dropped colorful decorative banners over the folded wings, hiding them from view. They could not let anyone ask questions or get suspicious. They could not take chances.

After a night of relaxing and camping out, they rode into Bluster, same as always, looking like they had traveled for days rather than hours. Their parade with the bells jingling, banners waving, singing, and the band playing was more extensive and joyous than ever. It surprised Edil to see Ronan was back again, staring him down from his spot in the crowd, but he did not let it bother him. He was too excited to be back in Bluster and to see his good friend Nick.

"Change of plans this year, Nick," Edil said as they greeted each other with hugs and pats on the back.

"Oh?" Nick replied with a smile. Edil noticed Nick had hardly any black left in his beard. It was almost completely snow white.

One wagon was completely covered, and Edil ordered it to be taken quietly into Nick's barn. There, Nick and Edil were left alone with the wagon. Edil untied and pulled off the covering.

"You will not believe this," Edil said with excitement. They already agreed among the people of the valley that only Nick would know of the flying reindeer.

"What's going on?" Nick asked. "What is with all the secrecy?"

"We need a vow from you, my good friend," Edil said quietly. "A promise that you will not speak a word of this to anyone."

Nick nodded, curious with sparkling eyes like a child.

"We fly," Edil began and then told Nick his tale of Buck flying home to escape the wolves and how all the reindeer fly and why they think they can fly. He ended his story by showing him the construction of the wagon and unfolding the hidden wings. He told him this was his wagon, and with a team of reindeer, he could deliver his gifts to towns quicker.

"Remarkable," Nick said, stroking his beard and walking around the wagon, inspecting it.

"You believe me?"

"Why, of course, Edil! You have never given me a lie before. Why would you now?"

"You do realize I am talking about flying reindeer that go up like a bird into the sky and defies all laws of nature and science."

"I do. I don't believe this has anything to do with science, though," Nick admitted. "I think that sometimes God just works in mysterious and imaginative ways."

"There's just one thing, Nick," Edil said, a sad note in his voice. "No one can see this. Can you imagine what would happen to the plight of reindeer around the world if the average man found out they can fly? Imagine if men like Ronan knew?"

Nick nodded. Edil was right. This was too great for people to know. Reindeer would be studied, used, and abused in unimaginable ways.

"What do you propose?" Nick asked.

"We would have to fly under cover of darkness. Leave the gifts for the children while they slept."

"Oh, Edil, I don't know," he shook his head. "To not see their little faces when I give them the gift…."

"I understand. But the tradeoff might be worth it. You will do several towns in a night. Perhaps fly further and further into the world. We can fly back and forth several times to Bluster and reload with more gifts. They are that fast. You might cover the world one day in the time we take to do a few villages."

Nick shook his head. It was so much information to take in. He could not imagine not seeing the children, but the idea of visiting more towns and villages and giving out more gifts to deserving children all over the world appealed to him.

"I don't know, Edil," he sighed. "I think I need to think about it."

Edil nodded, understanding his friend's dilemma. They covered up the wagon and headed to Nick's shop, where they found Effie, Lottie, and Pell pouring over the books and letters. They sat at a table with a pot of coffee and a plate of cookies. There was a flurry of papers being passed back and forth.

"Did you know they call you Santa?" Pell called out, holding up a bunch of letters, laughing.

"Santa?" Edil said, looking at Nick, who shrugged.

"Don't be so modest," Effie said. "It means Saint. The children think the world of him."

"Saint Nick, huh?" Edil teased.

"Yeah, and you're his elf!" Pell roared as Lottie glared at him and tried to shush him. "It says right here and even in this letter."

Edil frowned, taking the letters from Pell. Sure enough, the children were asking about Santa's elf that had traveled with him the year before. They wanted to know who he was and where he came from.

"This *elf* has a name," Edil grumbled.

"There are also children saying they will leave out trees for you to decorate," Lottie sighed. "They are writing about the tree of candy that one little girl received, and now it seems they want more."

"You don't say," Nick said, reaching over Lottie's shoulder to take a cookie. It was one of Byron's newest chocolate chip cookies.

"Oh, this is magnificent!" Nick roared in delight after taking a bite. Edil rolled his eyes and shook his head playfully with a smile. He never met a man who had such an obsession with cookies. "Byron's best one yet!"

The day went on, and they left to see Amelia and Johan. There were more people at the house. Edil and Gregor worried about how many more cabins they could afford to fit in the valley. The valley was vast, but there seemed to be no end in sight to the number of people that showed up yearly that needed a home there.

The Reindeer Games came and went as always with lots of gambling, celebrating, and some drinking. They spotted Ronan several times, but he kept his distance. He just watched, a permanent scowl on his face. Eventually, he disappeared with the crowds, never once speaking a word to Edil.

Edil stayed behind with a team of reindeer as the caravan rode out of town. He and Nick watched and waved. Edil felt good this time, knowing his friends, family, and neighbors would arrive home quickly and safely. They rode a half-day out, camped for the night, and then pulled up the banners, unfolded the hidden wings, and off they went.

Amelia and Johan once again stayed in Bluster. They had settled into their new role as ambassadors to the people who traveled with hopes to move to the unknown valley.

It took another two days before Nick came riding to Henrick's old house. Edil greeted him on the porch, waiting for an answer.

"We fly at night," Nick agreed, feeling sad, but he knew it was the best solution. The reindeer would be safe, and the children would still be happy.

That evening, they loaded up the wagon. When darkness fell and Bluster was still and quiet, Edil unfolded the wings. Nick held on tight, and Edil commanded the team to fly.

Across the dark sky, they went. If one looked up at the right moment for a brief second, one could see a dark figure streaking across the full moon. They were gone in a blink.

THE BIG MOVE

The trip went quickly with the reindeer. They snuck into homes and decorated empty trees with treats or left gifts by the hearth. Nick thought it would be fun to hide some small gifts for the children to find. He tucked trinkets in stockings, shoes, or under pillows.

They flew back and forth to reload the wagon over and over. They delivered gifts from early December and into the first week of the new year. They could even afford breaks between deliveries and sightseeing to barter for goods to bring back to Bluster and the valley. The world was getting bigger and bigger for them now that they could travel so much faster.

They returned to Bluster after their last trip for the season, invigorated in spirit but tired. Edil noticed Nick seemed slower. He watched as Nick and Effie bustled around the shop when he visited one last time before leaving for home. Effie walked as if her hips were a slight bother. Nick would grunt when he sat down in his chair. Gone were their dark hair and smooth faces. They still smiled with their eyes twinkling, but the lines were getting clearer on their faces.

Edil left Bluster worried for Nick, Effie, and the children. He wondered how much longer Nick could keep up with the travels.

He knew that there was a simple solution, but it was not entirely up to him. It was a decision that the entire valley needed to come together on.

As soon as he returned home, he called a council with Gregor, Lottie, Karina, Byron, Christoph, Benedict, and Robert. He presented them with his idea of asking Nick and Effie to join them in the valley.

"Giants? Here?" Robert said.

"Come now," Edil replied. "Giants? Really? We are talking about Nick and Effie."

"But doesn't it defeat the purpose of our home?" Christoph asked.

"They are not one of us. Not one of our kind," Robert reminded them.

"But they are," Edil insisted. "Look, if it were not for Nick, we would have no purpose. No children and their letters of wishes. No toy making. No wondrous little treats. No imagination. No creation. It would just be a typical village with tedious lives of farming and shopkeeping. Not much else. Nick gave us a way of life, and what a wonderful way of life it is, isn't it?"

They sat quietly for a moment, taking in what Edil had just preached to them.

"It was Nick that took us in and then convinced Edil and Gregor to take us back. It was Nick that said we deserved a good life just like everyone else," Benedict finally spoke.

"Personally, I think it's a fine idea," Lottie said. "We have many people living here from all over the world, and we manage just fine. What's a couple of giant people? They already contribute to our village. They are already family. Why not let them in and continue to contribute?"

"All those in favor of presenting this to the village for votes?" Gregor asked.

Around the table, all hands went up with nodding heads. They agreed they would appeal to the rest of the village to agree on moving Nick and Effie to the valley. They presented the case in the town square with little persistence. It was unanimous. They were going to ask Nick and Effie to join them in their miraculous community.

Gregor also needed to talk to Edil about another pressing issue he had been noticing. Their streams and rivers were becoming murky. The wildflowers trampled. Muddy footprints of both man and livestock seemed to be everywhere. The valley's air no longer smelled fresh of flora but rather laundry and cooking fires and other unsavory scents that only people can bring.

"Nature's system is breaking down," Gregor told Edil one morning as they walked about.

"What do you mean?"

"With all the people moving in and having families, building cabins, raising livestock, and taking up more and more room, I don't think the valley was meant for this. The valley is dying."

"Dying?" Edil asked, perplexed.

"It will be years, decades even, but if more and more people keep coming, it will destroy the valley. I think we have to move."

"Move? To where?!?" Edil exclaimed. "We can't just move. We can't go outside these walls. The wolves will eventually get the best of us and our livestock. The outside world will eventually find us."

"I've given it a lot of thought," Gregor said. "What about above the valley? Up on the ridge? It is so large up there. We can house many families and rebuild our village up there. Use the road to come down for the livestock to graze and farm small lots. We can watch the valley from up there. Can also keep an eye on the outside of the wall too."

"We can still be part of the valley," Edil nodded, realizing that Gregor was right. The only way to keep the valley from becoming overpopulated and eventually destroyed was to move everyone out and up. This was their best option. It would be cold up there, with ice and snow, but they would still have the valley for its true intent.

They once again had a council meeting, and the entire village agreed it was for the best to move up the ridge. They began almost immediately with clearing the ice and snow as best as possible to mark out lots and streets. One by one, families broke down their cabins, shops, stables, barns, and pens and had the lumber towed up the road only to rebuild everything. They drew plans up for a giant-sized home for Nick and Effie, should they decide to return with Edil after the next trip. They planned for a library to house all the books they gathered over the years, a little theater for the entertainers to put on shows, a post office to help file and organize all the wishful letters, and an office of records for Lottie and Pell to keep track of the children.

It was hard work rebuilding in the wind and cold. It was a slow process, but they worked on it as best as possible while keeping up with their daily lives and contributing to the year's inventory of toys.

When the Christmas Season was once again upon them, the work came to a halt. As was tradition; they once again traveled to Bluster with all the goods they made in the past year.

After their parade, the council sat down with Nick and Effie. Edil felt good about their decision to invite them back. Gone was some of Nick's hair, and he had grown quite a belly from slowing down. Spectacles sat on the edge of Effie's nose to help her read the children's letters better.

"What's with you lot?" Nick asked, noticing their serious faces.

"We wanted to talk to you and Effie," Edil admitted. "We had meetings over the year, and we would like very much if the two of you would come back with us."

"I don't understand," Effie said.

"Look," Edil sighed. "We don't talk about it much, but we know. We know that where we are from has some, I don't know, magic or science, but whatever it is, it slows our age down. We don't know for how long it slows down. All we know is that we don't age, we don't fall drastically ill, we don't know anyone who has died of natural causes or old age- not even our animals. And we know you are aware of this."

"Miracle. Not science. Not magic," Nick nodded.

"Miracle," Edil repeated. "We want you to be a part of this miracle."

"Oh, I don't know," Nick said, shaking his head. "I am not sure that is part of God's plan."

"He wouldn't have sent our Papa and Mama there many years ago," Gregor said. "He wouldn't have given Edil that itch to travel, and we wouldn't have met you. He wouldn't have inspired all this gift-giving in his name and celebration. He wouldn't have sent all those people to find us and help us grow. I would say this is all part of God's plan. God's great big plan."

"You're my best friend, Nick," Edil joined in. "We want you and Effie with us for a long, long time. The children of the world want you with us for a long, long time. What would Christmas be without Nick Claus? Hmmm? Come back with us."

"Where?" Nick asked.

They all pointed north and replied, "Home."

LETTERS

The Final Confrontation

After delivering that year's gifts, Nick and Effie cleaned out their shop and home. With Edil and Gregor's help, they packed up a lifetime of belongings and said goodbye to friends and neighbors. They locked the doors of their store and their beloved church with promises to be back the following Christmastime just in time for the blessing of the herd and the games.

They found the towering wall of ice impressive with its growing little city on top. Nick and Effie walked the fields of the valley, marveling in its miracle. The people were warm and neighborly, making sure they wanted nothing. Nick thought he knew his friend, Edil. Still, when he saw the workshops and warehouses, the bakery and storage facilities, the post office and records room, the reindeer stables and schools, and the church, he realized just how much Edil's heart he invested in the whole idea of Santa Claus and Christmas.

Nick arranged for Bluster's postmaster to deliver the children's letters every month to a secluded spot about a half day's ride north from town. Edil had the metalsmith built a large pole, painted with green and red stripes and a box to hold the letters and keep them safe from wind, snow, and rain. They placed the pole and box alone in the great open tundra so the Post Master could spot it easily and leave the letters there. Once a month, Edil would fly to the pole with Buck and pick up the notes sorted at their own post office.

It was an unseasonably warm day, and the construction was finally over on the top of the ridge when Edil flew to the pole to collect the latest letters. He came in as always, landing out of sight and riding by land, just in case anyone was lingering near the pole and watching. It was always a quick and easy errand, one that Edil enjoyed, having some alone time.

He rode Buck right up to the pole and dismounted. He opened the large metal box and smiled at the pile of letters. Every month the letters just grew and grew. On the last trip, he and Nick had crossed seas and continents to deliver the gifts. Children worldwide have now heard about Santa and his magical workers of elves who built toys for good little boys and girls. They called Nick by many different names, including Father Christmas, Kris Kringle, and Santa Claus.

"I don't understand it," he would say modestly with a chuckle. "I'm just Nick. A buddy. A pal. A fellow to have a mug of hot chocolate with. I'm nothing special."

But Edil and the rest of the people who lived upon the ridge knew better. Nick was indeed extraordinary. Not only to the children but them as well.

Edil bent down at the box, pulling the piles of letters out and stuffing them into his saddlebag when he heard hooves approaching him. He jumped up, startled. He had never encountered anyone at the pole before. He turned around, and his heart skipped a beat when he saw the horse before him and a man dismounting. The man was wearing the dreaded blue silk coat.

"Ronan!" Edil gasped. "What are you doing here?"

Ronan stood over him, looking down at him with that ever-present miserable scowl. He let out a grunt while Buck snorted with nervousness and pawed the ground.

"I heard about this pole in the north. I camped out for a while, watching it. Waiting for the likes of you," he snarled.

"Well, here I am, Ronan," Edil said, gathering his nerves and getting over the shock of seeing him. "What do you want?"

"You took Nick and the wife back with you to wherever it is you people come from?"

"True."

"Never took one of my kind back with you before," Ronan said.

"So?"

"So, I want to go back with you. I deserve what you and all you little circus freaks have," he growled.

Edil scoffed with a laugh and went back to grab the last of the letters. He stuffed them in his pack and buckled it shut.

"No," he said as he tossed the pack across Buck's shoulders.

"That's fine," Ronan smiled. "I'll just follow you."

"I'll stop you," Edil replied rather calmly.

"You and what army, little man?" he laughed as he mounted back up on his horse. "Do you even have an army up there, wherever there is? Are you equipped to battle for the rights of this magical land?"

"It's not magical. I don't know why you think that!"

"Ah, but it is!" Ronan suddenly roared with anger. "Do not lie to me! I see it. Everyone sees it! It's just that no one talks about it!! And now, Nick lives there too? He did not just suddenly decide a change of scenery would do him and the wife some good, did he? He's there for a reason, and I am going there for the same reason!"

"You're crazy," Edil mumbled as he mounted Buck. His mind was racing. He could not just fly off with Ronan to see.

"I'm crazy? Oh, am I crazy for seeing that you and the others have not aged a day in all the years I've known you? Am I crazy for seeing my reindeer are still as young as the day I lost them? They should be dead! And what about your parents? I've seen them, Edil. I saw them looking as young as you and your siblings. And now I see your father's hair thinning, your mother's hair greying, wrinkles around the eyes all because they no longer live up north in whatever whimsical fairyland you are from! Am I crazy for seeing that?"

Edil stared at him, seeing the madness in Ronan's eyes. He had to come up with a plan. A way to get Ronan out of sight so he could command Buck to fly away.

"You are crazy if you think I would ever tell you where I live," Edil finally said, nudging Buck to walk north. He could not fly yet. He had to take it slow and see just how far Ronan would follow him. He had to put some distance between the two of them.

He heard Ronan's horse behind him.

"As I said, I'll follow you. You can't stop me."

"It's a long and hard journey across this cold, barren land," Edil called over his shoulder.

"No matter," Ronan called back. "There's a treasure at the end. I know it. I feel it."

"Ronan, turn around. You are not prepared!"

"I'll risk it."

Edil continued to have Buck walk. He needed to figure something out. He realized he could just make Buck fly off and leave Ronan on the ground, bewildered, but he knew that the sight of a flying reindeer would just infuriate Ronan's insane jealousy even more. He imagined Ronan returning to Bluster with tales of the magical deer and people laughing at him. He could see Ronan wild with rage as he captured and tortured free-roaming reindeer, trying to prove that they could fly.

No, Edil shook his head to himself. He could not let that happen. The flying abilities of the reindeer were not only his people's secret but the reindeer's secret. He had to protect them.

He only hoped to outrun Ronan's horse. He needed to put enough distance between himself and Ronan that they could no longer see one another. Then, and only then, could he take flight.

"Ronan, go home!" Edil yelled as he kicked Buck to pick up speed. Edil's sudden move did not faze Ronan. He was expecting it and was ready. He made his horse gallop after him.

"There is no way you can outrun this horse," Ronan called after him. "He's the best of the best! Only the best of the best for me! You should know that by now!"

"You want to make a bet?" Edil teased with a smirk on his face. Ronan rolled his eyes and frowned.

"The only thing I want is your home!"

Edil ignored him and concentrated on putting distance between Buck and Ronan's horse, but Ronan was right. His horse was agile across the frozen ground.

Edil worried. The ridge was days away if he rode it back by land. He was not prepared. He did not have blankets or a bedroll. There was no food to eat or firewood to keep warm at night. He had only planned on picking up the letters and returning straight home. He was only supposed to be gone for a short time, not days. He might die in the open, cold elements of the tundra.

They continued to ride across The Great Nothing. Edil felt panicked, confused, and exhausted. He no longer knew what to do. Ronan, on the other hand, had determination. He was not giving up. His life depended on it.

With every mile, every hour, Edil grew more hopeless. He finally let Buck ease up on the running. Ronan followed suit, slowing his horse down. He grinned at Edil's slumped shoulders, his head hanging down in defeat.

Then, they heard the haunting call howling across the land, carried by the wind. Edil's head snapped up as he pulled Buck to a stop and scanned the horizon. Ronan pulled up next to him.

"What is that?" Ronan asked.

"Old Shadow," Edil said quietly. Ronan could hear the tension in his voice.

"Old Shadow?" he repeated.

Another call came across the land that sounded like hundreds of voices crying out from the great beyond. Chills crept up Ronan's spine.

"And his huge pack," Edil said, nodding to something in the distance.

Ronan squinted and could see a line of wolves slowly walking into view. They dotted the horizon in the distance. He had never seen such a large pack of wolves.

"Go home," Edil begged. "Please, return from the direction you came in. They might follow you, but they never go that far south."

"No," Ronan said. "I'm not giving up."

"We are not prepared for this. We have no food to give them."

"Food to give them? Why would we feed them?"

"We always do when we cross. Slows them down. Fills them up. Satisfies them," Edil told him. "Eventually, they let us cross in peace."

"You mean to tell me you and your people have been paying a toll to a bunch of mangy wolves all these years?"

Edil nodded. He did not bother to mention that they have not crossed in years, therefore, have not encountered Old Shadow and his wolves in quite some time.

"Ridiculous," Ronan snorted.

"Maybe, but I don't care what you think, Ronan. Never did. Don't think Old Shadow cares either."

With that, Edil kicked Buck to go into a flat-out run. He just needed to get the distance between himself and Ronan. Then he could fly away from the danger of Ronan and the wolves. He heard Ronan curse under his breath, and he also sped up his horse. Edil did not bother looking behind him as he listened to the wolves yip with excitement. The air became filled with the sound of hundreds of large paws thundering across the empty land.

Edil prayed. He prayed harder than he had ever prayed before. He had Ronan at his back. He had Old Shadow not far behind. He had to escape all of it. He could not believe his unfortunate luck.

Ahead, he could see a thick and cloudy wall towering up into the sky. It was not the wall to the valley because that was still miles and days away. He focused on it, realizing it was a perfect, dense fog to ride into that could prevent Ronan from seeing him. It could prevent the wolves from pursuing him. The fog was his only hope.

He raced Buck head-on into the wall of the fog, becoming enveloped by the mist. He could not see, but he could hear Ronan's horse not far behind him. Edil slowed Buck down so he could think about his situation. He looked around and tried to peer through the mist. He could see a large, tall, dark, shapely shadow not too far from him and made it out to be Ronan. He could hear the wolves loudly panting and occasionally calling each other as they entered the fog. He knew the wolves could not see him, but they did not need to see. They could still follow their noses.

Suddenly, everything became eerily quiet. The unnatural silence filled Edil's head and caused him to become dizzy. The hair on the back of his neck stood up as he breathed rapidly. He was not as safe as he thought he would be in a fog. He could feel danger around him. He knew he had to get out of there and fast.

"Fly!" he screamed, snapping the reins. Buck bellowed and leaped into the air, pumping his legs under and out. A sudden, loud growl came from under him. Higher, Buck climbed as more growls and yelping joined in. They suddenly filled the silence with snarls and howls, the voices of hundreds of wolves filling the blind fog.

The most inhuman, animalistic scream followed. It was the sound of a cornered monster coming face to face with his demise. Edil gulped as he urged Buck to fly in circles, trying to see what was going on down below him. Edil was not sure he even wanted to know. He could not see through the thick mist, but he kept circling. Eventually, the screaming stopped, and the wolves' voices quieted down.

Edil flew to the edge of the fog, then commanded Buck to land. He needed to catch his breath and recollect his thoughts and check his bearings. He needed to calm down and stop shaking. He had never been so frightened before in his life.

He took deep breaths, staring at the fog. Everything became still when Old Shadow suddenly appeared, walking cautiously out of the mist. Edil stopped breathing, and Buck stood stiff. They watched as the large, dark wolf continued towards them. He was alone. None of his pack followed him.

Old Shadow sat back on his haunches, his one eye never leaving Edil. They stared at each other, not a sound to be made. From Old

Shadow's mouth, a scrap of cloth hung. It was a small piece made from blue silk, its thread caught in his fangs. It was that unmistakable blue that Ronan treasured all those years.

Edil finally nodded, understanding. Ronan was gone, and Old Shadow had finally caught one of them on his chase.

Old Shadow finally became bored with their staredown. He rose, turned around, and simply disappeared back into the fog. It was the last time Edil would ever see him.

Edil returned to the ridge feeling victorious. He had survived his incredible adventure, and he was safe, his reindeer was safe, and his family and people were safe. That was all that mattered.

After a few years, Amelia and Johan eventually returned home. They were the oldest of the town, having greyed and wrinkled over the years. Even Onyx was slower with white around his muzzle. They returned because the people stopped coming. The world was changing, and people were more accepting.

The village continued to thrive and exist in secrecy. The years went by, and wars were fought and won around the world. Horses were replaced by cars, letters by phones. Through it all, children still believed in Santa and his magical elves that all lived in a magical land. They continued to write their Christmas wishes down, promised they were good all year and mailed them to the North Pole.

Edil, Nick, Lottie, Gregor, and the rest of the North Pole did their best. They fulfilled these wishes as best as possible, even if it took years to fulfill wishes, as it did with a little girl named Claire.

From

Epilogue: Edil's Gift

On Christmas morning, Claire McIntyre woke up in Gator Springs, Texas, to the sounds of the little feet of her grandchildren running down the stairs. She sat up, smiling and blinking the sleep out of her eyes. She stretched before putting on her glasses and throwing her robe around her shoulders.

She could hear her grown children and their spouses telling the children to wait while they made some coffee before opening their gifts from Santa. She climbed down the stairs slowly, her legs and hips still stiff from sleeping. She was not as young as she used to be.

The children were so excited, bouncing on the floor and urging their parents to hurry. Claire took her seat in a big, overstuffed armchair. She thanked her daughter when she handed her a mug of freshly brewed coffee from the coffee machine. They finally gave the kids the okay to open gifts.

Wrapping paper and ribbons went flying as the children shouted with glee. The parents laughed and took pictures with their phones. Claire's son tried unsuccessfully to keep up with the mess as he gathered the torn papers off the floor and stuffed them into a large, plastic, black garbage bag. It all ended as most Christmas mornings with children end with a pile of toys and paper all over the floor with happy, smiling boys and girls buried in the mess.

"I still see a box," Claire's daughter called out, pointing under the tree. "Whose is that?"

Claire's oldest grandson crawled under and pulled it out. He read the tag on it.

"Grandma. It's for you," he said, holding the box out to her. Claire's children looked at each other quizzically. None of them recalled putting the box under the tree and did not know what it contained.

"For me?" she smiled, delighted. She looked around, seeing the puzzled looks on everyone's faces. "I wonder who it is from."

She unwrapped the box and lifted the lid. Inside, wrapped in red tissue paper, was a book bound in leather. A note was carefully folded and rested on top.

"Mom, who is it from?" her daughter asked.

Claire lifted the paper and opened it. Inside was swirly handwriting that was addressed to her. Her eyes scanned the letter as she read it silently. Her family watched as her eyes became bigger and bigger with amazement.

Dearest Claire,

As a little girl, you had sent me a letter wishing for the gift of an elf on Christmas morning. While the letter amused me, I regret we lost the letter for many years, and I could not fulfill that wish. As you are more than likely aware, an elf would not have been a possible thing. Not then and not now.

However, I am sending you the next best thing. I have entrusted telling the story of my wonderful neighbors and family and how they came to be to my closest confidants. He was here from the very beginning, and it is he, not I, makes the Christmas magic possible.

It has taken him all year to write his memories, for they go back many generations. And here it is. His story. Our story. Share it with your grandchildren. Read it out loud.

We hope you enjoy it.

Merry Christmas!
Santa

Claire looked up from the letter in disbelief. She had forgotten she wrote it all those years ago. She looked down at the book. Its cover was red leather with gold lettering across the front that simply said *From Edil.*

"Well," she sighed, lifting the book out of the box. "Someone very special has sent me a Christmas story."

She motioned for her grandchildren to put down their toys and gather around her. Her youngest climbed up into her lap as she opened the book carefully. She cleared her voice, and then she read out loud from the book Edil wrote.

"There are things I've been told and things I remember...."

THE END

About the Author

Tina Bauer is an up and coming author. Born in Queens, New York, Tina has been writing and telling stories since she was twelve years old. She is a proud mom of two grown sons, happily married to her best friend, and adores all the dogs and cats that complete her family. When Tina is not creating a story you can find her cooking, road tripping around the country, reading, or watching movies and her favorite televisions shows. *A Gift From Edil* is Tina's first published novel. She hopes to have three other novels available within the next couple of years.

Tina Bauer is also the author of the children's book *My Big Cousin Ollie*, available now online where books are sold. More children's books are coming out soon, including *My Fun Aunt Millie*.

You can keep updated on all of Tina's books and story telling journey on Instagram @Tina_B_Storyteller and on Facebook @Tina Bauer Storyteller. You can also read her blog at www.tinabauerstoryteller.com.

About the Illustrator

Harley Dallojacono is an artist born and raised in NY who has not stopped creating since the moment she could hold a pencil. Being an artist has always been the dream. From taking high school art classes to attending Pratt Institute in Brooklyn, NY for a BFA in Fine Arts, creating art has always been her goal. Harley finds true inspiration from her surroundings which is why most of her artwork consists of portraits of her dogs, Bella and Thor. Without the constant support from her amazing family, Harley would not be where she is today. When she is not locked away in her studio creating, you can find her watching sitcoms, photographing landscapes while on a hike, at the beach, or at Walt Disney World.

To follow Harley Dallojacono's new art adventures you can find her on Instagram @harleydalloart.

www.ingramcontent.com/pod-product-compliance
Lightning Source LLC
Chambersburg PA
CBHW070542310726
48982CB00010B/1448/J

* 9 7 8 1 7 3 7 5 6 7 5 3 0 *